SECRET LETTERS

SECRET LETTERS

LEAH SCHEIER

HYPERION
NEW YORK

Text copyright © 2012 by Leah Scheier

All rights reserved. Published by Hyperion, an imprint of Disney Book Group. No part of this book may be reproduced or transmitted in any form or by any means, electronic or mechanical, including photocopying, recording, or by any information storage and retrieval system, without written permission from the publisher. For information address Hyperion, 125 West End Avenue, New York, New York, 10023.

First Hyperion paperback edition, 2013

10 9 8 7 6 5 4 3 2

V475-2873-0-13105

Printed in the United States of America

Library of Congress Control Number for Hardcover Edition: 2011024134

Designed by L. Lockett

ISBN 978-1-4231-2758-1

Visit www.un-requiredreading.com

For Eric, Aviva, Miriam, and Talia

CHAPTER
1

OUSIN ADELAIDE AND I were traveling to London to choose from the latest fashions of the season. There would be receptions, concerts and balls, evenings crammed with polite company and dinner parties, and I was simply dying to take part in all of it.

That was what my aunt Ina believed, at any rate.

The truth was that I had suggested our trip to my cousin, but not because I had developed a sudden need for hat pins or embroidered corsets. I had convinced Adelaide to journey to the city to consult Mr. Sherlock Holmes, the London detective, and plead with him to save her marriage. But that was our little secret, and if my plan succeeded, no one would ever know it.

As the train whistle sounded, my cousin quietly slipped her hand into mine and waved cheerfully to her husband.

"You needn't squeeze my fingers quite so hard, Dora," she whispered. "I know you're nervous for me, but you mustn't be so obvious about it. Give your aunt a smile, now; she's looking at you."

I couldn't help admiring Adelaide's perfect poise just then, her tranquil eyes, the waves of yellow hair in flawless coils beneath her stylish hat. There wasn't a hint of tears on her serene face, no trace of the night before when she had cried her fears out to me. In public my cousin would always be the model of a sophisticated lady. No one could ever guess what she was hiding behind her frank and easy smile, or how desperate she was to keep her secret from her husband and her family.

But then—we all had our personal mysteries, I suppose. Adelaide's husband didn't suspect that his sweet wife was being blackmailed by a criminal who'd purchased her old love letters from a servant. And Adelaide didn't suspect that her innocent sixteen-year-old cousin was hiding something as well. She never imagined that I had proposed this trip to the London detective not only because I wished him to help her, but because I had been waiting years for an opportunity to meet him.

And the reason that I had been waiting years to meet him? Well, *that* was the greatest secret of all.

It was dark by the time we arrived in London. As our cab sped away from Victoria Station, I caught a glimpse of ivory-columned buildings with sculpted rooftops and then endless rows of identical narrow houses, bordered by metal railings and illuminated by gaslight. The leaden taste of coal smoke made me catch my breath; the sloshing sound of hansom wheels against the pavement and the regular beat of horses' hooves against the cobblestones soothed and excited me. Every new sensation seemed to whisper promises of a great discovery and a dawning adventure.

My cousin pointed out St. George's as we neared our destination, and we were soon at her town house on Hanover Square. We were welcomed inside by Adelaide's house-keeper, and quickly installed in our respective bedrooms. I undressed, unpacked my bags, washed the coal dust from my face, and then settled into bed to listen to the city's sounds. Though I was tired from our journey, I could not risk going to sleep, because I was worried that I might miss my chance to steal away the following morning before my cousin woke. I knew that Adelaide would wish to visit the detective and present her case to him as soon as possible. And I would be there by her side, of course, to support her as she told her story. But I had my own reason for visiting Mr. Holmes and my own story to tell him, and so I had to reach him before she did—and I had to speak to him alone.

There were only a few hours left before daybreak, and the minutes ticked by more slowly as the night drew on. I tried to read a little to distract myself, but I found that somehow I could not concentrate on other people's plots. My eyes kept wandering to the framed portrait of my family that I had placed upon my nightstand. The painting was my most prized possession; it was one of the last mementos I had of my mother and father, for they had died of typhoid fever four years ago, after the picture was finished.

I reached my hand out and picked up the frame, running my fingers over the rough paint, over the gently smiling faces of my parents. It was such a lovely scene, my mother kneeling at my father's feet, her flowered dress spread out across the lawn, her face tilted upward gazing sweetly at us. I was perched proudly on my father's knee; one of his hands was on my shoulder, the other extended to his wife. It truly was a perfect picture.

Slowly, I turned the portrait over, grasped the corner of the frame, and tore back the folded canvas edge. It came loose with a snap of ripping thread, and a little packet

dropped out of the gaping hole into my hands. As I had
done a hundred times before, I carefully untied the linen
envelope and unrolled the single piece of paper on my lap. It
had been several months since I had looked over the letter;
the ink had faded slightly, but my mother's words were still
fresh and sharp in my imagination.

My dearest Dora,

*I do not know why I feel forced to write to you,
words that I know will only bring you shame. All
your life I have shielded you from a secret that would
have hurt you, and now, when I am no longer there
to comfort you, I feel compelled to transfer this burden onto you. There is no earthly reason why I should
not cast this page aside and let the secret die with
me. But the lies I've told you feel heavier than ever,
and I cannot bear to leave you without telling you
the truth.*

*Before my marriage, Dora, I was secretly engaged
to a man whom I had known since childhood. I knew
we could not marry for many years, for he could not
then support a wife, and my family would never have
consented to the match.*

*My father had invested very heavily in a business
venture with a friend. One night my mother found him*

unconscious in his study, a letter from the bank on the desk before him. He had had a paralytic stroke. The venture had failed, his friend had fled the country, and my father was ruined.

As my family was reeling from the shock and my father lay dying, an old suitor of mine stepped forward to comfort me. Philip Joyce was a good friend of my father's, a wealthy and respectable man. I had turned down his proposal the previous year, but when he renewed his offer, I broke off my secret affair and accepted Philip. The engagement was very brief, as you know, because my father wanted to see his youngest daughter married before he died.

Very soon after the wedding, I learned that I was with child. I wasn't certain then; I wanted to believe that you were legitimate, that I would have no doubts after you were born. But as I watched you grow, it became harder and harder to deceive myself.

If you had not been such a little, frail thing, Philip might have suspected that he was not your father, for you were born eight months after our wedding. But he never thought to question or doubt. You were our only child, and he adored you.

Dora, only a few months ago he learned the truth about my past—

I rolled up the paper and thrust it back into its hiding place, tucking the edge of the canvas over it to conceal it. At the bottom of the confession, my mother had revealed the name of the man who she believed was my real father. I did not need to read that part again. That memory—the squirming ink upon the page, my beating heart, the look upon my mother's face when she saw the letter in my hand—I did not want to think about that now. In my mind my mother's final good-bye would always be tainted by my own betrayal, for I had stolen that letter from her night table while she slept. And ever since that night I'd relived that awful moment every time I thought of her.

After my mother's death I'd been adopted by my aunt Ina and welcomed into her family. I had kept my mother's confession letter hidden from everyone, of course, for I never wanted anyone to discover her disgraceful past. And the name in my mother's letter meant nothing to me then; I had no idea who Sherlock Holmes was—and I didn't want to know. But the following Christmas Eve I would finally understand how Mr. Holmes and my mother's secret would come together and forever change my life.

I thought back over that day again, and once more felt the heat from the roaring fireplace in my aunt's parlor, saw the stacks of gleaming presents in the corner (my cousin had overbought that year in an attempt to cheer me up), and felt the pinch of my black crape mourning dress. Adelaide had placed a journal, the *Beeton's Christmas Annual*, on my lap. I'd glanced at it with little interest. The journal had never impressed me before, and there was no reason to think that the 1887 edition would be any different. I'd scanned the dramatic title, "A Study in Scarlet," flipped carelessly to the first page, and then froze.

There, black on yellow, underneath the chapter heading, was a name, *the* name in my mother's letter, the one which I would never forget.

It could not be.

He could not be the one.

I remember my cousin staring at me, calling to me. I heard her asking me if I was ill, and I shook my head, my eyes fixed unseeing on the page in front of me, my fingers trembling. She touched my shoulder, and I pulled away from her. Clutching the magazine to my chest, I dashed up the stairs and locked myself in my room.

There, by candlelight, I'd devoured the story, barely understanding the plot while I raced to swallow every scrap of conversation in the piece and inhale every word that the detective said. The narrator, a fellow named Dr. Watson, had written this first story about his friend and published it in this family journal.

I read the tale over and over, lighting candle after candle, crouching by the window until my muscles cramped, then stretching out on the floor like a child with a favorite toy. By the third reading, I had absorbed some of the mystery, shuddering at the gruesome double murder, grinning at the stupid inspector's confusion, and gloating over my detective's triumph. By the fourth time through, I was calmer, and I began to examine the details of Mr. Holmes's character. He sprang from the page to meet me, and a picture of the man formed in my imagination, a noble and kind figure, a hero who could support and encourage me as no one ever had. He was no longer just a name now, no longer a shadow from my past.

But although this secret opened up an interesting new world for me, it also marked the beginning of all my troubles with my aunt and my new family. After my parents' death, Aunt Ina had declared that she would raise me as she had raised her daughter, Adelaide, and so mold me into a proper lady. But, as it turned out, I no longer wished to stand straight, roll my *r*'s, or dance a waltz; nor did I understand why I ought to try. Every month the stays of my corset were slowly tightened to train my waist for its adult shape. Every afternoon my governess would instruct me on how to smile and breathe and say my vowels correctly. And every night I would tear the lacing from its buttonholes, pull apart the whalebone seams, and creep upstairs in loosened robes and slippers, to dream of improper adventures in a dangerous town.

But worst of all, I also began to "notice things," as Aunt Ina put it, things which an innocent young lady had no business noticing. "Your banker friend has just lost money at the races," I would declare at dinnertime. "He's had to sell his mother's jewels." Or "Our pastor thinks somebody is stealing money from the collection plate."

Amazingly, nobody seemed interested in these observations. And yet, I could never get enough of other people's mysteries. I collected secrets like stamps, and took pride in my collection. Instead of ladies' journals and embroidery squares, I saved newspaper clippings, cigar ash, and footprint samples, and stored them under a floorboard in my bedroom. It was all part of a grander purpose, of course: to train myself in the study of crime, so that one day I would be ready to meet Mr. Holmes himself.

Now, as I looked back on the four years I'd spent preparing for this day, I couldn't believe that I was almost there, that I was actually going to see him that very morning. Somehow I had pictured a grander presentation, with some celebrated individual in the background making the introductions. I wished suddenly that I was older, that I had done something spectacular to deserve this day. There was no guarantee that he would welcome me, I realized; he might resent me, or laugh at me, or deny the truth altogether. Or worse, he might smile indulgently, pat me on the head, and send me home to my diaries, my crime journals, and my silly dreams.

The clock struck four, then five, then six, and I slipped quietly out of bed and dressed before the mirror, shivering. It was an unseasonably cold spring day, and my fingers were stiff and numb as I buttoned up my collar. In the dim morning light I could just make out the outline of my small, thin figure wrapped in a brown plaid walking dress and velvet cloak. I traced the familiar contours of my reflection in the glass, the mass of dark, thick curls, my large gray eyes, my freckled nose, my pointed chin, and tried to imagine how I would appear to him.

Turning before the mirror now, I felt as if I were seeing myself for the first time, through the critical eyes of a distant stranger. I practiced different expressions to decide which one to wear. I rehearsed my smile and offered ten different greetings to the pillow on my bed. I tried out confidence and meekness and decided he would dislike them both. I pretended fear and stuttered, and felt his irritation. I gave brilliant examples of my criminal knowledge, and saw him yawn discreetly. I composed a heartfelt speech about my family, and then shuddered at his reaction to my mother's name.

Finally, I told my secret to the mirror and was met with icy silence. And as the morning dawned, I still sat terrified and undecided on my bed, clutching my little purse until my hands were numb.

I might have stayed that way forever had not a distant sound from my cousin's room motivated me to break the spell. There was no going back now, I told myself. I had traveled to London for this purpose, and willingly or not, I would meet him before the day was through. If I waited any longer, Adelaide would wake; and I would lose my chance to speak to him alone.

I went to my desk, drew out a sheet of stationery, and scribbled a brief note to my cousin. *Will be back by noon. Went for a walk around town.* By the time she found my message, I would already be there. I knew that she would fuss at me when I returned. Young unmarried women were not supposed to walk about alone. There was no way around it, though, and I wasn't really thinking about etiquette at that moment, anyway. I threw one last look at the mirror and then left the room, closing the door quietly behind me. The hallway was empty and, holding my skirts to still the rustling cloth, I stole down the stairs and into the street.

A yellowish gloom had descended over the city and obscured the morning sun. Beyond the haze, I could just make out the shapes of hansoms and broughams, and the hordes of street vendors and shop-men who were rushing past. A cab clattered toward me, and I stepped off the pavement and put out my hand. The driver asked my destination, and I hesitated briefly and cleared my throat before replying, "Baker Street, please."

That cab ride felt like the longest trip I had ever taken. The morning rush brought us into a thick knot of carriages, and the hansom swayed and pitched to avoid the swelling traffic. Above me, the driver cursed God, the city, and his horse, as if he had never seen a London jam before. I peered into the crowd and counted cabs to distract myself. And yet, when we finally arrived at his door, I wondered how the most important drive of my life could have been so short.

As I wavered undecided upon the step, the door swung open, and a man rushed past me; I saw that he was wearing a black mourning band around his arm, that his cheeks were gray and hollow, and his eyes bloodshot. Standing behind him in the doorway was an older lady who was gazing into the street and sobbing, clutching the railing in her grief as her tears fell unheeded upon the stairs

But still I did not see the truth; I did not dare to guess. And I could not move, not until the weeping landlady had closed the door, the unhappy gentleman had vanished around the corner, and a little newsboy had sauntered past me, hauling his stack of papers. Not until I heard the child's cracking voice, shouting out the latest headline, did I realize why I was shaking.

Not until I saw the words that he waved before me did I understand what I had lost.

Sherlock Holmes Killed in Switzerland

CHAPTER 2

I SANK TO MY KNEES before the startled child and grabbed the paper from him. I was afraid to read it; I did not want to know the details, for it would make it real to me and final. The boy was calling out to me, screeching, "A'right miss? A'right miss? Are you a'right?" in a dizzying loop, and the stream of passing carriages roared like gunfire in my ears. I could not breathe, my stays were like bands of iron across my chest, and the heavy stench of horse and greasy fog stifled me and made me gag. *We regret to report that the famous detective, Mr. Sherlock Holmes, has been confirmed dead by the Swiss police.* I closed my eyes and crushed the page between my fingers. "It can't be, it isn't possible," I moaned into the cracking paper in my hands. My skin was slippery with inky sweat, and the sharp, black odor of the newsprint stung my throat. "But I've waited years for you—" I murmured weakly into the spinning gray; and then the street went silent, and I dropped into the swirling shades and dust.

When I awoke my cheek was resting on something lean and rough, against someone who smelled of warm wool and cinnamon. There were two people calling to me now; the child's voice had faded slightly, and another, lower tone was whispering my name.

"Miss Dora, Miss Dora, please." I did not know the man's voice and I could not see his face; there was an arc of violet lights dancing before my eyes. I stumbled forward and heard him call to me once more.

"Miss Dora, please stay still a moment, or you'll fall on me again."

I felt him shift beneath me and raised my head; as my vision cleared, I saw that I was leaning on someone's arm, someone who was murmuring my name and patting me gently on the cheek. I jerked my chin away and pushed him back, my skin going dark with shame. Once more the sinking tug of nausea hit, and a veil of shifting colors blinded me; again the steady arm wrapped around my waist.

"Do you know this lady?" I heard the newsboy ask.

"A little," the voice responded. "I know that Miss Dora is in trouble, and that she has come to London to seek a detective's help. I know that she had something very important to tell him, and that no one knows that she is here." He plucked the newspaper from my fingers as he spoke and smoothed it out. "And I know that I am truly sorry for her sad discovery," he concluded softly.

I rose unsteadily to my feet and turned to face him; the haze was clearing, and it no longer hurt to breathe. He had released my waist, and I watched him as he stepped away from me.

He was quite young, no more than seventeen, but with the lanky height of a full-grown man. His skin was fair, the outline of his jaw was smooth, with only the faintest shadow of a beard. His eyes would have been very handsome ones if they had not been narrowed in a piercing stare, for they were green like sea foam, and flecked with hazel shadows. As he leaned back against the railing and readjusted his gray felt cap, a shock of straight, copper-colored hair tumbled out across his forehead.

I cleared my throat, shook the remaining shadows from my head and glanced over his figure once again.

"I appreciate your help, Mr.—"

"Cartwright. Peter Cartwright."

"Well, Mr. Cartwright, I see that you were running to complete an urgent task for your employer." I squinted at the leather pouch peeping from his pocket. "I do not wish to keep you. The first few months at a new post are the most important ones, after all. "

I saw him start; his lips fell open, and his eyes flashed with silent pleasure. It was quite amusing to watch the play of admiration and disbelief flicker across his features, and for a moment, it distracted me from my grief. I turned back to the newsboy and dropped a coin into his hand. "You may run along, please. I am feeling better now."

As the child shuffled down the street, my companion shifted uneasily in front of me and cleared his throat. "You are still very pale," he muttered, and handed me my crumpled paper. "It was quite a shock to you, this news."

I did not want to answer him. There was no way to explain my unhappiness to anyone, for why would I be mourning a gentleman whom I had never known? But the true facts were too shameful to reveal, and, more importantly, my story was dead now, and it no longer mattered what I said. A lie would do as well as any truth, for I did not expect to meet this boy again.

"Honestly, sir, I do not know what came over me just

now," I told him, wearily. "I had a long journey yesterday, and I am still tired, I suppose."

He could have pretended to believe me and let me go. A well-bred gentleman would have bowed politely and murmured something dull and understanding. Mr. Peter Cartwright crossed his arms, puffed his cheeks out, and whistled through his teeth. "Whew. That two-hour train ride from Eastbourne must have been *very* trying indeed."

He was grinning at me now, and his head was thrown back a little, like an artist expecting his applause. Clearly he was waiting for my surprise, for the inevitable "Dear me!" and the plea for an explanation. But I would not take the bait, of course. There was no mystery, after all, and besides, he had now stepped into *my* arena.

"Well, sir, I am sorry if your deductive powers have not left me speechless with amazement," I responded. "You see, I realize that my name is embroidered on my handbag, that there is a charm from Eastbourne dangling from my bracelet, and that you observed me reading about Mr. Holmes's death upon his doorstep. And, besides, you were wrong earlier about my traveling alone. I did not come up from Newheath on my own."

He raised his eyebrows. "I did not say you did. But your little trip to Baker Street this morning was a secret, wasn't it?"

I opened my mouth to answer him and stopped, alarmed.

He chuckled at my confusion and stepped closer to me, and I had to lean my head back to meet his gaze. I slowly ran my eyes over him again, more from fear than curiosity, for I was not used to strangers who could best me in observation.

He was neatly dressed, I saw, but his shoes were scuffed with years of wear, and his trousers appeared to have been recently rehemmed. A cravat had been tied very tightly around his collar, but it had slipped down when he'd caught me. Behind the shadow of the knot, I could see the edge of an angry, cross-shaped scar. He noticed me studying it, and his hand went quickly to his neckline; his eyes narrowed, and with a rough motion he pulled his collar shut and readjusted the tie to cover the mark.

We stared at each other for a little while without speaking, like two ragged knights over pointed lances. He finally broke the uneasy stillness with a laugh and backed away from me. "Well, do you give up?" he demanded.

"I beg your pardon?"

"Are you finished analyzing me? You've been scanning me from head to toe like a suspicious copper. Not very lady-like at all, for it makes a gentleman feel very vulnerable to be examined so." He sighed and shrugged his shoulders. "I daresay you are preparing a witty little speech to put me in my place. I'm all ears."

I suppressed a smile. No one had ever encouraged me like

that before. "I promised my aunt that I would not do that anymore."

"Nonsense, that isn't it at all. You simply haven't found out anything interesting, and you aren't ready to admit it. There, now, I'll give you another chance." He took a step toward me, turned about slowly, and extended both his palms before my face. "How about now?"

I did not understand what this brazen person wanted from me. Did he go about taunting every strange girl he met upon the street, or was I the first unfortunate? At some other time I might have liked to meet his challenge; but today I could see nothing but a teasing boy, and for once, I did not care to look much further. These games felt trite and meaningless now, and my skill seemed rather silly. "I am sorry, Mr. Cartwright, but I cannot care today—" I began and stopped, exhausted.

His arms dropped to his sides, and his smile faded; with a shamefaced look, he shoved his hands into his pockets and stepped aside. "It's more than just disappointment, isn't it?" he ventured, after an awkward silence. "Did you know Mr. Holmes well?"

I thought about the letter tucked inside my picture frame and shook my head sadly. "No, I didn't. I never met him."

"Oh, I thought perhaps you had, for you looked ready to cry a moment ago. I was just trying to distract you a little, as best I could." There was an earnest sympathy in his smile now, and my grief was reflected in his eyes. "You see, I *have* met Mr. Holmes, and I was very sorry when I heard the news."

I glanced back at him with renewed interest. "You consulted him on a problem?"

"No, but for a short time I worked as his assistant."

"His assistant! And what happened?"

"Ah, now suddenly I'm interesting to you. Well, Miss Dora, if you must know, Mr. Holmes solved the case."

"Well, of course he did," I retorted. "But that's not what I was asking. What I meant was—what I wanted to know was—" I paused for a moment and swallowed uncomfortably. Peter Cartwright was staring at me now with a bemused expression on his face and shaking his head. Had I seemed too eager? I wondered. And did it really matter if I had? He certainly thought that I was odd already. Besides, I would never get a chance like this again. "What was Mr. Holmes like?" I ventured after an awkward silence.

He laughed shortly and crossed his arms. "What was he *like*?"

"I've read the stories, obviously," I told him. "But I've never spoken to anyone who's met him, who's actually worked with him. What was he like?"

He shook his head and shrugged. "He was—smart."

I nodded patiently. "And—?"

"Masterful."

"I beg your pardon?"

He smiled absentmindedly, as if recalling an amusing memory. "Sherlock Holmes could silence a hardened criminal with a single look."

I didn't know how to respond to that. And Mr. Cartwright seemed to be watching me closely, as if waiting for my reaction. I thought it best to distract him for a bit, before he asked me why I cared so much about a man I'd never met.

"You enjoyed working with him, then?" I inquired.

"I did. In fact, I became rather enthusiastic about his line of work. I was only fourteen then, and quite impressionable. Perhaps you will read about the case in Dr. Watson's chronicles one day. At the end of the investigation, I offered to extend my services and become his apprentice. Needless to say, he declined, and I was—disappointed. I was very unhappy for a time, though I did not swoon in the street, as you just did." He gave me a wicked grin and rolled his eyes dramatically. I had a sudden, unladylike urge to knock him down.

"Well, I am glad to see that you have recovered, sir," I responded coolly. "I cannot imagine why anyone would reject you, truly I cannot. Your talent for deducing a lady's name from her handbag is quite astonishing; I know that I am still all aflutter. I'd best run home before I collapse again."

"Don't you want to hear what I did after that case?" he inquired with a wounded air.

I was still smarting from his jibe about my fainting spell, and so I answered him more brutally than I intended. "No, not particularly. I really don't see why I should care."

"Because I want to offer my help. Mr. Holmes was not the only private investigator in London, you know."

"No, but he was the best. And now you want me to bring my problem to you—a sixteen-year-old boy?"

"Seventeen. And I wasn't recommending myself, though perhaps one day I will be. I was referring to the gentleman for whom I work."

"And who is that?"

"Mr. Neville Porter. He is an investigator as well as a private agent. Until recently, he handled Mr. Holmes's 'overflow' cases, but it seems that now we may have more business than we bargained for. Oh, and by the way, *don't* tell Porter that you went to Sherlock Holmes first. He *hates* to hear that. May I give you his card?"

I took the slip of cardboard and dropped it into my handbag without a glance.

"I will have to ask my cousin. It is her case, after all, not mine."

He gave a short, triumphant laugh, as if I had just confirmed his guess. "Ah, and yet you came here this morning, without consulting her. I find that very curious."

"Mr. Cartwright, I already told you that I came to London with my cousin. Why do you assume that my visit this morning was a secret? Why would I deceive her? Isn't it more likely that she sent me here?"

"No, it isn't more likely, Miss Dora. Not unless your cousin is blind, that is." He flicked his index finger at the nape of my collar. "The two open buttons on the back of your dress force me to conclude that you made your preparations today before daybreak, and that you were anxious, alone, and in a hurry. As to why you decided to travel across the city without a chaperone—why *that* I have yet to discover. Perhaps I will, in time. *If* you give me a chance." There was a demure insolence in his voice and a playful gleam in his sober eyes that begged for a reaction, that taunted me to answer him. A proper lady would have frozen this impudent fellow immediately and stalked away. But I was not angry, or even irritated. It was exciting to talk to a man who did not treat me like a porcelain flower, who appeared to relish an intelligent retort as a special treat, and who seemed able to predict my thoughts before I myself was conscious of them. I decided that I would beat him at his little game—and then I would walk away.

"Thank you for your kind offer," I began in a bored and

patient tone. "You clearly have good intentions and you seem to be an intelligent boy, though perhaps lacking in humility. Unfortunately, I must decline your offer." The expression on his face did not change at all, but his shoulders began to droop a little. "I see that you have *some* skill, but I'll wager that you miss as much as you observe. Can you tell me where am I staying, for example? No? Well, this smear of clay across my boot heel is unique to the area on Hanover Street where they are laying the electric line. Can you guess if I am familiar with London? No answer? Well, it should be obvious that I am not, for if I was, I would have known that walking was far more efficient at this hour than riding in a cab. But I clearly did not walk, for the hem of my skirt is clean. Honestly, I am not impressed, Mr. Cartwright, and I truly doubt that you can help me. So, in the end, I believe that I am better off alone," I concluded shortly.

It was the final sentence that scored the hit, for I saw his pale cheeks flush red, and he drew back as if I had slapped him. His lips tensed for a moment, and he swallowed twice before he answered. "I thank you for your frankness, and I am truly sorry to have bothered you. Good day, Miss—"

"Joyce."

"Miss Joyce." He paused and his brows came down. "Miss Joyce?" he repeated, and his mouth fell open in surprise. "Not Miss Dora Joyce, of Newheath?" he inquired in an awestruck whisper. I nodded dumbly. "Little Dora, who's known the secrets of her entire town since she could talk, who sometime back shocked even her sweet old pastor? The same Dora Joyce whose aunt insisted that she stop her 'prying,' if she wished the family to be welcome in society? I believe you've even solved a mystery or two in your little village, have you not?"

It was my turn to blush now, and I admit that I did, happily and completely. It seemed incredible that my reputation was known in London, but this boy seemed absolutely overwhelmed, and he had just recited my little history as if it was the stuff of myths and fairy tales. It was true that I had located a missing puppy some months ago and later found a bit of jewelry for a distant relative, but I had never imagined that the news of my small accomplishments would have traveled to the city. And that my name should actually cause this peculiar boy to gawk! I was very sorry that I had tried to hurt him and resolved to make it up to him immediately. He looked quite meek now, and his tone had been at once gentle and appealing.

"Thank you for the compliment," I murmured sweetly. "Really, Mr. Cartwright, I am very flattered that you have heard of me. People truly speak of me here, in London?"

His jaw snapped shut, and he grinned at me with gritted teeth. "No, they certainly do not. And I've never heard of you until today. Everything I said just now I learned from you, my conceited little friend. The famous Dora Joyce, indeed! And yet you accused me of lacking humility?"

I was entirely crimson now; I could feel the heat pulsing from my forehead to my collar. And he was laughing, easily and without mercy. I hated him, hated him with an intensity that shocked me, with a force that numbed my sadness. But I did not drop my head; I would not admit defeat. I simply could not let him win, not after I had been beaten by my own bad luck and wasted plans. *Today is only the beginning*, I promised silently, as I glared at my opponent. I felt the blood drain from my face, and my lips went taut. *This is only the beginning.*

I never expected a reaction, for I did not say a word just then. But as I glowered at him, his laugh strangled in his throat and his eyes came open in blank surprise. He shook his head and glanced away as if to clear his sight, and when he turned back to me his face was drawn and rigid, with the faraway look of a wakened memory. I heard the whisper of an exhaled breath and then the words, "Dear God," and nothing more.

We stood and watched each other for several moments, and when I could no longer bear the tension of the silence, I broke the spell.

"Good morning, Mr. Cartwright, and good-bye."

He seemed to have the lost the ability to speak. He nodded absently and played with the edge of his lapel. As I stepped off the pavement and turned toward home, he coughed suddenly and called to me.

"Miss—Joyce?" Was it my imagination, or had he put more emphasis on the pause than on my surname?

"Yes?"

"You will come back?"

"I—I'm sorry?"

He smiled wistfully, but his eyes were shining like twin jade fires. "Forgive me, Dora, and come back."

Somewhere, someone would have known the correct response. Adelaide would have found some feminine and honest words for him; my aunt would have cut him with a moral.

I sputtered for a second and shot out, "If I do, you'll probably regret it, sir!" and sped away with the sound of his laughter ringing in my ears.

CHAPTER

3

ADELAIDE WAS PACING back and forth over the parlor rug when I returned. She rushed forward when she saw me and grabbed my hands. "Dora, why didn't you wait for me?" she exclaimed. "How could you go out alone?"

There was no need to answer her question, I decided. She would forget all about it anyway when I gave her my sad report. I threw the newspaper down, sank onto the windowsill next to her, and laid my head against her shoulder. "I'm sorry, Adelaide, I didn't know," I whispered. "Sherlock

Holmes was just killed in Switzerland."

I felt her flinch beside me.

"He was—he was *what*? My goodness, Dora, how did you find out?"

"It was in the *Times*. I have the article here—if you want to read it."

"Oh, you can't be serious! I can't believe it," she gasped and reached out for the paper by my side. "How *could* this happen?"

"It doesn't say," I answered wearily. "The report is very vague. They say he drowned; that he was attacked by an old enemy at Reichenbach and was pushed into the waterfall."

She nodded and ran her fingers absently through my hair. "It is a tragedy, of course, but I wasn't speaking of Mr. Holmes. I meant, how could this happen to us? We've traveled up to London for no purpose. Oh, Lord, what will I do now?"

I didn't know what to say at first. I had not yet absorbed the shock of my discovery, and what I wanted most just then was comfort and sympathy, not more dilemmas. But Adelaide had already moved on to her own concerns, and honestly I couldn't blame her. Sherlock Holmes had been a potential solution to her problem, nothing more; and now that he was gone, she had to find another. I loved my cousin more than anyone, but at that moment she seemed so far away from me. It was not her fault; I knew that very well. I had chosen to keep my secret from her. She could not sympathize with my grief if she was not aware of it.

Still, if I had to mourn, I realized that I would have to do so on my own time. I had come to London with my cousin because she needed my support. I couldn't withdraw it at the moment when she needed me the most. And yet—how could I help her now? Would she be interested in speaking to someone else about her problem? I wondered. Was it worth telling her about my meeting with Peter Cartwright?

And—more importantly, was all of this really worth the trouble? Adelaide had never really explained to me why these letters were so crucial to her. In fact, she had only confided in me because I had accidentally stumbled into her room just after she'd received the blackmail threat. I'd been shocked to find her weeping on the floor—my cool and confident cousin was actually sobbing out her fears to me! It was the first time in our lives that I had been the calm one, the one offering support instead of the one receiving it.

But what if Adelaide's case wasn't really as dark as she imagined it? She'd only mentioned that the letters were old love notes that she'd written to her young music tutor some years ago. How incriminating could they be? Perhaps in the end she could reconsider consulting a detective and return home to Newheath.

"I don't understand why you're so worried about these letters, Adelaide," I told her finally. "Is it so important that you get them back?"

She paled a little and nodded grimly. "I can't tell you what was in the letters, Dora. I'm afraid you'd never trust me again."

I sat up and took her hand in mine. "You don't really think that, do you? I wouldn't love you any less, no matter what was in those letters. And surely your husband would forgive you if you were honest with him. It was so long ago, before you even met him."

Her jaw tightened, and she shut her eyes. "You don't understand. Richard sees me as a lovely innocent angel, pure as a child until our marriage. I believe he loves that image of me more than he loves me. He's so proud of me, Dora. It may sound ridiculous to you, but I can't bear to lose that."

"But that's absurd!" I cried. "You're telling me that he's proud of someone that he doesn't truly know."

I knew that I had gone too far even before the last word had left my mouth when I saw Adelaide's eyes harden over with hurt.

"Dora, I'm supposed to be an example, a model of virtue, don't you understand?" she cried. "Not just to him, but to everyone around me. Don't you know how hard it was for me to admit this shame even to you? Do you know how many times I've regretted telling you?"

I smiled. "Why? Because *I'm* the one always getting into scrapes? Really, Adelaide, you've spent most of your life defending me. At least let me show you now that I haven't forgotten that. Trust me just a little, and tell me why you're so terrified of a couple of ancient love letters."

"I *cannot*," she said miserably. "Just believe me when I tell you—Richard will leave me if he reads them. I'm certain that he will. Oh, Dora, you know how much I love my husband. And maybe one day you'll understand what I'm saying to you now. I hope that one day you will meet someone whom you will care for more than anyone. And you'll want him to honor and respect you—and to see only the best side of you. When that day comes you'll understand exactly why I'm so afraid right now."

I did not believe what she was saying. My cousin had always been a model lady—the one whom I was meant to imitate and admire. And I *had* tried to follow her example, as best I could. But did I want my own life to turn out like hers, to become some desperate and elaborate charade? I was already tired of pretending sweetness and innocence in front of Adelaide and my aunt. And yet now it seemed that I would be expected to pretend forever, even in front of my future husband. Just like my cousin was doing now—and just like my mother had done until she died.

"Adelaide, you know I'll stand by you just the same, even if I don't understand," I told her finally. "I only wish that you had more faith in me."

"I do have faith in you," she replied miserably. "If I didn't, do you think I would have confided in you? But I should never have dragged you into this sordid business in the first place. You should be practicing your dancing lessons and thinking about dinner parties and receptions, not blackmail threats."

"But that's exactly what I want to think about!" I blurted out. "You must know that about me."

I'd said the wrong thing again; I saw Adelaide's eyes cloud over and her figure tense.

"I'm glad to hear that my troubles are entertaining for you," she remarked coldly.

"Oh— No, that isn't what I meant—"

"No, I understand you now," she interrupted bitterly. "You've been waiting for a chance to show off your little hobby, haven't you? All those months collecting bits of cigar ash, analyzing footprints, and tracking homeless kittens through the snow 'for practice'? Tell me honestly, Dora, was my problem just another exercise for you?"

I would have reassured her, for I could feel that she wasn't truly angry at me, that she was simply frightened and vulnerable. But somehow I couldn't find the words just then; I was suddenly exhausted. I wanted the comfort of my pillow, the darkness of the sheets over my head. And I didn't want to listen to this speech about my "hobby" anymore. I had heard it so many times before. My odd behavior, my hopes, my studies, they were all so *strange*, so alien to everyone I loved. And they all agreed that I ought to change: my aunt, my pastor, even my dearest cousin, everyone except—

Except—

"I met a boy outside," I told her quietly. "He handed me this card and invited you to call. Do as you please, Adelaide. I am going back to bed."

I opened up my purse, threw the card onto the table, and left the room, shutting the door behind me.

CHAPTER 4

ora."

I think I answered her, but my voice was muffled by my comforter, and all she heard was "Burrrrrrr?"

"Dora, I am very sorry for what I said."

"Burr."

"Dora, please come out. I've written to this Porter fellow, and he has agreed to meet us—meet me. But—you will come with me tomorrow when I go? I'm sorry if I hurt you.

I didn't mean to talk to you like that. Please, Dora, I cannot bear to go through this alone."

I thought of Peter Cartwright's impish grin, his piercing eyes, and heard again the swell of his sudden laughter. He had gotten the best of me in our first meeting. But I had not really been myself that morning. Surely I deserved another chance? I could not leave him laughing at me, could I? Even in the safety of my room the memory of his mocking challenge made me flush, and my throat went tight with anticipation. *Forgive me, Dora, and come back.* Quickly I pushed the memory of his words away and roughly shoved my pillow to the side.

"All right, Adelaide, I will come along," I answered in an even voice. "If it means that much to you."

We set out for the investigator's rooms the following morning. The flat was only a few blocks from Hanover Street at the northern corner of Portman Square. A little bronze plaque with the man's name and profession was the only detail that distinguished it from the row of identical brick houses with their whitewashed doorways and iron railings. A pretty maid ushered us into the hallway and into an empty sitting room. "Mr. Porter and Mr. Cartwright will be in shortly. They like to enter after their guests are seated," she told us with a patient smile and then departed. Adelaide and I seated ourselves on a sofa by the window and stared at the unusual sitting room.

There is no simple way to describe Mr. Porter's home, for it was a study of opposites rather than a simple living quarter. The left side from the large bay window to the door was decorated in a baroque and ornate style; from the cherub paintings to the vase of roses on the baby grand piano, the little London flat seemed to mimic the grandeur of a country mansion. The bookcases boasted a library of leather-bound volumes arranged alphabetically in perfect rows; the letters on the writing desk were stacked in self-conscious little piles of precisely ten envelopes per group; and every item from the folded newspapers to the iron coal tongs had been placed exactly in their correct spot in accordance with geometric harmony. But for a half-empty bottle of claret, it appeared that the area had been designed for display only and had never been soiled by human fingers. That describes the left side.

The right side appeared to have declared war against the left. I could have traced just where the division of the room began, for a pile of debris seemed to grow from this imaginary line in a majestic mountain. Torn trouser legs, bits of journals, stacks of shoes and papers lay strewn about the floor as if half a hurricane had struck the flat. A little faded armchair sat like a battered throne amid the wreckage, with a halo of tidy carpet as the only sign of order in that area.

"It's a little like a scene from a Lewis Carroll story, isn't it?" my cousin whispered to me. "I wonder which side belongs to whom."

I had opened my mouth to answer her (for I was fairly certain that it was Cartwright who ruled the clutter) when the two bedroom doors swung open, and the gentlemen entered. Mr. Porter strode slowly into the tidy section and bowed gravely to my cousin. Mr. Cartwright stumbled over an overflowing rubbish bin and collapsed awkwardly into his armchair.

"Lady Forrester, Miss Joyce. A pleasure."

"Good afternoon, Mr. Porter. I want to thank you for seeing us on such short notice."

"All my clients come to me on such 'short notice,' madam. It is the nature of my work. I understand from your note that your case is a very sensitive one, and that you have come to London to resolve it *without* your husband's knowledge." There was a shade of sourness in the agent's rumbling baritone, and I saw my cousin flinch beneath his gaze. "Pray begin by telling me what happened, Lady Forrester."

Adelaide cleared her throat and glanced from Porter's impassive face to his young assistant's. Cartwright was sitting forward in his chair, elbows resting on his knees, a tense, alert expression in eyes. He smiled at her and nodded, and I saw her form relax and the fingers in her lap unclench.

She exhaled slowly and began her story. As she recounted her history with her music tutor, their romantic letters, and her recent blackmail threat, I studied the two investigators quietly. It was interesting how their surroundings complemented each of them. Mr. Neville Porter was solid, dark, and dignified, with a drooping mustache, modest whiskers, and the traditional flared nostrils of a nobleman. Everything about the man was crisp and proper, from the ironed creases of his trousers to the small Masonic tiepin beneath his collar. He seemed to be quite at home amid his little luxuries, and I found it difficult to picture him dashing to a manhunt or sniffing out a murder trail.

Peter Cartwright, on the other hand, seemed very comfortable in his cheerful squalor, as if he had planned the placement of every bit of rubbish. There was a broken sword hilt wedged between the cushions of his chair, but he seemed entirely oblivious to it, even though the edge was making a jagged indentation in his thigh. During my cousin's speech he did not break his attention once, but kept his gaze fixed upon her as if his life depended on his concentration. Though our eyes had met briefly when he had first come in, there had been no flash of anything within their depths, no mirth or mocking, not even a flicker of recognition. I was careful not to watch him, because I was certain that he would notice; but it was soon obvious that it did not matter where I looked, as he seemed so intent on ignoring me. So throughout the interview, we pretended not to see each other.

When Adelaide had finished, Mr. Porter looked languidly at his assistant and waved his hand. "Go ahead."

Cartwright gave a quick nod and shifted forward in his chair. "Lady Forrester, I presume you brought the blackmail letter with you."

My cousin shook her head and dropped her eyes. "No, I'm sorry, I do not have it anymore. I was quite upset, you see, and I'm afraid I threw it in the fire."

The two men exchanged looks, and Mr. Porter let out an irritated sigh. Cartwright threw me an exasperated frown.

"That wasn't wise," he muttered under his breath.

"If it helps—I remember what the writing looked like," I ventured after an embarrassed silence. "I could describe it to you."

But Cartwright had already turned back to Adelaide. "The blackmailer had signed his letter with the initials 'J.F.' Is that correct?"

"Yes."

"No address, I presume?"

"Just a London postmark."

"And the man to whom you wrote the letters? Your music tutor?"

"He died a few months ago. But before we parted for the last time, he promised me that he'd burn my letters. It turns out that he didn't keep his promise. But, then, neither did I."

"And this J.F. has both sets of letters?"

"So it seems."

"And how are you to pay the fellow?"

"He indicated that he would contact me by the thirtieth of the month and name the place of the exchange. He suggested that I use the time to raise the money. I don't have anywhere near the sum which he is asking. What do you think I ought to do?"

Porter shook his head and shrugged. "I'm afraid, madam, that I recommend you do just what he said. If you are absolutely certain that this man really has your letters—"

"He quoted a passage from one of them in the middle of his note. He has them, I am sure of it."

"Then, unfortunately, the next move is his. You say that your servant, the one who stole the letters from you—what was his name?"

"Thomas Dyer."

"That Thomas Dyer has already left your employ. We might have tried to trace the blackmailer through him, but even if we found him, we would still be no closer to your letters. Our only hope would be to discover something actionable, something criminal about this man 'J.F.' to use against him, for if we try to arrest him for his current crime, he will carry out his threat and mail the letters to your husband. When the time comes, we can attempt to negotiate with him and bring the price down, but short of that, there is not much that we can do now."

Adelaide sank against the cushions and closed her eyes. "I know you're right; that is what I expected you would say."

"And what did you expect, Miss Joyce?" Mr. Porter asked, turning suddenly to me.

"I—had no expectations, sir," I responded. "I came to accompany my cousin."

"Indeed," growled the agent. "How irregular. This is quite a sordid business for one so young."

"Dora is not easily shocked or overwhelmed, Mr. Porter," Adelaide countered icily. "She has been my support through this sad affair."

Porter shrugged and rose abruptly from his chair. "Cartwright, you may look into this matter as you please. There is not much for me to do here."

I half-rose to face him, and, ignoring Adelaide's heavy hand upon my shoulder, cried out, "But, sir, you have dismissed us without even trying! What of Hunt's, the servants agency that recommended Thomas Dyer to my cousin? Should you not inquire at Hunt's registry and see if he has put his name back on the lists? If the blackmailer and the servant have worked together in the past, then perhaps we can use that knowledge."

I might have stopped there if Porter had given me the briefest nod or murmur of acknowledgment, but he had picked up a newspaper and had started thumbing through the pages without looking in my direction. "Lady Forrester, your cousin is quite an excitable little thing," he rumbled. "It is none of my concern, of course, but I have always felt that young girls cannot be too careful about their surroundings. They are so innocent, you see, and their innocence makes them both blind and vulnerable. Perhaps she would have been better off at home."

I had not expected that. It was true that I had not liked this so-called "detective" from the first; he was not the man I had hoped to meet. Still I had been prepared to sit quietly and judge him as favorably as he deserved. After all, it was not his fault that he was not Sherlock Holmes, and he was not responsible for my disappointment. But there was no reason to be silent now. My blood had been slowly rising to my face throughout the agent's speech, but it was his final words that brought me to my feet. I was vaguely conscious of Adelaide's restraining hand and the chagrined flush on

Cartwright's cheeks, and then my world went red. All of my cousin's gentle training, all of my aunt's good manners slipped from me like a threadbare cloak, and I let my outrage and hurt spill over.

"I may be small, Mr. Porter, but I can see as far as you, and even farther," I retorted. "A girl is better off nurturing her blindness, that is your position, is it? But then, sir, I could not give you the benefit of the doubt. I would be forced to think that this poor temper is your natural state and not due to the fact that you have not had a drink for near two days. Oh, don't worry, the tremor in your hand is very fine, and you hide it rather well. An *innocent* girl would never notice it."

"Dora!"

I really should have ended there. But I had discovered more about him, and he was staring at me now with such a look of baffled rage that I could not stop myself. "You were critical of my cousin from the first!" I continued furiously. "Why did you judge her like that and turn away? She never injured you. And yet the story of her old romance obviously upset you so much that you could not speak to her impartially. I wonder why? Could it have something to do with the fresh imprint of the missing wedding band upon your finger? You took the ring off less than a year ago, judging by the fair strip of skin above your knuckle. And yet, sadly, you aren't wearing mourning. I am very sorry for you, sir, and because I am not blind, or innocent, I will conclude that you are a good man who is very angry at some other lady who has badly wronged you."

I had never experienced a silence like the one that followed that declaration. I had a vision of Adelaide's white face, and two dusky, throbbing veins across the agent's temples. Peter Cartwright appeared to be strangling on something; he kept swallowing and turning his head away as if he were choking on a laugh. I sank heavily into my seat and waited for the storm to hit. No one said anything for a moment; no one dared even to breathe. Then Mr. Porter calmly folded up his newspaper, readjusted his cravat, and turned gravely to his apprentice. "This morning you asked me for a case, young man, and now you have one. I wish you the best of luck. Lady Forrester, Miss Joyce, good day."

He bowed crisply to us, smiled frigidly at me, and left the room.

After he had gone, Adelaide moaned softly and pulled me to my feet. "I am so sorry, Mr. Cartwright. I should not have brought her with me."

"Not at all, madam. I am delighted to be of service—to you both. Mr. Porter is still involved, you understand, but he is allowing me to manage the details—under his supervision,

naturally. I hope that will be agreeable to you." There was a
glint of satisfaction in the young man's eyes, but his face was
drawn and sober.

"Mr. Cartwright—" I began timidly, and stopped, for
Adelaide had just savagely pinched my arm.

"Not another word, Dora, do you understand?" she hissed
at me.

"It's all right, Lady Forrester, technically she did follow
my instructions. I asked her not to mention Mr. Sherlock
Holmes in Mr. Porter's presence, and she didn't. Unfortunately, she chose to mention *everything else*. Next time I will
try to be more precise in my directions."

"There will be no next time, sir. I am sending her home
tomorrow."

"Adelaide!"

"Hush, Dora. Mr. Cartwright, I will stay in London
until I hear from you. You have my address in town. Good
afternoon."

A grip of iron closed around my elbow, and I felt myself
being propelled steadily toward the door. There was no
point in protesting anymore; I had been wrong, and there
was nothing I could say that would change her mind, in
any case. But I could not leave like this; I had to say good-
bye properly and squeeze at least one pleasant memory from
my sorry trip to London. I did not want to be remembered

as the girl who had stupidly lost her temper and been sent home in complete disgrace. There was one last thing I had to do.

So I left my purse behind.

As my cousin started down the stairs, I glanced back and saw that Cartwright was standing by the sofa and staring at my little handbag with a perplexed look upon his face. He seemed about to call to me, but then his eyes met mine and he smiled broadly. I gave an innocent little shrug, put a finger to my lips, and shut the door behind me.

CHAPTER

5

ADELAIDE HAD A LOT to say to me when we got home. It was all true, really, and I knew it. I was honestly sorry for my outburst and ashamed that the two men had seen me at my worst. "Curious and quick-witted" was what I had hoped to be; I had never wished to earn the title of a "sixteen-year-old shrew," as Adelaide now referred to me. I tried to apologize and show her that I regretted my behavior, but my repentance did not change a thing. I was to go back to Newheath the moment she found a chaperone to escort me there. In the meantime, I was to spend my free hours repenting my many failings.

When she finally left my room, I paced about and considered the best means of escape. I could have asked to call on a fictitious friend, or requested a shopping or a library trip, but Adelaide would certainly have insisted on accompanying me. At my "tender" age, even a brief stroll across the street was considered improper, and a visit to an unmarried gentleman's quarters (even to retrieve a missing handbag) was quite unthinkable. Disobeying my cousin was wrong, of course, but I would be returning to the country the following morning, and I would have the remainder of a dreary lifetime to atone for my behavior. So I waited until Adelaide went out to pay a call, and several minutes later I quietly scurried out the servants' entrance.

"Hunt's registry office," I told the cabbie, and moments later I was off on my own private investigation. It would likely end in nothing and I knew it, for the task was difficult enough without the added handicap of my gender. I had no freedom to explore my findings, and even if I discovered something, I would be forced to hand the details over to our male protectors. But I could begin, at least; I could begin what I could not finish. And I might see Peter Cartwright one last time and show him that angering adults was not my only talent.

The servants agency was located in the heart of Marylebone with two adjoining offices functioning as the

male and female branches of the organization. A solemn old
gentleman presided over the men's department, and three
middle-aged ladies acted as the agent's scribes. On the desk
in front of them lay several oversized ledgers that contained the names and references of prospective servants and
employers. I approached the lady in the center and stated
my cousin's name and town address.

"I was wondering if you could help me," I began sweetly.
"You see, our footman, Thomas Dyer, recently left our service rather unexpectedly, and we never had a chance to settle
our accounts. He is still owed his quarter's wages, and I was
hoping that you had his information in your records. He
was referred to us through your agency while we were in
London, and I thought perhaps he might have put his name
back on your lists. It would have been less than a fortnight
ago. I hoped you might remember him. He was a very tall
gentleman, freckled skin, bright red hair."

The woman shrugged and began to leaf through her giant
notebook. "Dyer," she murmured. "We have a Drewer here,
and a Dyner, but I do not see a Thomas Dyer. I'm very sorry."

And so ended my brilliant spree as a detective.

I sighed, and began to walk away.

"One moment, miss!" cried her assistant. "Did he speak
with a little lisp?"

I turned about to face her. "Why, yes, he did!"

"Oh, I remember him! He was in here just over a week ago. But I never wrote his name down because he wasn't looking for a place at all. Don't you remember, Annie?" Her companion shook her head wearily and shut her book. "Well, it was a bit unusual, so maybe that's why I remember. We don't usually have people in here searching for old friends," the girl continued. "But that's what he was after. He was looking for another servant who had registered with us."

"Do you remember the servant's name?"

"Oh, I forget—it started with an 'F.' Just a moment, please—" She turned the pages to the spot and read the entry out. "There, you see, I marked it. James Farringdon. Took a place as a valet at Hartfield Hall, six months ago."

The other lady nodded. "Now *him* I remember very well. Handsome as the devil, and proud of it, too. He was a strange one, certainly."

"Why was that?"

"James? Well, we simply could not work with him. He turned down several of our suggestions because they were not noble enough for him and then finally came in here to let us know that he had found the perfect place. And yet a week earlier, he had been offered a better spot, as first footman in a viscount's home, and he had refused it. There's no accounting for the whims of these 'aristocratic' fellows."

Now, *this* was information I could use. Thomas had been looking for this Farringdon after he'd discovered Adelaide's letters. This noble valet had to have been his buyer.

James Farringdon, I repeated to myself.

J.F.

I thanked the secretary and left the office smiling to myself. I had learned the identity and the address of my cousin's blackmailer in twenty minutes. That was as much as anyone could do in London, and I could not help feeling just a little proud. It was now time to retrieve my purse from Cartwright's study.

When I arrived at Portman Square, the maid appeared surprised to see me. "Master and young master are not in just now, miss. Would you like to leave your card?"

"Oh, I only need a minute. I accidentally left my purse here earlier. Is it all right if I go upstairs and fetch it? I can let myself out."

She motioned me upstairs with a little shrug. "Certainly, if you like."

I climbed the stairs and shut the door behind me. I was very sorry that Cartwright was not at home, for I had wanted to relate my findings to him personally. Now it seemed that I would have to tell him about my trip in writing and then go away without another word. I had hoped to see once more his startled smile, the flush of laughter on his face, even the flame of emerald mockery in his eyes. Somehow I did not want to leave the city without that memory. And yet, this was to be my final visit.

My purse was sitting by the sofa where I had left it. I picked it up, walked over to the desk, and began to write my note. As I scribbled my message down, a sheet of paper slid from off a pile, and a folded slip of stationery on the table fluttered open. My fingers froze around my pen. I had not meant to look at the private letter, but the signature at the bottom had jumped off the page at me.

It was impossible.

I could not understand it.

There upon the monogrammed paper, in precise and stately script, the following words were written:

May 8, 1891

Mr. Porter,

I would like to call on you this afternoon at three in order to consult you about a disturbing event which has recently occurred at my estate at Hartfield. I trust that I may rely upon your secrecy and discretion. Please confirm the appointment at the Carlton Club, if this time is agreeable to you.

Charles Frederick Dowling, 4th Earl of Hartfield

There was no earthly way that this note was a coincidence. I had just learned that my cousin's blackmailer was serving at the earl's country home, and now some "disturbing event" had upset this nobleman so much that he had traveled up to London to consult a detective. The two events were connected, they *had* to be connected. But what had happened at the estate? Was the earl also being blackmailed? And, more importantly, how would I find out?

As if on cue, there was a distant rumble outside the door, the shuffling thud of feet upon the stair; and then I heard the muffled sound of Mr. Porter's voice. "I want to assure Your Lordship that I have found Mr. Cartwright's collaboration to be invaluable, especially in cases that require the most discretion."

His last words had barely registered before I had decided on the second bedroom as a hiding place, and hurried to it. His Lordship was not going to find me gawking at him when he entered, that was certain. I could at least spare Mr. Cartwright that uncomfortable explanation.

As the men entered, I shut the bedroom door and crouched by the keyhole to peer into the study. Mr. Porter was standing aside to usher in their client, and I could see at once why his lips were set in such an awed and guarded smile. Anyone would have recognized their visitor; Charles Frederick Dowling, the 4th Earl of Hartfield, was a true celebrity, a man famous in the political world as a prominent Conservative and member of the Privy Council, and in society for his lavish parties and his yearly regatta ball. My cousin's blackmailer had attached himself to one of the wealthiest landowners in England.

He was a giant man, almost as wide as he was tall, with broad shoulders that spanned the doorway. Everything about the earl declared his power and his wealth, from the fur-trimmed mantle that brushed against his thick blond beard to the onyx studs that gleamed in the cuffs of his perfectly tailored suit. Mr. Porter offered the nobleman a drink as Cartwright took his cloak, and the two older men sauntered over to the sideboard.

Peter Cartwright was walking toward the sofa when I saw him freeze and stare pointedly at the writing desk. In my haste, I had left my half-finished note on his table when I fled and tossed the inky pen beside my purse. With grim determination he strode over to it, picked up the handbag, and turned slowly toward his bedroom door. He was glaring at the keyhole now, his eyes narrowed, furious, as if he meant to burn a passage through the wood and expose me to the world. I held my breath, waiting for him to call me out, dreading the moment when I would have to creep into the light and explain myself. Already I could hear my cousin's outraged wail: "You found her *where*—?!" and the thump

of my aunt collapsing to the floor in shock. I was certain it
was over, and I had moved to rise when suddenly I heard
him murmur, so softly that only I could hear, "Well, there
goes my reputation—" A resounding thud cut off the ending as he tossed my handbag with vicious strength against
the keyhole.

Then he turned sharply on his heel and walked over to the
window as the nobleman and the investigator were settling
into their armchairs with their drinks. It seemed that I was
safe for now. Afterward I would have to make Cartwright
understand that I was actually *protecting* his reputation. If
I came out now, he would have to explain why there was
a sixteen-year-old girl hiding in his bedroom. So, until the
interview was over, I had no choice but to crouch by the
keyhole and listen to the earl's case.

I admit that it wasn't absolutely necessary to eavesdrop. I
could have stopped my ears. But Adelaide's blackmailer was
living now on the earl's estate, and I was, so far, the only one
who knew that. It was obviously my duty to listen in.

"I can hardly stress the importance of absolute secrecy
in this matter, Mr. Porter," the earl was saying. "Even my
presence here is a compromise. My wife and son were of
the opinion that I should wait, but I could not rest until
I had some explanation. Going to the police would have,
of course, led to the very scandal that we wished to avert,

so after some debate, Lady Hartfield and I agreed that you should be brought in."

Cartwright had come to stand opposite the earl's chair, and he shook his head as he dropped into his seat.

"You are convinced, then, that your daughter is beyond saving?" he inquired.

The nobleman gave him a startled look.

"How could you—?" he began.

"When Your Lordship removed your cloak earlier, I caught a glimpse of a cabinet-sized portrait that was tucked into the inner pocket. The young lady in the photograph bears a striking resemblance to Lady Hartfield. Even the fondest father does not regularly carry a portrait of that size about with him. It would have been unnecessary to bring a picture if we were shortly to meet the young lady herself, so you must be here to consult us about her disappearance. The discovery must have been embarrassing for your family, and so you have concealed her flight from everyone."

Mr. Porter inclined his head slightly and gave a little sniff of satisfaction. "*My protégé*, Your Lordship, *as* you can see." I had a sudden urge to throw something at his puckered face.

The earl relaxed his posture and smiled. "Well, he certainly is a credit to you. And it is true that I've come to consult you about my daughter."

"Your Lordship, perhaps you could tell us a little about

your family," Mr. Porter suggested. "And then continue on to your recent problem."

The earl nodded and settled deeper into his chair. "I have two children, Mr. Porter," he began. "The eldest, Alfred, or Lord Victor, is the only child from my first marriage to Lady Gwendolyn Lennox. Lord Victor's mother died when he was quite young and he has few memories of her, and so he regards the current Lady Hartfield as his mother. Lady Rose is my daughter by my second marriage. She has lived most of her eighteen years at Hartfield, my country estate, with the exception of the Season months, which we frequently spend in the city. Several days ago I traveled alone to town to attend to a business matter, leaving my wife, son, and daughter at Hartfield Hall. It was during my absence that Lady Rose disappeared. Two nights ago, late Wednesday night, she vanished from her bedroom. Her bed had been slept in, and a large satchel, several articles of clothing, and her best jewels were missing from her bureau. There was no sign of a struggle, and nothing else in the house was missing. My wife and I believe that she fled from the house in the early hours of the morning before the servants were awake.

"When Lady Rose did not appear for breakfast on Thursday morning, her brother suggested they go look in on her. They found the door locked, and there was no

answer from within. Lady Hartfield has a duplicate set
of keys, which she retrieved, and when she entered, she
found Rose gone. The window was open, and our daughter's keys lay upon her writing desk. My wife telegraphed
to me at once, I rushed back home, and we searched the
room together. When we discovered the missing clothing
and jewels, we immediately recognized the horrible scandal
that would ensue if her flight became known. After some
discussion, we agreed to consult you privately, while circu-
lating the story at home that the young mistress had gone
to stay with her aunt in Brighton. My son, as you may have
read in the papers, is shortly to be married to the daughter
of the Duke of Wellsborough. Her family is of the strictest
and most religious standards. Any shadow of impropriety in
our household would serve to break off the match."

Mr. Porter nodded briefly and cleared his throat. "Was
your wife the only one with a key to Lady Rose's room?" he
inquired.

"No, I myself have a master key that fits all the locks in
the house. No one else has access to it, as it sits on my bedroom dresser with my other keys and does not leave my side
while I am awake. Rose does not normally keep her door
locked, but that night she chose to fasten it, and then left
her keys on the table behind her."

"How did she leave the room, then?"

"There is a tall tree outside her window. As a child, she used to climb down to the garden every morning until her mother finally ordered the branches trimmed. They have since grown to their original height and are easy to scale."

"How would you describe Lady Rose's character?"

Lord Hartfield shifted uneasily in his chair. "I think most men would claim to have trouble understanding their daughters. Young girls seem to act on whims and moods that are a complete mystery to their parents. And yet I would say that my daughter has never been as excitable as the majority of her acquaintances, nor as capricious or spoiled. She was always a devoted child and a loving one, if a little quiet and awkward. This Season was her coming out, and even I must admit that so far it has been a complete disaster. She hung about in the shadows during the dancing, answered company in monosyllables, and was finally declared by the family physician to be suffering from an 'attack of nerves' and so unable to participate in the remainder of the social season. My wife was quite unhappy over it."

I couldn't help feeling sorry for the missing Lady Rose. Perhaps the strain of disappointing her family over and again had proved too much for her. I could not blame her for running away, and I wondered if I, too, might one day wish to disappear in the middle of my "coming out." It had certainly crossed my mind during many a dinner party. Still, for a well-bred noblewoman to vanish so suddenly without a warning—? But Cartwright was already asking the question on my mind.

"Your Lordship, can you recall any recent unusual events or any change in her behavior?"

"No, I cannot. My son, however, informed me that during my absence he saw her speaking to a tall young man in the garden by the solarium. They were at some distance from him and he was unable to see the man's face, but the fellow's dress was that of a gentleman, though not of her station. It was the first time she has done anything of the sort, and the fact that it occurred the morning before her disappearance seems significant to me. I am truly shocked that she would behave in this fashion and at such a crucial time, just weeks before her brother's marriage. To bring this shame upon us now . . . I have been struggling to understand it, and I cannot."

"Do you have any idea who the gentleman might be?"

"I do not. Indeed I was surprised by my son's report."

"Was Lady Rose opposed to her brother's marriage?"

"Not to my knowledge. She barely mentioned it at all."

"Can you tell me what was missing from her room?"

"Several dresses, a pair of shoes, some articles of jewelry, and a large suitcase, one of a pair. The personal belongings that one packs for a journey. And yet she left behind one item that surprised me."

"What was that?"

"For her sixteenth birthday, I gave my daughter a small crucifix necklace encrusted with diamonds. She loved the gift and swore to keep it with her always. I remember laughing at her enthusiasm but, true to her word, she never left her room without it; when it did not suit her gown she would tuck it into the bodice of her dress and wear it as a sort of talisman. And yet, the morning of her flight, she left it untouched in the drawer. I cannot believe she would have left it behind voluntarily."

"You believe she may have been abducted, then?"

"It is the only explanation other than a deliberate deception."

Cartwright shook his head and frowned. "The kidnapper would have had to scale the tree outside her window, have woken her, have waited patiently while she packed some clothing, and then forced her to climb down the tree carrying a large satchel. A descent down the staircase and out the front door with a struggling or unconscious girl would have been risky, even at night. Besides, the bedroom door was locked from the inside, and her keys still lay upon her desk."

"I confess I cannot think of an explanation."

"You have received no ransom note?"

"No, thank heaven."

"Have you questioned the servants? Did anyone observe anything unusual?"

"To question the servants would have been to admit that something was amiss, and was therefore impossible."

"Has the room, at least, been left untouched?"

"Again, how could we ask her parlor maid to neglect her mistress's quarters without arousing suspicion?"

Cartwright leaned further forward in his chair, and I saw that his pale face was flushed and he was vibrating with a suppressed energy. "So now Your Lordship wishes us to investigate your daughter's disappearance from her bedroom *after* the maid has destroyed any trace of that evening with her duster. If you were concerned about a possible abduction, why did you wait two days before coming to consult us?"

The nobleman flushed and looked helplessly at the older agent. "We thought only of the scandal at first, Mr. Porter, and we prayed that she would return home before any damage was done. It was my recent discovery of the crucifix that prompted our decision to consult you and risk this exposure. We are now quite prepared to assist you in any way that would not compromise our privacy."

Mr. Porter seemed to consider a moment before replying, "Frankly, Your Lordship, I wonder if you are attaching too much significance to a piece of jewelry. A woman in the throes of a romance often forgets even her most sacred duties—so I admit that this abandonment of the necklace does not surprise me. Still, I must examine her room before making a final decision on the matter. I would be willing to go down to Hartfield under some other guise in order to avoid gossip, if you like. You may inform your housekeeper that you are expecting workmen this evening. That will explain our visit."

With a satisfied nod, the nobleman rose to go.

"One more thing," remarked Cartwright as Lord Hartfield gathered his cloak and hat. "It would be helpful if you could send us the names of your household staff, along with their dates of hire, agency, or references. And also, please leave your daughter's portrait behind."

There was a grim silence after the earl had left, and I was certain that my moment had finally come. There was no longer any reason to keep my presence there a secret, and I felt sure that Cartwright would immediately throw open the bedroom door and drag me out into my shame. I waited miserably for the summons, my head pressed against the wooden doorpost. When nothing came, I sank back onto my heels and exhaled slowly. It seemed that I would be a happy prisoner for a little longer. Outside the door, Mr. Porter and his apprentice had resumed their conversation.

"Well, Cartwright, you seem to be lost in thought. What do you make of it?"

"The man seems less anxious about his daughter's welfare than about the wedding preparations."

"That is not fair. Consider his position, his reputation, the concerns of his wife and son. Surely you do not believe that he would be indifferent if his daughter were in any real danger?"

Cartwright rose to his feet and paced in front of his mentor. "And yet, if the daughter left of her own will, I wonder she did not leave a letter for her father. They seemed to have had a decent enough relationship."

"Ah, but that means nothing to a lady who fancies herself in love. Girls of that age will often act in a perverse and capricious manner and may even shock the men who trust them."

Cartwright glanced at my keyhole again, smiled briefly, and resumed his pacing. "Well, you may be right. Nevertheless, it is our duty to find her, even if she does not wish it."

Mr. Porter folded his arms. "I am not likely to shrug off an earl's request, my boy. We will go down this evening as I promised, and then we can put this case to rest . . . or not. In the meantime, I have several other matters to attend to. Be sure to meet me at Paddington at six—and do not forget to bring the two disguises."

"Yes, sir."

There was a scraping sound of shoes upon the carpet and the creak and slam of the front door. No sooner had the agent gone than the bedroom door upon which I was leaning swung open, and I tumbled into the room at Cartwright's

feet. I scrambled upright, brushed off my skirt, and stood in
serious attention before him, as if I had been summoned on
a secret mission and was now prepared to trot out my report.
He was staring at me with a look of teasing disbelief, like a
comedian who has just been handed several tricks at once
and is trying to decide which one to use. Finally he leaned
against the wall and jerked his chin in the direction of his
room.

"So, Miss Joyce, you've had half an hour to poke around
my bedroom. What *scandalous* things have you found out
about me? Or must I wait until we are in a more public place
for you to announce my story to the world?"

I was tired of blushing before this boy, of feeling silly,
small, and female. So I threw my head back as if our conversation was quite natural and gave him a triumphant smile.
"I am sorry to disappoint you, Mr. Cartwright, but I have
no interest in finding anything out about you. I do, however,
have something to say about the Hartfield case, if you care
to listen."

There was a brief struggle in his eyes; the desire to pro-
long the joke was strong but curiosity won out in the end,
and he crossed his arms. "Well, what is it, then?"

"I thought it strange that Lady Hartfield and her stepson
went up together to the girl's bedroom when Lady Rose
didn't come down to breakfast."

He opened his mouth to answer, and then paused as the idea dawned on him. "And why is that?"

"I would expect that they would have first appealed to one of the servants to inquire after their mistress."

He nodded briskly. "And what does that suggest to you?"

I had not thought that far ahead, so I chose a safe reply. "I cannot theorize without talking to them first. I'd like to speak to their servants, too, I think."

He sauntered away from me and collapsed wearily into his armchair. "You would like to interview them, would you? What on earth has this to do with you?"

I moved quickly to stand before him and leaned over him with solemn gravity. (At my height, I did not get the opportunity to tower over people very often.) "It has everything to do with me, Mr. Cartwright. It might interest you to know that Mr. James Farringdon, the blackmailer who has my cousin's letters, has recently taken a post at Hartfield Hall. Or perhaps you already knew that."

I had been waiting patiently for that look, the staring eyes, the trapdoor mouth, the blankness of surprise. That look was what I lived for, honestly.

He inhaled sharply and sat up in his chair so suddenly that I had to jump back to avoid being knocked over by his head. "It *cannot* be a coincidence," he murmured to himself.

"Of course it can't. That is why we need to speak to

servants, butlers, ladies' maids, anyone who knows him."

He shook his head and threw his hands out. "And yet we—*I* cannot interview them. Their servants are under the impression that Lady Rose is enjoying a visit with her aunt in Brighton, and we cannot truly question them without exciting their suspicions."

"*And* the savvy Mr. Porter has all but dismissed the case. Before it has even started."

His eyes flickered ominously. "So?"

"Well, his conclusions must be your conclusions; he is your master, after all."

"Oh, so naturally I must obey my master," he snapped. The mocking grin had left his lips, and there was a cool tension about him now, like the wariness of a fencer. Something told me that I was about to tread on dangerous ground, that he would resent any further comments. But the clues were literally lying at my feet, impossible to ignore. The boy's shameless clutter, his forthright manner, the *equality* between the apprentice and his master were entirely unnatural. There was no way he could deny it.

"Mr. Cartwright, you do not respect Mr. Porter as a teacher or even as a colleague," I declared. "Why on earth did you choose to work for him?"

His jaw set and his brows came down; there was an angry glitter beneath the white surface of his smile. "And why,

Miss Joyce, are you still mourning Sherlock Holmes's death?" he demanded suddenly.

"I am not—"

"Oh, stop, I beg of you. I know that you are lying, I can see the sadness in your eyes."

I could not answer him. There was no way that I could speak about my history or my loss; he would simply have to bear the mystery. "We were talking about *you*, sir."

"No, Miss Joyce. We were talking about subjects that are not to be discussed. You have yours, clearly, and I have mine. Let that be enough."

"I cannot mention Mr. Porter in your presence?"

"We do not talk about my post, how I came by it or why. As far as you're concerned, I was born the day I moved here, I have always been a detective's assistant, and I have no other aspirations."

If I had not already been interested in his past, those instructions would undoubtedly have sparked my curiosity, for his apprenticeship and manner were not the only remarkable thing about him. I glanced at his collar, remembering the cross-shaped scar that I had seen when we first met. Its shape and depth was that of a deliberate injury, and yet the location of the cut was quite unusual. Self-inflicted gashes are usually closer to an artery or a vein, to ensure maximum blood loss, while neck wounds from an attacker are typically located near the jawline, a straight slash beneath the chin made while seizing the victim's head. This one was different; it was its own story, a crimson brand, his tiny, livid secret.

He saw my puzzled look and followed the direction of my eyes. His cheeks flushed scarlet, one hand traveled halfway to his collar as if by instinct. I quickly turned my head and focused on the window, but he had already risen and walked away from me. "Good day, Miss Joyce," he told me shortly. "I trust your cousin will forgive you for this last infraction."

I grabbed my purse and joined him by the door. "I slipped away when she was out."

"Well, then you'd best be going now, before she realizes that you're missing. Otherwise you won't be able to come back tomorrow."

"Tomorrow! But—"

"At half past two. Mr. Porter will be out."

"But—I—"

"Oh, and if, by chance, I haven't yet returned," he added with a little smile, "please try to wait for me in the study, on the sofa, like a normal girl. Not beneath my bed, or inside the chimney, or hanging like a kitten from the curtains. *Please.*"

CHAPTER

6

ADELAIDE WAS NOT at home when I returned, and so I was able to greet her innocently at dinner. Cook had let me in the servants' entrance and had stared pointedly at my muddy boots before nodding me upstairs. Though she knew that my three-hour absence and my dirty boots were not the result of a "little stroll" across the street as I had claimed, I knew about the "extras" that the cook purchased every week, bits of candle, fat, and sugar that she later sold in secret by the tradesmen's door. Cook would never reveal my secrets out of fear that I would respond in kind.

Adelaide and I had a peaceful dinner with no further mention of my returning home, which I hoped meant that the subject would remain closed. Even so, I was no longer certain about my role in London or in this investigation. Cartwright and Porter would be taking over now; they were at Hartfield Hall already. Perhaps they would solve the case that very day, and I would hear about it in a letter, or through my cousin. Who was I that they should include me in their adventure? I was a child who made startling observations, who occasionally terrified her relatives and frequently flouted every decent rule. But most importantly, I was a *girl*.

And yet—he had asked me to come back. Perhaps that meant something after all.

I retired early that night, but I found that I could not sleep, for our final conversation played over and again in my imagination. Why had he asked me to come back—*again*? What exactly did he want of me? Did he wish to see me because I stimulated him, because I challenged him? I had always thought that young men hated that quality in a lady. I edged over to the dresser mirror and studied my reflection in the glass. Surely it had to be my mind that had charmed him, and nothing else. I was so slight and simple, after all, my cheeks so thin and pale. If I smiled just right, there was a sweet, coy glitter in my eyes, and if I held my breath, my figure rounded out a little—almost like a woman's, but not quite. And that hair, the wayward coiling curls, that mass of fog around my forehead—my hair did not improve the picture. I pulled the covers around my shoulders and sank back into my pillow. It *had* to be my mind, I decided finally. There could be no other explanation.

I ought to have been proud of the distinction, of being recognized for my intelligence. That was what I'd worked for all this time. I wanted to be proud, to fall easily asleep with this new confidence wrapped tight around me. But somehow, I could not manage it. It was not a fitting thought, perhaps, especially for the daughter of the great detective, but I couldn't help wishing that just once I could be seen as more than a useful brain.

The following morning, I was hovering by the fireplace like a nervous sentry, waiting desperately for my cousin to declare her schedule for the day. I was hoping she would announce a shopping trip, a stroll across the park, or perhaps another social call; I could refuse any of those plans, and they would take Adelaide from the house and leave me free. It was not until our lunch was finished and she had settled into her armchair by the fire with a book of poetry that I realized that my window for escape had completely vanished. I shrank miserably into the sofa and tried to read her thoughts. She could not possibly intend to sit there for the entire afternoon; it was her second day in London. The Season had already started, and there were shops to visit, people to meet in drawing rooms. What was she *doing*?

Already it was two o'clock, my appointment with Cartwright was drawing near, and still she had not moved. I watched her flip, flip, flip those pages, counted clock strokes, and gnawed the lace around my sleeve. She wasn't planning to go anywhere; that was obvious. This was my last chance to see Peter, and there was nothing I could do.

I did not hear Cook enter, I was too busy being furious. She shuffled for a bit and cleared her throat. Adelaide looked up at her, and Cook glanced slyly at me before she spoke. "Lady Forrester, I was wondering if you wanted soup this evening. Or will you be going out?"

"No, I had no plans today." My cousin shrugged. "You may put the soup up, if you like."

I suddenly hated soup. Poetry, too, and downy armchairs, and fires, and London. I glared my feelings at our servant. She winked quietly at me and then turned back to Adelaide.

"I've just heard of a new milliner's shop in Knightsbridge. Supposed to be the latest styles from Paris, better than Fineman's here on Oxford Street. Today is opening day, ma'am."

"That sounds rather interesting," Adelaide responded,

thumbing through her volume. "Perhaps I'll take a look. Knightsbridge is not so very far. Dora, what do you say?"

"Well, you ought to go, surely. Your riding hat is just a fright. But I have a little headache, so I think I'll stay in today."

My cousin shrugged and slid lazily off the chair. "I will be back for supper, then. Why don't you try Dr. Brown's elixir? It is just the thing for headaches. You will find it on my dresser."

"Certainly, Adelaide," I breathed and scurried off to fetch it.

My cousin took an age to dress, and it was nearly half past two when she was ready to leave the house. In the meantime, I had thrown a little jacket over my walking dress and had styled my own coiffure (a snaky bun with fifteen little pins to keep the curls down); but it did not matter that it sagged a bit, for when the door shut behind her, I knew that I was finally free.

As I flew through the servants' entrance, Cook grinned at me and waved me on my way. "Thank you," I called to her. "I won't forget this!" That woman could sell the entire kitchen for all I cared; I would never breathe a word.

I was at Cartwright's flat in little less than a quarter of an hour. A cab was hardly necessary: it was only several blocks away, and I ran the distance. I wish now that I had been less eager in my entry, for I practically barreled through his door. He was lounging on the sofa when I entered, his long legs stretched out before the fire, a tent of newspapers covering his eyes. As I came in, the sheets slid off; he pushed himself forward on his elbows and regarded my breathless, glowing face with some amusement.

"All right, Miss Joyce, I missed you too," he smiled. "Won't you sit down?"

I caught a glimpse of my reflection in the mirror on the mantelpiece and sank into the chair in mute embarrassment. My cheeks were shining from a thin film of perspiration that extended to my collar, and my hair had blown into a cloud of charcoal dust beneath my hat. There was a streak of something inky across my brow. I looked like I had rolled across the city.

"It was hard to get away. You needn't laugh," I gasped out angrily.

"Well, well, I'm sorry. A drink of water, maybe? You look a little—gray."

"No, thank you, I don't know how long I've got." I paused for a moment and took a ragged breath. "And this is certainly my final trip. Please just tell me what you found at Hartfield."

"Your final trip? You do not mean that, surely?" His tone was light and playful, but there was a glimmering of something else behind the sea-green depths—a silent question. "Why, then we must speak of pleasant things, Miss Joyce. Music, maybe, your favorite books, the weather? Let's not spoil this moment with talk about kidnapped daughters and other scandals."

"Then—you believe that she was kidnapped? Truly? Oh, you must tell me, please!"

He heaved a dramatic sigh and leaned back against the cushion. "I suppose you'll want to hear all the details, what everyone was wearing, the color of the curtains, the size of the salon—oh, stop frowning, and I will tell you everything from the beginning."

I folded my hands patiently and watched him with suspicious eyes. There was still something goading and deceptive in his look, like that of a child extending sweets which he intends to snatch away.

He shook his head at my expression, gave another sigh and began his statement. "We arrived at Hartfield Hall yesterday evening and were instructed to wait for Her Ladyship in the drawing room. Porter and I were both disguised as workmen, come to consult on alterations to Lady Rose's bedroom. I was dressed in a *very* fetching number, brown plaid with patches at the elbow, and my colleague was all in gray, with a red scarf for accent. The room was *simply stunning*, Miss Joyce, for it was decorated in the Oriental

fashion, but with a curious assortment of English antiques."
His voice had risen to a comic pitch during this description;
his mocking falsetto tone resembled a chirping schoolgirl's.
"Oh, and next to the piano there was a charming little Ming
vase which I was simply mad over— All right, where are
you going?"

I had risen to my feet and grabbed my purse. "I am going
home. You clearly do not need me here, and I am tired of
being treated like a funny pet. Good day, sir."

He leaned forward, grabbed my wrist, and pulled me down
into my chair again. "I'll stop, I promise. Please don't go."

"Then tell me only what you would tell a male colleague.
In your regular voice, please."

He cleared his throat and began again, hesitantly this
time, but in his natural low, soft murmur. "A portrait of the
missing Lady Rose smiled at us from over the fireplace—
a duplicate of the one that the earl had given us. I was studying it when the door opened to admit the lady of the house
and her stepson, Lord Victor.

"Lady Hartfield was quite handsome, petite and blond,
with the same clear eyes as the ones that gazed upon us from
her daughter's portrait. Her face was pale and composed, but
there was a tightness to her lips and a tense alertness in
her posture that expressed her cautious pride. She smiled as
she glanced over our workmen's attire and thanked us both

for coming in disguise and for the effort we had made to preserve their privacy—"

"One moment," I interrupted. "Would you mind telling me exactly what everyone said? It's more accurate than a summary."

He raised his eyebrows and laughed quietly. "Just as you wish, sergeant," he murmured. "Let's see, I believe Lord Victor spoke next, and he echoed his stepmother. 'I admit that I was opposed to calling in a detective at this sensitive time,' he said, 'but my father has assured us that you have pledged to locate my sister quietly and without causing any scandal.'

"Lady Hartfield smiled and nodded approvingly. 'My son expresses our concerns exactly. I would be devastated if any harm were to come to my daughter, but I recognize that she has brought this on herself. As a mother, I must also consider her brother's future and recognize how his sister's shame will affect his happiness.'

"The son murmured his agreement. They were an interesting contrast, sitting there next to each other, nodding almost in unison. She was fair and small; he had a swarthy complexion, a thick mane of black curls, and deep-set dark eyes.

"'I assume you wish to question me about the meeting I observed between my sister and the gentleman in the garden,' remarked Lord Victor after a short silence.

"'I would like to hear your account, of course,' Mr. Porter replied.

"'I wish I could give you a more detailed description of the man, but I only saw them from my bedroom window, and that is some distance from the garden. I realize now that I should have paid more attention, but at the time I thought she was simply speaking to some visitor of my mother's, and I did not think to question it. The interview was a long one, though, for when I looked out again nearly half an hour later, they were still there.'

"'You did not mention the incident to anyone?'

"'Not until she went missing, no. I hadn't attached any significance to the meeting. My sister was such a quiet sort that it never occurred to me that she might have a lover.'

"'I assume that you have not received any message from her since she left?'

"Lady Hartfield shook her head with a wounded air. 'I wonder that she has not written to us, to at least ease our minds. We have had our differences, it is true, but I would not have imagined that she would have been so unkind.'

"'Has an inquiry been made with your daughter's friends?'

"'I myself have paid social calls to the families of the young women she was close to. In each home I learned that no one has heard from her in several weeks. I also discreetly questioned her servants, to learn if they had observed any unusual activity around her disappearance. Her lady's maid was quite surprised that a sudden trip took place without her knowledge and attendance, but, thankfully, she is not over bright and did not question the situation too closely. She did not mention anything out of the ordinary.'

"'May we examine your daughter's room?'

"'Of course. I will be happy to show you upstairs.'

"Lady Rose's bedroom was situated to the left of the winding staircase on the second story of the great house," Cartwright continued. "Behind me, I caught a glimpse of a lavishly furnished dining room, about which several house-maids and footmen were milling, setting the long table with crystal glasses and gleaming silver.

"As we were ascending, one of the servants called his mas-ter's name, and Lord Victor left us with a promise to return if he was needed."

Cartwright stretched himself and reached out for a glass of water on the table. "Well, that is enough free informa-tion for the moment. You shan't get off that easy—not today, Miss Joyce. I'd like to hear what you would have looked for in Lady Rose's bedroom. Where would you have started?"

"The bed, certainly."

He winked slyly at me. "Ah, but the bed was turned by the parlor maid before we got there."

"I would still look underneath it, sir. And pat the mattress down. Girls frequently hide things inside their mattresses, you know."

"Very true. Well, there was a feather underneath the bed. Now, what?"

A single feather? I thought. Had the mattress been cut open?

"You examined the seams, I hope? Were there any holes?"

He smiled and nodded his approval. "I looked for holes in the covers, of course, and in the seams. I found a single thread, of a dark blue color, adhering to the mattress. The seam was absolutely intact and was sewn together with the same blue thread."

"Oh, but—that is impossible. If the bed was turned and pounded, as you said, then the thread would have floated off. Unless—unless someone cut the mattress and searched through it before you got there. *After* Lady Rose was gone, and after the maid had cleaned the quarters."

"Exactly. Very good. You have a curious talent for this sort of thing, I see." He looked away from me for a moment, and I saw his lips tense briefly. "One of your relatives used to be an officer, by chance? An investigator, possibly?"

"No, of course not," I retorted stiffly.

"Ah, well. I thought perhaps—deductive skills are frequently hereditary, you know. Well, never mind. So what do you suppose I looked at next?"

I sighed and silently scanned the imagined room. How I wished that I had been there! Would I have seen something that he had missed? Did I dare hope that I might one day be the eyes of the investigation, instead of a passive listener, like a child begging for a bedtime story? "Well, Mr. Cartwright, I would have opened all the dressers and the wardrobe first."

"Indeed. The latter was filled with clothing and trinkets, but the bottommost drawer of the dresser was empty. I asked Lady Hartfield what the drawer had contained.

" 'My daughter kept all her correspondence, as well as her diaries there,' she told me. 'She must have emptied it and taken them with her.'

"I did not say anything at the time, Miss Joyce, but it seemed strange to me: that bottom panel sagged very markedly in the middle, as if it had held the weight of many pounds of paper. Why would a girl take all her correspondence with her when she fled?"

I shook my head. "And how could she scale a tree with so much weighing her down? Perhaps she hid her diaries somewhere before she went, or someone else took them after she had gone. But what did Mr. Porter think of all of this? What was he doing while you were crawling about the floor?"

Cartwright took another sip of water and stuffed a bit of cinnamon pastry into his mouth. "Talking to Lady

Hartfield, mostly. Lady Rose had a strange collection of clocks displayed on one of the bookcases, and they were discussing those, I think."

"Was there something special about the clocks?"

"They were set to different time zones, actually, corresponding to the cities of their origin. Most were very beautiful and made of porcelain or silver. There was one old broken wooden one in the back that did not match the others, but there was nothing particularly interesting about them, no. Mr. Porter likes that sort of thing. I believe they would have talked about ceramics all that evening—if I had not fallen out the window."

"You fell?!"

"All right, I jumped. Lady Hartfield and Mr. Porter got very excited."

"Oh, I see. You were trying to re-create Lady Rose's supposed flight."

He rolled his eyes and slumped back against the sofa cushion. "You could at least *attempt* to be mystified, Miss Joyce. Just once in a while. It would really help my ego."

"You appear to mystify the rest of the world, Mr. Cartwright. I think that should be enough for you. But what I want to know is: Did you take a suitcase with you when you leapt courageously out the window? You should have done."

"Yes, of course. I stuffed it with the appropriate weight of clothing and tried to descend the tree outside her window. The branches were slick with rain and it was near impossible. I slipped, in fact, and might have broken my neck if Porter hadn't caught me by the collar."

"Ah, so he is good for something, then. But you haven't told me about the ground below. Were there any marks upon the soil?"

"A pair of footprints, yes."

"No imprint of a suitcase?"

"None."

"Then she could not have lowered her suitcase from the window with a rope, nor tossed it to the ground."

"Exactly."

"Did the footprints match a pair of Lady Rose's slippers?"

"Not unless the lady chose to wear men's boots that night. And the only shoes that have gone missing are Lady Rose's ballroom pumps. Not the best choice for a stealthy flight by dark."

"Oh! But I do not understand—how did she escape her room without help, and without leaving any marks beneath her window? And if she was kidnapped—how could her abductor carry her down a tree against her will? Or through the house, for that matter? How could he be sure that none of the servants would see him?"

"That was what I asked myself before I even arrived at Hartfield. Unfortunately, after I had combed the room and the soil outside, I was no closer to answering that question. So I am afraid that I am at a dead end—for now."

"But the servants? Surely you could speak to someone—as a workman, stir up some gossip, whisper in a few ears. You are so very good at winking at strange girls, after all."

He looked offended. "I only winked at you because you seemed to appreciate it. All right, don't pout, I'll take it back. The truth is, I was only able to speak with the housekeeper for a little while, and I'm afraid I did not get any useful information. She was a gossipy sort and was more than happy to relate all of the sins and troubles relating to her house staff, however. I found out that one of the scullery maids has come into a bit of money from an old uncle and so has left their service. Two of the upper housemaids have gone off to better themselves in Australia, and one unfortunate laundry maid was obliged to leave abruptly due to an affair with an irresponsible gardener. The housekeeper even informed me that she suspects another maid of being in the same 'situation' (a valet is responsible this time), but there are no grounds yet to warrant her dismissal."

"But you learned nothing at all about James! And why do the love affairs of scullery maids matter to us?"

"Oh, they don't matter to me. But I did note that the

recent romances beneath the stairs have brought about a staff shortage at Hartfield. A *severe* staff shortage."

I laughed and rose slowly to my feet. "Perhaps you should put on a servant's cap and apron and apply for the position, then. You'd make a very pretty maid."

He did not smile at my little joke, and I thought for a moment that I had offended him again. For a few minutes he sat quietly, chewing thoughtfully on a thumbnail and staring past me out the window. I was wondering if he had heard me or noticed my movement toward the door when he cleared his throat and murmured wistfully, "But—Miss Joyce, they already know *my* face at Hartfield."

His words fell like lead into my lap. I gasped beneath their weight and dropped heavily into my chair. There was a throbbing silence, the blood was beating slowly in my ears, and I felt my hands go cold and numb. I must have misunderstood, I reasoned quickly. He was certainly joking, mocking my enthusiasm, daring me to answer him. And yet, there was no laughter in his eyes. His shoulders were bowed and tense, his fingers clasped, his lips drawn tight. He would not look at me.

"What do you mean—?" I exclaimed desperately. "Mr. Cartwright, you *cannot* think—please, you *must* tell me what you meant." I was choking on the words; my voice was harsh and dry as gravel.

He rose slowly from the sofa and moved to sit across from me, pulling up the opposite chair so that his feet almost touched my skirt. Leaning toward me, with his elbows resting lightly on his knees and his fingers clasped together, he *looked* at me, not at my ashen face or shaking hands, but deep into my eyes as if he would read me, fixing me with a gaze that stopped my breath.

I realized suddenly that I had not misunderstood his meaning; I knew finally what he wanted from me, what he had been hoping for when he had asked me to return. And I could not think of anything to say to him. A hundred voices screamed their protest in my ears, a hundred judgments against my reputation, a hundred reasons to refuse. It was unheard of, impossible, and shameful. My family would reject me if they ever learned of it; my cousin would never even think of giving her consent.

The minutes pulsed by slowly and still he watched me, saying nothing, his eyes a timid question fixed on mine. *Are you ready?* they seemed to say. *Will you accept the challenge?* Inside me a tempest raged, pounding me with doubts. How could I leave the city without my guardian's approval? How would I even claim this post? What if I failed completely, and the case was lost because of me? Who did he think I was—?

But then suddenly I knew my answer: it had been inside me all the time. There was no other choice; I had been praying for a chance like this. The words came very calmly when I answered him, the words which I had waited years to say.

"I can go, sir. Let me take the case."

The tension melted in a moment, his triumphant smile mirroring my own. "I thought I knew my Dora Joyce," he murmured.

I put my chin up and crossed my arms, suddenly annoyed by his audacity. "I am not *your* Dora Joyce, sir. You did not enter into my consideration. My cousin needs my help, and that is why I have agreed. I am doing this for her."

"Are you sure about that, Miss Joyce? So you haven't been dreaming about this moment all your life? Oh, never mind, don't answer. We have more important business to discuss, and there are still a few details to consider before we begin. The Hartfield housekeeper is already expecting an application from my 'friend's sister.' I will draft the letter for you and provide you with the references and the uniform which you will need. While you are at the estate, I will, of course, be as nearby as possible; but we cannot be seen talking to each other without exciting gossip. Before you arrive I will station a young friend of mine named Perkins near the house, and we will communicate through him."

"But I cannot simply vanish! What shall I tell my cousin?"

"You know her best, Miss Joyce. I will leave that bit to you."

I considered the problem for a moment and nodded slowly. "Very well, then. I'll want a chaperone."

He threw his head back and barked a laugh. "You're not serious? A scullion with a chaperone?"

"I'll need an older woman to escort me from Adelaide's home and to the train, that's all. This 'chaperone' will be my alibi for the next few days."

He pursed his lips and frowned. "And what exactly do you plan on telling poor, unsuspecting Lady Forrester?"

I shrugged and gave him a playful smile. "I will tell her that the criminal Underworld is suddenly very interested in my movements."

"Ah. Someone has been following you, perhaps? You must go into hiding because you're—"

"—in mortal danger, yes. You will confirm these terrible suspicions, naturally."

"Naturally."

"I presume Mr. Porter will not be hearing of this development?"

"No, Miss Joyce, not unless you embarrass all of us by your performance. At present he is very busy trying to locate Lady Rose and her supposed lover. He gave me leave to work out my theories on my own. I am lucky that he never asks about my methods; he cares only about results. In any case, you will be at Hartfield for a mere day or two. Scrub a few grates, learn the servant gossip, and then disappear into obscurity. I assume that you can act a little? The accent, for instance, a maidservant's manners—these are all familiar to you?"

I rose briskly to my feet. "You forget that I have been surrounded by servants all my life. I would never have volunteered if I could not play the part, sir. But now I must be going, for if Adelaide finds me here our adventure ends before it can begin."

He chuckled and strode over to the door. "*Our* adventure, Miss Joyce? You do not mean that you are including *me* in your investigation? I am truly honored."

I shrugged and picked my purse up off the ground. "Laugh if you like, I cannot care; I know that you'll never understand. This is just a job for you, something to do to earn your bread. It obviously means nothing to you."

He smiled deliberately, pushing up his lips into a tense, fine line, while the humor drained slowly from his face. A light of protest stirred briefly in his eyes; I saw the flash of wounded honor flare and die. My comment about his work had hit the mark, and it had hurt. Detection had never been a dry career for him; and even as I said the words, I had known that they were false. But I had meant to dig a little, to touch his pride. I hoped that he would argue with me and let his guard down for a moment. I wanted to know the story that he had sworn never to tell, to hear about the "subjects that were never to be discussed." And yet now as I watched the fight in him freeze over, I knew that I had lost the gamble. He would never speak to me and give himself away.

"Ah, yes, I'd forgotten how important your cousin's case is to you," he remarked in a sweet voice. "Is that why you swooned so dramatically into my arms when we first met?"

He *would* bring up that humiliating scene every chance he got. That morning would never be allowed to fade; I would relive that swimming darkness every time I saw him. And yet my fainting spell was not what I remembered first when I looked back at it. That moment had merged somehow with the memory of my waking to the brush of his wool jacket on my cheek and his clear voice calling out my name. But I could not think about that now, not while he was studying me with those mocking eyes.

"Well, I did not come to London to meet *you*, at any rate," I retorted as I swept past him toward the landing. "I just have really rotten luck, I think."

"Perhaps you do," he called out softly. "Or perhaps you've been waiting for a figment of your imagination." His voice was gentle, low, and dark, like a whispered confidence. I was already halfway down the stairs before I heard him, but I turned and faced him now and waited, doubtful and uneasy, for his meaning. *He could not know*, I told myself. There was no way he could have guessed my secret. And yet—

"I am sorry that I am not the man you hoped to meet," he concluded in the same soft, sympathetic tone. "But, really, Dora, do you honestly think that *anyone else* would be giving you this chance?"

And before I could think of answering, he had shut the door behind me.

CHAPTER
7

WHEN I RETURNED HOME, Cook was waiting by the servants' entrance with wide eyes and drawn lips. "She came back twenty minutes ago, miss," she whispered anxiously to me. "I told her that you'd just slipped out for a bit of air, but I ought to warn you—she's awful mad now. That's her pacing, up there."

As she spoke, I could hear the angry march of boot heels tapping back and forth above our heads. "I'll slip into my bedroom now, and after a few minutes I'll need you to call her for me. Would you tell her that I want to speak with her?"

She smiled patiently at me and shrugged her shoulders, and I hurried up the stairs to start preparing for my trip. I did not need to pack much clothing, for a cast-off dress would be my servant's walking outfit, and my maid's uniform would be provided by Mr. Cartwright. My task now was to perform a lie, a dramatic, tear-filled falsehood, the first of many that I would have to tell.

I had only moments to prepare, for Adelaide would be coming in to reprimand me soon. I threw open my dresser, pulled out all my dresses, and threw them in a pile upon the bed, then dragged my suitcase out and tossed it by the door. With a rough motion I disarranged my hair, then smudged my face, and sprinkled my handkerchief with water from the washing basin. When I was satisfied with the atmosphere of chaos all around me, I wrapped myself in a blanket and began to cry, quietly. And so Adelaide found me, my cheeks streaked in red and white, my eyes swollen and damp with tears. She had entered with a thunderous brow and a scolding on her lips, but she paused when she saw my face.

"You were right," I whimpered to her, as she hurried over to sit beside me. "I should never have gone out alone."

Her breath caught, and she gripped my hand. "Dora, what happened to you? Where did you go?"

"I only meant to go out for a little, little bit, just around the corner for some air. I was but a block away when I saw the man. He was standing beneath a lamppost watching me, simply staring at me. I thought at first that I was imagining it, but when I turned in the opposite direction, he moved to follow me. Adelaide, this man has been tracking us since we came to London. He knows about the letters and knows that you have consulted Mr. Porter."

I watched her cheeks go pale. I was so sorry for the lies that I was telling and embarrassed by her honest pain. It could not be helped, I reasoned with myself as her arms tightened around my shoulders. Perhaps one day I would tell her the truth but, for now, I had to do this.

"I walked this way and that, trying to convince myself that I was mistaken," I continued, my voice sinking into a whisper, "but he was always there, not fifty feet behind me. I finally darted into an alleyway and through a store and so got rid of him. On my way back home I ran into Mr. Cartwright, and I immediately told him what had happened. When I described the gentleman who had followed me, Mr. Cartwright was quite upset. He told me about a great network of criminals, Adelaide, and terrifying stories of what they can do to their intended victims. He suspects that there may be more men involved in this blackmailing scheme than he had thought. And if they are not successful, if their demands are frustrated, Mr. Cartwright is afraid—"

I let the unfinished sentence hang between us. She shuddered and put her face into her hands for a moment, then lifted it again with new resolve. "You must get away from London," she told me firmly. "You have to return home."

"And bring this danger back with me? To the aunt who trusted me, who took me in? Adelaide, I cannot."

"What then? You cannot stay here. They will not harm me, because they are hoping for their payment, but how can I protect you? And when will this nightmare end?"

"I have to hide," I murmured. "Until it's over. That is what he thinks, at least."

"What do you mean? Where would you go?"

"He has a distant relative," I told her. "A single woman, who lives in the country, in a cottage near Swindon. I could stay with her until this has passed. She only keeps one elderly servant, and they will be discreet and will not tell tales after I am gone."

She stared at me for a moment in disbelief. "Mr. Cartwright's found a hiding place for you? Just like that? When—when did this happen?"

"Well, this is not the first time a client has been threatened, apparently," I explained. "Mr. Porter has run into this problem before. He has represented several witnesses who had to testify against criminal organizations, innocent people who were being pressured to keep silent. Mr. Cartwright's relative has taken in women in the past and watched over them until their court appearance." I was making this story up as I went along, spinning a yarn of convoluted lies and hoping that it sounded reasonable. But she was still shaking her head doubtfully, her eyes clouded in worried thought.

I had to argue now, I realized. I had to make her think that this was her idea, her recommendation, not mine, or she would never agree to it.

"But I do not *want* to go, Adelaide," I shot out desperately. "I don't care how dangerous it is! Please, I want to stay with you."

My protest made her wince, and the tears started to her eyes. "No, no, he's right, Dora, you have to go," she told me sadly. "I would never forgive myself if anything happened to you. I was supposed to be guiding and protecting you, but instead I have actually put you in this danger. You have to go."

"Oh, but—"

"*No*, Dora. I have already made up my mind."

I sighed and wrapped the blanket tighter around my shoulders. "Then I'll write to Mr. Cartwright and let him know of your decision, Adelaide," I told her wearily.

"No, I will write to him. An unmarried girl does not write

letters to a young gentleman, Dora. No matter *what* the circumstances."

I dropped my head to hide my smile. Until the last, through blackmail schemes and looming scandal, even beneath the shadowy threat of the lurking Underworld, my cousin would always remain the perfect, proper lady.

CHAPTER

8

Dear Detective in the Sky,

After my mother passed, my cousin suggested that I write letters to her as if she were still alive. She said it might help the grieving process if I pretended that she was still with me.

So now as I sit here waiting for my "chaperone" to take me to my new assignment, I'm thinking about Adelaide's advice and realizing that I want to speak with you more than ever. I know we've never met, that we will never meet, but I think I need you even more now than I ever have. So much has happened in the last few days, and I find that I have no one to confide in. To start with, I have deceived my family and frightened Adelaide. And yet somehow I do not feel as badly as I ought. I admit that I'm excited, more excited than I've ever been. I've thought this over carefully, and I've come to the following conclusion: I have you to thank for all of this.

Here are the facts:

If I had not learned of you, I would not have studied crime detection.

If I had not known about you, I would not have come to London with my cousin.

If I had not come looking for you, I would not have run into Mr. Cartwright.

If not for you, I would not have had the courage to step into my first adventure.

Thank you, sir, for these beginnings.

Yours gratefully,

Dora Joyce

P.S. By the way, you should know my feelings for Mr. Cartwright are strictly professional.

I folded the letter, slipped it into the flap inside my picture frame, and settled back to wait.

The woman who came for me the following morning was something of a surprise to me, but she fairly took my cousin's breath away. I had expected an elderly spinster or a stately matron, but the iron spike who introduced herself as Miss Mina Prim was so respectable that she was nearly unbelievable. With graying hair and pointed bun, hooked nose and steel spectacles, black crape and high, stiff collar, she looked like a schoolmistress from a Dickens novel come to whisk me away to a distant nunnery. I wondered where she had hidden her wooden ruler and if she would soon start smacking me across the palms with it.

"Well, Lady Forrester, I presume that *this* is my unfortunate young girl?" she demanded in a reedy, nasal whine, waving a bony finger in my face like a baton.

"This is Dora, Mrs. Prim," Adelaide replied and put her arm about my shoulder. There was a look of pity in my cousin's eyes, and she patted my hair sympathetically.

"*Miss*, Your Ladyship, *Miss* Prim. Now, if Miss Joyce is ready, my instructions are to take her directly to my home and to keep her with me until I hear from you or Mr. Cartwright. Is that correct?"

My cousin nodded, and I stepped forward meekly.

"Very well. My address is known to Mr. Cartwright. Any letters to her may be sent to him and he will deliver them to me. That way, no one can trace them, do you understand?"

Adelaide nodded once again and kissed me on the cheek. "I'm sorry, Dora," she murmured sadly. She was looking at the terrifying spinster as she said it.

"I don't want to go," I whispered to her, and began to back away; but the cabbie had already grabbed my bag and turned his back to me. Miss Mina Prim solemnly linked her arm through mine and pulled.

A final smile, a brief embrace, and I was pushed across the house, out the door, and into the waiting hansom in the street. The driver flicked his whip and we were off, and my cousin's figure faded quickly into the fog.

My plan had worked; I could scarcely believe my luck. Just four days ago I had been someone's pesky ward, a misplaced nuisance, my good aunt's burden. And now I was completely free.

"I want to thank you—" I began, turning eagerly to my stern companion. "You certainly put my cousin's mind at ease—"

"Confound this bloody dress!" my new companion snarled, tearing convulsively at the lace around her neck. "Blasted thing is killin' me. Can't bloody breathe!"

Miss Mina Prim's nasal whine had vanished, and my "lady" spoke now in a rumbling bass, punctuated with expressions that I would never be able to repeat. "Ah, that's better," my chaperone declared as the collar buttons came undone and a rather prominent Adam's apple breathed its freedom. "These corsets are bad enough, but I'll never understand why you women insist on wearing chokers all the time, too."

I blinked at him. "First time in lady's clothing, sir?"

The fellow gave me an offended sniff and spit loudly into the street. "Certainly not! I'm an experienced actor, miss, and so I'm *quite* familiar with women's clothing. Unfortunately, business has been rather slow recently, so I was obliged to take this little escort job. You needn't worry, miss, I'm quite discreet. I make my 'deliveries,' take my payment, and ask no questions. It's not *my* business where you're going."

He grinned and gave me a confidential wink, then pulled a flask out from under his dress and began to drain it in loud, contented gulps. Two odorous whiskey belches completed his performance, and he finally slumped against the cushion and fell asleep. I stared at him for a moment and smothered a smile. This person who was now salivating on his hat was the one charged with protecting my respectability and reputation. The irony of my position was both terrifying and amusing. Somewhere in my imagination, I could hear Peter Cartwright laughing heartily.

Our driver halted a few feet from Porter's door. My soused companion roused himself, swore briefly, and stumbled from the hansom. I moved to follow him, but he waved me back into the cab and instructed me to wait until Mr. Cartwright signaled to me. Then he vanished down the street, and I settled back to watch patiently for my summons.

The signal came after Mr. Porter's exit from the flat. Barely a quarter of an hour after my arrival, Porter hurried out his door and hailed a passing hansom. As he stepped into the carriage, the window shutters opened, and Cartwright peered down at me through the gap. I waved at him and jumped out of the cab.

He was hovering by the doorway when I came in, and, as I extended one hand to him in greeting, he grabbed me by the wrist and pulled my glove off with his fingers.

"White leather!" he thundered before I could say a word. "And this season's lavender chiffon? Are you posing as the richest scullery maid in England?"

"But these are the oldest clothes I've got."

He sighed and tugged briskly at the bellpull. "Janet," he told the little maid when she appeared, "please bring Miss Joyce something unattractive to wear at once."

The girl ran off without a word and returned immediately, bearing a faded Worthing dress, which she laid reverently at my feet. She gave me an apologetic curtsy and then vanished as I tried to thank her.

"You may dress quickly in the spare room there, Miss Joyce," Cartwright muttered and turned away from me.

There was a weird tension in the air around him, an

unnatural electricity that I could not understand. He had not smiled once since I had come; he had barely met my eye. I was glad for the excuse to get away, and I slipped gratefully into the empty chamber to change my costume.

As I struggled with the row of buttons and the ragged bows around my wrists, I examined my new form before the mirror, frowning at the shapeless sleeves, the high, pinched collar, and the lumpy skirt. The bodice was cut for a bulkier girl, and I used the opportunity to loosen the stays and lacing of my corset. I took a shallow breath, relaxed my ribs, stretched out my back, and exhaled happily, enjoying my unexpected freedom. I looked terrible in the cast-off dress, like a sagging gift box wrapped in tattered ribbons, but I did not care. It felt so wonderful to breathe again.

When I re-entered the sitting room, Peter Cartwright was pacing by the window, chewing alternately on a cinnamon pastry and his thumbnail. The tension in his face had not eased at all; he appeared more distant and uncomfortable than before. I curtsied casually, but he stared helplessly at me without responding to my smile; even when I lisped out, "Well, Your Lordship?" he did not move.

This was not the careless boy I knew; he seemed so awkward now, so raw and restless. I wanted to call out to him, to bring him back, to shake him, to be bold and silly so that he might mock me one more time. This creeping quiet troubled me, not just because it was unnatural for him but also because I was beginning to suspect that I was actually the cause of it. Was he doubting my abilities? I wondered suddenly. Was he was going to change his mind and send me home?

I had to act immediately. I had to say something, anything; I had to show him what I could do, *now*, before he spoke and it was over.

If the driver had not entered at that moment, I might have lost my chance. But as Cartwright reached past me to grab my suitcase, I darted forward and pulled it from him, stumbling toward the startled cabbie in my eagerness. This young coachman would be the first witness to my disguise, I decided quickly, and my final chance to prove myself.

I smiled shyly at the cabbie as he reached out for my valise and allowed our fingertips to touch briefly before drawing my hand away with a little blush. The young man seemed startled by my gesture and slightly pleased, and I held his look, my confidence growing as his color deepened.

"You will help me at the station, sir?" I murmured sweetly to him. "I've never been out of the city before, and I'm terrible scared of gettin' lost."

From beneath lowered eyelids, I watched him stammer and wag his head, his lips hanging open, his fingers playing nervously with his lapel. "O' course, miss, o' course," he said.

"I'll see ye onto your train myself, ye needn't worry . . ."

"That will be all, sir!" Peter Cartwright cut in, sharply. "You may wait for her downstairs."

The coachman shrank back into his overcoat, muttering his apologies. He gave me a final timid glance, grabbed my suitcase, and scurried out the door. After the man had gone, I turned confidently to my companion and waited for his reaction. He had asked me earlier if I could act the part, and I had just proven that I could. And yet there was no satisfaction or approval in his eyes. In truth, he seemed rather shocked and not particularly impressed. There was a rising color in his cheeks, and his lips played nervously with each other. He raised his head slowly and looked at me, his features drawn and wary, his hands clenched together behind his back.

"What *was* that, please?" he muttered between his teeth.

"I—was trying out my character," I faltered. "Was it not convincing?"

"Convincing? The fluttering eyelids, the perfect helplessness—the pouting lips?" He paused suddenly and cleared his throat. "Yes, it was *quite* a show."

"Thank you. I'm glad you liked it. May I go then?" One of my hands was already on the doorknob.

He moved to stand in front of me and placed his palm upon the handle, his fingers came to rest beside my own.

"Wait a moment, please, Miss Joyce. There is something I must say to you."

His voice was low and troubled, his head was bowed, his hand shifted slightly back to cover mine. He was standing very close to me; I could feel his shallow breath warm against my skin.

"I can see you're worried about sending me to Hartfield," I began. "But I promise that you won't regret it. I know that I can help you solve this case . . ." I paused, uncertain, swallowing the ending in my confusion.

"What are you talking about?" he shot out irritably. "I wasn't thinking about the case! I am only thinking about—" he stopped suddenly, undecided, and exhaled slowly.

"You have to promise me—" he continued in a softer voice. "You have to promise to be more cautious. I've seen how innocent and thoughtless you can be." I started to turn away, but he grabbed my hand and pulled me back. "Wait, Dora, I'm begging you, just this once *listen* to me—please." He was looking directly at me now, his skin deepening to a dark, unhappy scarlet. "You've been so sheltered from the world; perhaps you'll think that I am simply trying to frighten you. I may not be much older than you, Dora, but I have seen some things, some men—brutal, vicious men, who will think nothing of—" He paused again and shook his head. There was an uncertain, wandering expression in his eyes, like a child waking from a bad dream.

"Please," I whispered to him and moved to draw my hand away, for his grip had tightened suddenly, and my fingers had gone cold. "Please, Peter, let me go."

His hand slipped suddenly from mine. I pulled my throbbing wrist away and leaned my back against the door. Three livid fingerprints stood out in red upon my skin, and we both stared at the marks in silence for a moment.

"Dora, wait, I'm sorry—"

But I had already turned away, throwing off the arm which he'd extended, as I hurried past him to the street.

CHAPTER 9

I FOUND A DRIVER waiting for me at the train station. He threw my little suitcase on the back of his dogcart, jerked his thumb at the space next to my bag, and climbed up into his seat without a word. I jumped on, and he flicked the reins and we were off.

On the way to Hartfield Hall we passed several small tenant farms that belonged to the estate. Sheffield Green, Whitelands, and Donnanfield were just a few of the villages that paid the earl to live on and work his lands. Besides his investments, the farmers were Lord Hartfield's chief income source, so he acted as both their landlord and their manager. They looked like charming little homesteads, nestled between acres of rolling pasture, with the spire of a chapel poking out behind the hills.

By the time my hired dogcart had reached the edge of the estate, the mist had lifted, and I was able to view the great house in all of its grandeur. We approached the south side of the sixteenth-century mansion via a paved drive bordered by tall elms. Around us stretched acres of perfectly manicured lawn and a garden ornamented with ivory statues of Roman gods in heroic poses. Two steeple towers connected by a pillared, ivy-covered stone mansion comprised the main part of the Hall. We passed through an arched gateway and pulled up to the tradesmen's entrance.

A young urchin ran to take the horse's harness and was promptly warned off by the stable boy. The little fellow took a cuffing from his superior and moved to the back of the cart, where only I could see him. He touched his hand to the brim of his dusty cap, winked broadly at me, and disappeared. This, I gathered, was little Perkins, the boy who would be my messenger.

I was escorted to the servants' hall by the butler, a tall, taciturn man with a red snub nose, who eyed me with distaste. I caught only a glimpse of the winding oak staircase and the crimson and golden dining room beyond before I was hurried by the back passage to the basement and placed in the housekeeper's charge.

Mrs. Bentney looked me over with a critical eye, and her greeting consisted of a sniff and a comment about my thinness. "I trust you're not consumptive or sickly," she demanded severely as she led me on a brief tour of the home. "We will need a good deal of help in the coming weeks with the reception for the wedding. The event was supposed to take place at the bride's home, of course, but an outbreak of typhoid fever among their staff necessitated a change of plans. As if that's not enough, tomorrow night Lady Jane and her family are dining with His Lordship, so you'd best look smart and learn your duties quickly. I understand you come with the best references, though I wager you've never served in a home this grand."

I prayed that she would not inquire too deeply into my résumé but a simple "No, mum" and an awed stare seemed to satisfy her. She puffed her cheeks out with an air of self-importance and proceeded to describe my chores and the intricate rules that applied to my attendance of the noble family.

My duties were those of any under-maid and consisted of the "lower work," cleaning grates and lighting fires, scrubbing floors, and all other occupations that were beneath those of the upper-house servant, who attended to the standing work (curtains and such). I was one of seven girls of a similar status in an estate that boasted forty house servants, as well as a dozen men to tend to the stables and the grounds.

A girl in my position could, after years of dedicated service, aspire to the post of a cook's assistant, or if she was especially pretty and well-spoken, a parlor maid. I could never hope to achieve the status of a woman like Bertha, Lady Rose's lady's maid, whose main purpose in life had vanished with her mistress and whom we occasionally observed wandering about the house with a lost look in her vacant eyes. These servants were recruited from good families and were much more cultured and literate than the ignorant under-staff. The snobbery below stairs was one of the most frustrating obstacles to my real occupation in that home, as I could not easily converse with those girls who had the most contact with the lords and ladies.

Mornings for the lower staff began at five-thirty when I, along with four other girls, would polish and light the kitchen range. The reception hall and breakfast room were then dusted, and the grates black-leaded and fireplaces lit. The latter was the most difficult of all my chores; it was lucky that one of my fellow under-maids was patient with me and helped me with the task until I learned the trick. Finally, before mealtime, I would empty the dustbin into the rubbish container behind the stables and carry out any other refuse which remained from the evening before.

I was shaking the bin to make room for my odorous bag of kitchen scraps when a large metallic object sailed out from the overloaded tub and knocked me on the temple. I leaned over to pick it up, wondering lazily why someone would throw out the mechanism of a clock instead of attempting to repair it, and chucked it back into the pile. "Careless, wasteful noblemen" was my assessment; and, wiping my hands on my dress, I hurried to complete my errands before the upper-maids joined us for tea.

I had completed the sweeping and was heading toward the servants' hall when I encountered Agatha, a young parlormaid, who was carrying a tray of cutlery to the dining room. As I passed her, I noticed her pallor and dilated eyes; but in my rush I paid no heed until I heard a wretched gasping sound behind me, and the clatter of falling silver. I ran back in time to catch the poor girl from falling to the ground, and a moment later she was sick into a potted houseplant in the corner. When she had recovered from her spell, I helped her to her feet and indicated that I would fetch some assistance, but to my surprise, she clung frantically to my sleeves and begged me to stay with her a while and help her set the silver. I looked appropriately shocked at her suggestion, for dirty scullery maids were not permitted near clean linen.

She glanced about her and whispered hoarsely, "They

can't know that I was ill again. I'll be let off for sure. It's the fourth time in two weeks. I can't lose my place yet, not 'til I'm sure of the other."

I shook my head. "Have you seen a doctor?"

She looked embarrassed. "There's nothing they can do for me. They'd only—"

We were interrupted by a tall footman bearing a steaming food tray to the dining hall. As he passed us, Agatha and I scurried backward into the shadow behind the plant. A pungent aroma of boiled kidneys lingered behind him and caused my miserable companion to hold one hand to her mouth and grab helplessly at mine with the clammy fingers of the other. She doubled over the hibiscus tree, and as I wondered if she would anoint its leaves once more, the cause for her anxiety became suddenly clear to me. By the time she had regained her composure, I had understood what her condition was and was sorry for her. She would lose her place immediately when it became known, that much was certain—and, if she had no family to help her, would end up in the workhouse, or worse.

She gave me a wan, guilty smile and allowed me to lead her into the dining hall.

"Does the—father know?" I inquired hesitantly as we set the side table.

"I can't speak to him," she murmured sadly. "Not after he was so angry with me."

"Why was he angry with you?"

"Well, he'd been so quiet, not like himself at all, and I got worried, you see. I thought perhaps there was someone else, and that was why he was avoiding me. So a few days ago I went into his room when he wasn't there, to look around a bit. And he caught me. Ah, he acted something awful, like I had committed murder. Me, the woman he promised to marry, and soon to bear his . . ."

She glanced down at her waist and blushed.

"Did you find anything in his room?"

She shook her head and groaned. "I know I oughtn't to have done it, I shoulda trusted him. He's different from the rest of them, mind you. He thinks greater thoughts than all of us put together, and he's read more than the master himself, I daresay. It's what I noticed about him from the first. Every time I entered the study, there would my James be, with a different book in his hands, leafing through it like his soul depended on it."

"James, the valet?"

She blushed again and frowned, realizing that she had given away his name without intending to. I imagine she would have come to it eventually, but girls like to reveal such things on their own terms, after a little breathless expectation from their audience.

"Yes, who else would I risk my good name for? I fell in love with him the moment I saw him, same as all the other girls did. He's been here but a few months, and I don't think there is a single maid below the age of fifty that wouldn't give her eyes just to be noticed by him. That's why they speak so meanly of me, you understand."

"Is he so very handsome, then?"

"It's more than that, you'll see. But they'll all be here in just a moment, and then afterward you can tell me what you think of him."

I realized that in normal circumstances Agatha would never have addressed me as a friend; my status as a scullery maid put me below her notice, just as she was below the master's. But I shared her secret now, and in her eyes, her shame made us equal.

I put my hand about her waist and smoothed her damp hair from her forehead. "I won't tell anyone," I promised. "And I'll help you any way I can."

There was a sound now from the hallway, and Agatha shrank back against the wall. "Stand there behind that post," she instructed me, "and if anyone notices you, just slip out through the door. You look clean enough, and I'll just tell Mrs. Bentney that I had called you in to light the fire. Just mind you don't stare at them too hard, for you ought to be below stairs with the other scullions."

I slipped quietly into the shadows as Lord and Lady Hartfield and their respective footmen entered the room quietly, without regarding one another; and their son, Lord Victor, soon followed. A sharp nudge from Agatha drew my attention to the servant behind him, though I scarcely needed her encouragement to watch him, for he was a key suspect in my investigation. Agatha had just told me that James had recently been hired, and now he seemed to be hiding something from his curious fiancée. He might very well be the mysterious "J.F," I realized.

What would Adelaide think if she knew that I was staring at her blackmailer at that very moment? I wondered. I was supposed to be nestled safely in a spinster's cottage miles away from here, reading novels, and waiting patiently to rejoin my cousin. Instead I was a detective's spy, dressed as a maid, hovering dangerously near a mystery and a handsome criminal.

My suspect was a pleasure to study, I must admit. Tall, blond, with large, heavily lashed blue eyes and full lips, it was no wonder that every heart beat for him as he passed. He glanced briefly at Agatha, and I was suddenly and irrationally angry with him. I preferred my criminals to be ugly and unromantic; it was easier to pursue someone with hairy ears and brown teeth than one who looked like a Greek god.

Still, it should have been no surprise to me that he was handsome, for valets were kept in only the richest households and, like footmen, were frequently chosen for their looks and height. His duties would have been quite specific in that household, requiring more patience and devotion than intellect. Thanks to his valet, Lord Victor's bootlaces were carefully ironed, his newspaper scented, his slippers always placed at the appropriate distance from the fire. When the pair would go hunting, the young lord's leather breeches would be expertly powdered and his rifle loaded so that he always appeared to advantage in front of the ladies. It was not a difficult post, but a stifling one to any man with brains or ambition. As I watched him, I wondered how he could bear his lot, if he was indeed as intelligent as Agatha had claimed.

Lord Victor was no less handsome than his servant, but he was as dark as James was fair. The earl's son glanced briefly in my direction, and I forgot for a moment that I was a scullery maid and returned his look. His raised eyebrows brought me back to my senses, and I stepped backward into the shadow and dropped my head. I was supposed to be an objective and quiet observer, a timid under-maid, I reminded myself, not a debutante at a ball. It would have been easier if Lord Victor's eyes had not been so very black and he had looked a little less like a pirate captain.

It was a frustrating meal for me. No one said anything suspicious at all. In fact, there was almost no conversation between the lord and lady, and the son ate quietly, staring in front of him in distracted silence. James carefully avoided Agatha's eye, and I watched her shrink slowly against the wall in helpless disappointment. And standing there like a mute and rumpled statue, I could not do anything to comfort her.

After the noble family had finished the meal, they departed, and Agatha and I were joined by a stream of servants. While we cleared the table, I encouraged the other girls to chatter about the masters of the estate. It did not take much for the gossip to start flowing. Everyone seemed anxious to bring me up to date on all the happenings and on their theories regarding Lady Rose's rapid trip to an aunt in Brighton.

"If you ask me," declared Agatha, "I think Her Ladyship is hiding something, for all the brave smiles she puts on for us. If Lady Rose was going off to a trip, why was it so secret-like, in the middle of the night, with her maid left behind? Young miss is in some kind of trouble, and her mother knows it. They're covering something up, you mark my words."

Flora, a pretty, rosy-cheeked scullery maid, snorted and arched a sarcastic eyebrow. "Tell us more about this here trouble, Aggie. What kind are you meanin' exactly? Indigestion, do you suppose? Perhaps she got her 'indigestion' from you? I suppose you could be very helpful to her, and teach her all about lady's *indigestion*."

Agatha winced under her malicious smirk and seemed to cower before us. The other servant girls giggled and exchanged meaningful glances over their brooms. Encouraged by her reception and by the prospect of humbling her social superior, Flora continued her assault. "I've heard tell by the midwives that 'indigestion' can lead to horrible things. Your feet swells up, and then your belly and even your bosom"—she wagged her own for emphasis—"and before you know it, you're walkin' down Old Kent Road with your hair hangin' down and your skirts pulled up over your ankles, asking the drunken touts if they're looking for a friend for a night." The tittering was more pronounced now, and several of the younger girls had dropped their tasks altogether to stand in judgment, hands on hips, before their victim.

"You know what I heard?" interjected a spindly red-faced little maid named Lydia. "That *indigestion* is caused by eating too much food from the *valet's* trays." Her joke brought fresh cackles of laughter. But Flora was not to be outdone. "I always say, ring first"—she waved her bare fingers in front of Agatha's miserable eyes—"and crumpets later."

The girl visibly shrank before them, and one hand slid in

an unconscious, defensive motion over her belly. I could not bear to watch Agatha's suffering, and I cast about for some fresh bait to toss to the sharks.

"I got a little indigestion myself this mornin'," I ventured, with a silly giggle, "when I caught a look of the young master. Perhaps it *is* catching." Their reaction was just what I had hoped for. Several of the upper-maids raised their arms in mock dismay, and Flora screamed with laughter. From the corner, Agatha sent me a pathetic look of gratitude.

"Aye, there's a man after my heart," Flora sighed, pursing her full lips. "He don't waste himself on just anyone."

"You've seen him already, then?" inquired Ellen, a little stillroom maid. "That dark hair and those black eyes that look straight through you." She shivered as if she enjoyed being "looked through."

"That's it exactly, isn't it, girls?" Flora put in, in a wounded tone. "Lord Victor never really looks at anyone, does he? He'll smile and brush your cheek as pretty as you please, but it's all honey without anything beneath. We've nothing to complain about from him."

I got the feeling that Flora wished she had something to complain about. Indeed, all of the young maids looked wistful and disappointed, as if recognition from their handsome master was something they all wished for.

"I think maybe he's lonely," mused Ellen, rubbing her

cheek absentmindedly. "For all his charm and good looks, he don't have friends, really."

"He's got a temper on him, Ellen," remarked Judith, an older housemaid, who had been listening to the conversation with a superior frown on her face. "He scared off the one friend he had, remember? That gray-haired squire from Lambley, Mark Fellows? They were close as wax for months, though there was twenty years between them in age at least. Then one day, the man was gone. Left his family, his friends, without a word. Our young lord was never the same, I tell you."

"That's not what I meant, Judith. I just think he needs a good woman, is all," replied Ellen, checking her reflection in a silver spoon.

"Aye, Cinderella, perhaps you ought to drop some more napkins on the floor when he's about. I don't think he noticed your rump the first ten times!" The girls whinnied with delight as Flora bent over in a mocking, exaggerated demonstration and shook her bottom in the air.

"But what of Lady Jane?" I suggested when they had quieted a little. "He must love his fiancée." My ignorant remark set off fresh hoots of laughter.

"Lady Jane indeed! That biddy! He cares more for his hunting dogs than he does for her. I heard he refused to marry her at first. But his father's estate was in such a way, and the young master's debts didn't help. And then there was poor Lady Rose, and her miserable first Season. There's no telling if they'll ever get her married off. In the end, I suppose Lady Jane's lovely dowry made her look a little more attractive after all. But he is not happy over it."

"Does Lady Jane know?"

Agatha gave me a lofty look. She had obviously recovered from the teasing and was now happy to rejoin the gossip, as long as she was no longer the subject of it. "Lady Jane is so thankful to finally hook a husband that she's screwed her eyes shut for good. Not that they'd do her any good open, that stupid cow. Even her mother knows that it isn't a love match, though she's been preening herself over her daughter's conquest. I tell you, when Lady Jane finally realizes what her charming fiancé thinks of her, she will bust her corset!"

The remainder of the conversation consisted mainly of imitations of ripping fabric and cow bellowing.

CHAPTER

10

AT THE FIRST opportunity I stole away from the cackling girls and hurried down to the toolshed behind the stables where my little messenger was scheduled to wait. I had yet to officially meet him; my first afternoon on the assignment had been too busy to send messages. This evening, however, I had written the following letter to Cartwright:

Dear Detective (or the closest thing to one),
My beginning as an investigator has gone better

than I could have hoped. My suspicions about James are all but confirmed. According to one of the servants, he acted strangely the day before Lady Rose's disappearance; I am certain he knows where she is.

I am encouraging all the servants to gossip about the family, but so far I have only learned that every young maid here is pining for either Lord Victor or for his valet, both of whom are really very handsome.

I keep wondering what my cousin would think if she could see me now, elbow deep in ashes and grease, with coal dust in my hair. I hope you are sending her reassuring messages about my well-being. I hate to think that she is worried about me. There is no reason to be concerned; I am muddling through my tasks well enough to keep my fellow servants from becoming too suspicious. I feel that I was meant to be doing this— the investigating, that is, not the floor scrubbing.

I hope that by tomorrow I shall have more news for you. At this rate, perhaps I'll not need your assistance in the end.

Yours,

Dora Joyce

It was hardly the brilliant message that I had hoped to send; on close examination there was really only one bit of new information in my letter. Still, I hoped it would distract Mr. Cartwright for a little while I continued my investigation.

I found young Perkins sitting cross-legged by the "meeting" rock, gazing intently at the manor house. As I approached, he leapt quickly to his feet, doffed his cap, and stood rigidly at attention, one small hand extended. He was a sweet-faced little fellow, fair-skinned and freckled, with large hazel eyes and auburn curls. Cartwright had indicated that the boy was near fourteen, but to me he looked no more than twelve. I smiled at his formal posture and urged him to be seated.

"You must be Perkins," I said. "Mr. Cartwright has hired you to be my messenger."

The boy nodded briskly and put his hand out a little farther. "Oh, he didn't hire me, miss. But I'll be here every morning and every evening like he asked. We're old friends, you see, and I'm happy to do this favor for him."

"Have you known him long, then?"

"About three years. We started together at the express office, and we used to see quite a bit of each other before he went to work for Mr. Porter."

"And you're fond of him?"

He nodded. "Well, I miss him now he's gone. He's always been straight with me and stood up for me. So I'm straight with him."

"He's defended you against the older children?"

The child grinned proudly and relaxed his posture slightly. "Oh, yes, miss. He's no chicken, I can tell you that much. A couple of the other boys learned that right quick."

"Oh, did they? I wish I'd been there! Quite a show, was it?"

I had clearly hit on a favorite topic, for the boy now pushed his shoulders back and puffed his chest out in happy recollection. "Oh, he fairly took us by surprise, he did. He was such a curious fellow, you see. Barely spoke to us at first, lurked about in corners, reading newspapers, piles of books, anything he could get his hands on. I think I was his only friend, and even I couldn't say I really knew him. He was a great worker and all that, and the boss had even talked about promoting him to clerk or operator, for he could take dictation by ear after only two months on the job. But he didn't seem to care for anything. And he was so sad, too, all the time. Those first few months I think I only saw him smile once, and that was after he had beaten Drummond's face into a mess."

I wondered for a moment if we were talking about the same young man. I had never seen Cartwright without laughter on his lips, and as for violence, I simply could not picture it.

"What had this Drummond fellow done to him?"

"Oh, no one blamed Cartwright afterward. That bully had

had it coming to him for months. But I could not believe
it. After everything that boy had said to him, after all the
teasing and the torture, it was such a little, little thing that
did it."

"What was it?"

Perkins scratched his cheek thoughtfully and sighed.
"Well, you know Mr. Cartwright pretty well, I think, so you
must remember how miserable he used to be?"

I nodded shortly. There was no need to tell this boy that
I had only met his friend that week. His story was becoming more interesting by the minute, and I did not want my
little fountain of information to dry up. "Of course, Perkins,
I remember very well. Go on."

"Well, Drummond found him in the supply closet one
afternoon, hunched over by the ink bottles. Lots of us boys
used that room for sneaking cigarettes or catching little naps
between message runs. Well, Drummond had—pictures he
wanted to show the rest of us. Prints, you know. At first we
didn't even see poor Cartwright in the corner, 'cause it was
awful dark in there. It wasn't until I lit the lantern that we
realized he was there, and then it was too late for him to
hide himself. I think he had been crying, miss, for his eyes
were all red and swollen. I felt sorry for him, honestly. But
for Drummond it was like he had won the lottery."

"What did he say to him?"

"Oh, the usual. Called him a baby, made little sucking noises with his lips, the sort of thing that you'd expect."

"And Mr. Cartwright hit him for it?"

"*No.* That was what was curious. He said nothing, not a word, just started to walk away from us. There didn't to seem to be any life in him at all. It made Drummond fairly desperate, of course, because he was looking for a rise. So he made the stupidest little joke, blurted out one desperate last shot."

"What was the joke?"

The boy's brow furrowed in concentration, and he crossed his arms. "He called out, 'Eh, chicken! Where you going? Running to your sister so she can rescue you?' It was so silly, you see, the kinda thing dumb boys say to one another all the time. So none of us could understand why it turned Cartwright stark raving mad like that."

"What did he do?"

"He turned on that boy so quick that Drummond never had a chance. It took the five of us to pull him off. I never saw such a face, I'll tell you that, and I've been in a few good fights myself."

"That sounds awful. I suppose he must be very sensitive about his sister."

Perkins shook his head and laughed. "He doesn't *have* a sister, nor brothers neither. I asked him about his family when we first met and he told me so. He's an orphan, I think, and he was living with an uncle then. That's all I know, at any rate. He never spoke about his family to you?"

I shook my head. "He's rather private, isn't he? I never dared to ask him."

Perkins's face clouded over and he ducked his head in sudden shame. "Oh, I suppose I've said too much again. Cartwright says I need to mind my tongue. You needn't tell him that I told you all of this. I'll just take the message, then, as I shoulda done before."

I slipped the note to him, and he pulled a letter from Adelaide from his cap and handed it to me. "Good day, miss."

"Oh, Perkins, before you go—"

"Yes, miss?"

"I was wondering—that scar on Mr. Cartwright's neck. Do you have any idea how he got it?"

The boy shrugged and pursed his lips. "The cross? Nah, he's had that ever since I've known him. I wouldn't ask him about *that* if I were you. I made a comment 'bout it once and he looked red murder at me."

CHAPTER
11

THE HOUSEKEEPER was waiting with her hands on her hips when I returned, tapping her foot next to a full coal scuttle. Luckily, before she could ask where I had been, the butler came in with urgent news about a broken vase that she needed to attend to. I grabbed the heavy scuttle and hauled it upstairs, unloaded half the coal into the dining room fireplace, and then proceeded to the drawing room.

A little of the dust had floated onto one of the brightly upholstered pink divans by the pianoforte, and as I swept it up, I studied the gold-framed portraits of the Dowling family on the wall above me. The largest painting showed the earl and his second wife in formal wear, staring proudly into the distance. Nearer the harp in the corner hung a portrait of Lady Rose, which showed her leaning forward against a column, dressed in a flowing Roman gown, a harp balanced on her hip. She was a beautiful girl, pink-complexioned and full figured, with large, heavy-lidded green eyes and a sweet pout on her lips. She appeared graceful and innocent among the flowers; the artist had erased the awkwardness which had troubled her parents. On the opposite wall, Lord Victor's picture presented a vivid contrast to his sister's smiling one. Shown with one hand holding a horse's reins and the other a hunting rifle, the young lord's confident pose was true to its owner's real image. Judging by what I had heard so far, the brother's and sister's charms were equal only in their portraits.

I was gathering up my brush and scuttle when the red baize door suddenly swung open, and Flora entered, bearing a basket of rags and a heavy broom. She did not see me standing in the corner, and I was about to greet her when the sound of a familiar voice stopped me.

A tall, roughly dressed workman was standing behind her, his shoulder against the doorpost, his arms crossed across his chest. He grinned broadly, clicked his tongue, and murmured something that made the girl drop her basket and giggle. I shrank slowly behind the pianoforte and watched, barely breathing, as Peter Cartwright sauntered into the room, swinging a workman's cap. He saw me, of course, and winked while her back was turned, then directed his attention to the maid, who was abstractedly brushing a rag over an already spotless table.

"Now, sir," she protested, as he circled her. "We're expecting a houseful of guests tomorrow, and I'm already late on the sweepin' and dustin' that I were supposed to have done this morning before breakfast. You'll be causin' me to get my notice, sir, and me with my poor mum to support."

Cartwright leaned forward, the fringe of his wool scarf brushing her reddening cheek, and whispered hoarsely, "Naw, Miss Flora, I don't see how any gentleman in his right mind would have the heart to bring a tear into them blue eyes, not over an harmless bit of gossip, when your work's mostly done."

"It's the housekeeper that does the firin', and much she cares for me eyes," Flora shot back, tossing her head and looking pleased. Cartwright murmured something in her ear and indicated the portrait of Lady Rose. She jumped backward, jabbing at him playfully with the handle of her broom, and let out a sound between a laugh and a snort.

"Oh, my young mistress is most lovely, sir, and no plain

workin' girl like me could hold a candle to her."

"Ah, miss, I'd like to see the girl that's prettier than the one in front of me, that's a fact."

Flora sniffed and shrugged. "Well, you won't be seein' her today. She's gone to her aunt's place quite sudden-like. The servants have all been talking about it. We all say she's in some sort of trouble. As for me, I think I know what it was that started it."

"How's that?" Cartwright inquired blandly.

"Mind you, I heard it meself, but I haven't told anyone yet," she informed him. "I was cleanin' the rug outside His Lordship's study on Wednesday, and I sees young miss storm past me into the room. Her face is that pale, but her eyes are wild, not meek and sad, like they usually is. And as she opens the door I see that her fingers are dirty, cov-ered in mud—she that is always so proper and clean. She shuts the door, and I hears her speaking to someone inside. Then I leans against the keyhole, you know, as I was headed that way in my cleanin', and I hears her say, 'You don't really expect me to keep this a secret, do you?' If the missis hadn't called for me, I'd have heard the rest. Now, what do ye think o' that?"

Cartwright shook his head and smiled. "I think, my dear, that you are not the only little spy in this place. That pretty one there behind the piano has been standin' there with her mouth open for nigh on five minutes." And he pointed to me.

Flora spun about to face me, her cheeks an angry crimson. I gave her a shamefaced grin.

"I didn't want to interrupt—" I began, but she turned on her heel and flounced from the room, leaving the rags scattered behind her.

Cartwright bowed gravely to me as if to say, "Now, *that* is how it's done," closed the door behind her, and then collapsed dramatically onto the sofa.

I was glad to see that he had lost the tension of our last encounter. Perhaps watching me in my role had eased his worries somewhat. I was clearly managing at Hartfield decently enough. He could see that I was safe, despite my fragile gender; the demons of the Underworld had not yet swallowed up my maiden's innocence.

"Well, so *I* must be discreet at Hartfield, Mr. Cartwright, but you may leave a trail of broken hearts behind you?"

"Come now, don't be so dramatic. I doubt that I made much of an impression on that pretty maid. Girls like her are used to being courted. *You* seemed to be more affected by my performance than she was."

"Oh, I was absolutely captivated, sir."

He gave me a guarded smile. "Were you, really?"

"Yes, indeed. I would never have thought that you could charm a pretty female, even a brainless one like Flora. And yet it was *quite* a show."

He frowned and shoved his hands into his pockets. "Let's talk about the case, shall we?"

"Oh, yes, let's. Did you get the message that I gave to Perkins?"

He pulled a slip of paper from his pocket. "I just met him outside. What 'suspicious behavior' were you referring to?"

"James was behaving oddly before Lady Rose disappeared. One of the maids was concerned about it."

"Is that all?"

"Well, no, actually. The maid, you see, is carrying his child."

He blinked at me. "Unexpected fatherhood makes most men behave oddly. But that is not the mystery we are investigating."

I shifted uncomfortably and bit my lip. I really had *nothing* else to offer, and he was going to make me feel my failure.

"Well, what do you make of Flora's statement, then?" I remarked after a brief pause. "Do you believe that James is blackmailing Lady Rose? Flora overheard her speaking of a secret."

He shook his head. "If we are to believe the maid, Lady Rose looked triumphant, not meek, before confronting the person in the study. Any other theories?"

"Well, I did think it rather odd that Lady Rose vanished on the very day that her father happened to be away from home. It seems rather a strange coincidence."

"Yes, I was wondering about that as well. So while you are rummaging through the coal dust here, I plan on investigating the earl's alibi."

"And I will examine the family bedrooms next."

"I have already covered the daughter's chamber, but you may feel free to go through it again, in case I missed anything." His sarcastic smile was a little too much to bear. I immediately decided that I *would* search Lady Rose's room and find something he had overlooked. I made my resolution quietly, and felt a little better for it. Without looking at him, I rose to my feet and grabbed my coal scuttle.

"Miss Joyce."

I glanced over my shoulder to find that he was watching me with an intent, disturbed expression; his light eyes flickered for a moment, and then his jaw set. "You understand that we are investigating a serious crime, the kidnapping of a young woman?"

"Yes, of course. I already told you that I'd be careful."

"I'm glad to hear it. But don't be so careful that Lady Rose dies while waiting for us to find her."

I flinched and turned quickly toward the door. He had spoken in a hushed, bland voice, without a trace of mockery or conceit. I could always protest when he teased me and easily cut into his arrogance, but there was no way to argue with the truth.

So I simply left the room.

CHAPTER
12

I T WAS TIME to break the timid maidservant mold, that was certain. As important as it was to remain inconspicuous, it would be useless if I learned nothing that Cartwright did not already know. It was already twilight by the time I had finished with my tasks. I would have to begin afresh the following morning, I decided.

Despite my determination it was early evening on my second day at Hartfield before I could get away. All morning I was sent on errands—first to Sheffield Green, the tenant village, to purchase replacements for the buns that the cook had ruined, and then to scrub the front steps white with shale-oil soap in preparation for that night's dinner party. Setting the servants' table was my final chore, and after I had finished, I fled upstairs for my real work. One of my duties was filling fireplaces before bedtime; so for the second time that day I hauled a heavy coal scuttle up the winding staircase. I began my researches in Rose's bedroom, partly because I was eager to fulfill my little promise to myself, and partly because I knew it would not discourage me too much if I failed. After all, the trail was five days old by now, and Cartwright had already canvassed the area.

It was a sad, cold little chamber, lavishly decorated but barren, as if its owner had taken the warmth with her when she vanished. There was a desolate eeriness to the place, and I found myself looking over my shoulder, as if the missing girl might suddenly spring upon me and demand to know what I was doing. I crept about the floor for a while, dove under the bed, hung out of the window, and went through every drawer, but I discovered nothing new. A tall bookcase laden with some twenty timepieces was the only unusual feature of the room. Only one clock caught my notice, however, for it did not match the others. It was the simple wooden one which Cartwright had mentioned briefly to me. It was unique only for its size, and for the fact that its minute hand pointed to the hour, while the rest of the clocks pointed to the half hour. Lady Hartfield had told Cartwright that her daughter had set the clocks to correspond to time zones, but this one seemed to have stopped entirely. I remembered the broken clock mechanism in the rubbish bin and shrugged. It was the plainest piece in the collection, and the girl had simply not bothered to get it fixed. The discovery did not seem to be worthy of a report.

I was discouraged, of course, but I passed hopefully on to Lord Victor's bedchamber; it had not yet been searched, and perhaps I would uncover something. I crept into his room, closed the door behind me, and lit the gas lamp. From corner to corner, from bedspread to desk, birdcage to ferret pen, I inspected every inch of the entire area. Half an hour later I had discovered that the heir of Hartfield enjoyed smoking in bed, reading questionable literature, and feeding chocolate truffles to his ferret. I was fairly certain that Cartwright would not be interested in any of these details, assuming he was not already aware of them.

The fireplace was my final hope. A careless maid had forgotten to empty out the grate, for it still contained some glowing embers at the very back of the hearth. It appeared that Lord Victor had recently been burning something in his room. Carefully, I plucked out the blackened slips of paper with coal tongs and examined them beneath the gaslight. The writing was illegible, for the faces of the pages were charred, but the article that I had rescued appeared to have once been a bound notebook. The string that held it was still intact, but as I strove to separate the pages, the entire package crumbled in my hands and fell in ashes to the floor.

This was beginning to feel hopeless. Burnt paper meant nothing; many people discarded their old documents by throwing them in the fireplace. I was kneeling by the hearth to sweep up the mess when a sound upon the landing outside brought me to my feet. I glanced at the fireplace and groaned at my own foolishness. My full coal scuttle was still in Lady Rose's chambers, and my excuse about lighting fires was no longer believable. The hot water and towels for washing had already been set by the valet. There was no credible explanation for my presence in the room at this hour. It would be bad enough if I was discovered by Lord Victor, but if it was James, I would be alone with a suspected blackmailer and kidnapper. I dimmed the gas lamp, scrambled onto the windowsill, undid the latch, and threw open the shutters. The turning knob on the bedroom door glinted in the moonlight, and the hinges creaked their warning. As the door swung open, I slid out onto the ledge and crouched outside the casement between the shutters and the open windowpane. The large embroidered curtains hid me from view, but since I had not closed the glass behind me, I could hear and see everything that passed within.

James had entered his master's bedroom and turned up the gaslight. As I watched, he drew a small sliver of paper from his pocket and then walked over to the fireplace. He stood there for a few moments; I could not see what he was doing for the curtain was in my way, but after only a minute he stepped back into the center of the room and gazed with satisfaction in the direction of the mantelpiece. Then he wiped his hands carefully on his handkerchief and shoved the slip of paper back into his pocket. I shivered and pulled my shawl tighter around my shoulders. It was unseasonably cold that night, and my knees were aching from kneeling on the marble ledge. I hoped that James had done whatever he had come for and that I would soon be able to sneak back into the bedroom.

Unfortunately for me, however, someone else was also very interested in James's movements. There was a soft tapping at the door, and James spun around and quickly reached out to lower the flame in the gas lamp. "Who is it?" he called out.

Agatha entered; she slipped into the room like a frightened ghost and then shut the door behind her. They gazed at each other for a moment; even by the dim lamplight I could see the color rising in his cheeks and the tremor in her lips. I groaned inwardly and slumped against the shutter. There was a scene coming, anyone could feel that. And I certainly had no desire to be a witness to it.

"I've been waiting to talk to you," she said, her voice barely over a whisper.

James seemed to waver for a moment; then, with a smooth motion he shifted a little closer to the desk. I noted that he had now positioned himself to stand between Agatha and the fireplace, and was blocking her view of it.

She didn't seem to notice his movement, though. She was attempting to speak again, but something seemed to have stuck hard in her throat. I was truly sorry for her then, and I prayed that her lover would take pity on her and say something to make her stop shivering so pathetically.

But it was soon clear that her misery had touched him too. When Agatha had first come in, James's entire body had been taut with caution, ready to spring to action. But as he watched her quake in front of him, his expression brightened suddenly. He was grinning at her now; all the tension drained away from him in a moment. He seemed totally at ease and in control, as if he was drinking in her embarrassment and actually enjoying it. With a fluid, gentle movement he stepped over to her, reached his arm out, and drew her close. His hand slid over her waist and up her spine; her body stiffened in surprise and then relaxed against him. With one finger he lifted up her chin and kissed her, then traced her lips with his, trailing slowly across her blushing cheek down to her collar.

She shuddered and tried pull away, but his arms twined more forcefully around her back; he murmured something in her ear, and she ducked her head and laughed, her face resting against his shoulder.

"Did you have something you wanted to say to me, darling?" he whispered, twisting a coil of her hair around his forefinger. She reached up and took his hands in hers, then slipped out of his arms. He moved closer to her, but she stepped back, one palm outstretched in front of her.

"I did, James," she answered in a shaky voice. "And I cannot wait a moment longer."

"Well, then, tell me quickly, and afterward let me kiss you again," he begged her, with a silky pout. "Oh, sweet girl, you have no idea how hard it's been for me out there, pretending to ignore you. You drive me absolutely mad, my darling."

She was still trembling, but the color which he had kissed into her cheeks had darkened to a flaming scarlet. I couldn't blame her for the feeling; there was something so vital and sincere about him now. He was not a cool criminal at all, not in front of her. All of his worries seemed to have vanished in that moment, and his thoughts were only about her. In spite of myself I actually envied her then, just for a second. What must it feel like to captivate a man like that?

"So—you've been pretending not to notice me?" she asked him in a hopeful voice.

"Of course, what else could I do?" he exclaimed, throwing his hands out in front of him. "Do you want me to lose my place, Agatha? Do you want to lose yours?"

She glanced down at her waist and blushed. I could see what she was thinking, and I gritted my teeth in anticipation. *Don't tell him*, I begged her silently, *please don't tell him now.*

"How much longer, James?" she asked him finally. "What exactly are we waiting for?"

His jaw hardened, and he crossed his arms. "Not much longer," he told her grimly. "There's an old injustice that I have to set right. But I promise you—it won't be long."

"What are you talking about?" she demanded. "What injustice do you mean? The earl has been nothing but good to all of us. Lord Hartfield is probably the best master you've ever had."

"Oh, yes, he's certainly a perfect *master*," James retorted through his teeth. "Kind and generous to everyone, isn't he?"

"*I* think he is. And I don't understand why you seem so angry at him sometimes. It makes no sense. He doesn't owe you anything."

"Oh, no," he responded carelessly. "*He* doesn't owe me anything. We're not waiting for him."

She looked confused. "Then what—who are we waiting for?"

He chuckled to himself and reached his hand out to her in a sweet gesture of submission. "We are waiting for Lady Rose to come back home," he said. "She is our ticket to a real life, dearest, a life without masters and their slaves. So we are waiting for that unhappy girl to find her way back home—back home to her loving family."

She stepped back from him and shook her head. "What do you mean, James? Lady Rose is on a visit to her aunt's. That's what everybody says."

He laughed shortly and leaned back against the desk. "Oh, come on, Aggie, when have you ever heard of a noble lady traveling without her maid? In the middle of the night? Are you joking?"

"Well, then, where do you believe she's gone?" she demanded sharply.

"I have no idea," he shot back. "But I expect to find out soon."

"You expect—"

"And I also expect that you'll trust me and be patient. No more sneaking into my room, no more meetings behind the greenhouse. *Nothing* can change between us until I'm ready. No one can suspect."

"But I can't wait—"

"You *can* wait, and you will," he interrupted firmly. "Or we can end this now. I can't risk losing everything at this point."

"But—"

"And if I'm distant for a while, or even if I smile at another girl, I can't have you flying at me in a rage. I know what I am doing, Aggie. And I promise that you won't regret it in the end."

She seemed about to protest, but he pulled her close again and put his lips up to her ear. I leaned forward a little and held my breath, straining to hear what he was saying. "You have no idea how long *I've* waited, dearest," he murmured sadly. "You have no idea how hard I've worked to get here. But every other effort, every other scheme has been so small, so *insignificant* compared to this, that I can't believe that I'm actually getting close now. If in the process I make a few pounds, close an important deal, then so much the better for us. But I will *never* lose sight of my goal. I know you don't understand, and you probably never will because no one's ever really hurt you. But if you trust me and don't let me down, I promise to make you happy, just as I always have."

She nodded mutely and hastily brushed her sleeve over her cheek. "You know that you can trust me, James. I'll do whatever I have to do—"

Her hand slid down to rest briefly at her waist, and she took a deep breath. She might have spoken then, she might have confessed everything to him. But it was obvious now that James was no longer listening. He kissed her forehead and turned her toward the door. "We'd better go now before they miss us, Aggie. And remember what I told you. Nothing can change until I say so."

He turned the lamp off as he spoke and then quickly led her out into the hallway and closed the door behind him. I breathed a short prayer of thanks and scrambled to my feet. I had to hurry back to the kitchen; the housekeeper would be missing me and I had no excuse to offer her.

CHAPTER

13

B

UT I WAS NOT destined to exit quite so easily that evening. My feet had barely touched the floor when the knob creaked ominously again, and I sprang quickly back into the gap. And so once more I found myself crouching on the cold stone ledge—but this time I could not see a thing inside the room. Whoever had entered had not turned the lamp back on, and there was no way to guess what they were doing. Had James returned to Lord Victor's bedroom? I wondered. How long was he intending to stay? I couldn't possibly let him see me now; he'd know that I had overheard his conversation with Agatha, and would guess that I'd been spying on them—even though I couldn't possibly know what any of it had meant.

What had all of that been about? I asked myself. What schemes had he been speaking of? Could he have been hinting at one of his blackmail plots? Was he thinking about Adelaide's letters and the "deal" that he was about to strike with her? But then—what injustice was he referring to? Why had he seemed angry with the earl?

Somehow I felt instinctively that he had told Agatha at least a portion of the truth. He had admitted that there were certain things he could not explain to her and had begged her to be patient. If he had been trying to deceive her, he could have simply invented a convenient lie. No, I felt sure that he had actually been honest with her then. And if he really had been truthful, why had he said that he had no idea where Lady Rose had gone? And if he didn't know, who did?

And more importantly, how on earth was I going to get back into the house? The minutes ticked by and nothing changed. There was a sighing sound from inside the room and the groan and shuffle of someone sinking into an armchair. This did not bode well for me. There were only two possibilities remaining to me now. I would have to risk a descent down the flimsy tree branches or resign myself to a lonely night upon the narrow ledge and many uncomfortable questions in the morning.

The gravity of my situation dawned on me as I tried to grasp the branches in my hand and felt them give way beneath me. There was a thick bough looming in the darkness some ten feet below, but the limbs closest to me were too flimsy to support my weight.

I untied my shawl from my neck and, bending forward, wrapped it around the thickest branch that I could reach. Then I tugged twice at the cloth, testing its strength, and with a quick jerk, pushed myself off the ledge and dropped down onto the bough below. It was slick with moss, and I grabbed onto the trunk as my feet slid off the branch. After I had steadied myself, I flung the shawl over a nearby branch and prepared to lower myself onto a lower bough.

I do not know whether it was the stem that snapped or the cloth that tore, but I had no sooner leaned over than a terrible crack and a ripping sound splintered the still night air, and I felt myself falling through the darkness. The branch beneath me broke my fall and cut short the scream which had burst from my lips. I lay there for a moment, conscious only of a nauseated, swimming feeling, until a loud shouting somewhere above me brought me unsteadily to my feet.

Lord Victor was glaring at me from his open window and gesturing with his hands. He vanished into the darkness

of his room, and I leaned heavily against the tree trunk,
wondering if he planned to inform the household of the
new maid's lunacy. Presently I could discern a faint glow of
lamplight and a white flutter at his window. He had fash-
ioned a rope of bedsheets and was lowering it down to me.
I grasped the end and was slowly pulled back into the room.

We stood opposite each other for a moment, breathing
heavily and shivering from the night air. Some explanation
was due, of course, and I pointed to my shawl, which still
fluttered on the tree outside. "I had come in to see if the fire
was ready for Your Lordship, and I opened the window for
some air. The wind blew my shawl out onto the branch and
when I leaned out—"

I stopped and looked down at my feet. He was clearly
not listening to my explanation. He had barely glanced at
me while I was speaking, and now I saw that he was gazing
past me and that his face had hardened into an expression of
blank surprise. He was staring at the fireplace, but it was not
the sooty pile upon the floor that fascinated him. His mouth
was hanging open, and his eyes were fixed in widened terror
upon the ivory mantelpiece. Slowly he stepped over to the
wall and turned up the gas. There upon the mantel were several clear streaks of coal dust. At first glance they appeared
to be careless smudges, marks that had been made by dirty
fingers against the paint. But after a second look, I saw that

they formed letters, a string of V's, X's, and I's that seemed to have no meaning. Yet somehow these symbols had paralyzed him; the brash confidence had gone and he actually trembled before me. Finally he gasped out, "It's not possible!" in a horrified whisper and grabbed a nearby chair to steady himself.

Then he turned on me. "Did you see who did this?" he demanded, his voice rising. I shook my head dumbly and wondered why he hadn't thought to blame me, as I had been the last one in the room. And yet his look was not accusing, just panicked and wild, like that of a hunted man desperate for shelter.

"Sir," I faltered, "I can ask the other girls if they heard or saw anyone—"

"No!" he shot out. "It—it doesn't matter, really. I just—I just don't like to have my things disarranged or dirty, that is all." But his voice cracked as he said it, and he reached a shaking arm out for a book on the table. He clutched it to his chest for a moment in distracted agitation and then started madly turning the pages. "I don't understand," he muttered to himself, and as he moved toward the light I saw that he was holding a leather-bound copy of the Bible in his hands.

I looked at the fireplace and considered the gray marks. The first were three vertical lines followed by a V and three

more vertical lines. I glanced over at the Bible and saw that
he was gazing intently at the chapter of Leviticus that discussed leprosy and the burning of contaminated clothing.
This was what he was reading in a time of crisis? Either the
lord had become suddenly deranged or—

The solution came to me in a triumphant flash, and I
understood what I was witnessing. I smiled in spite of myself
and then quickly composed my face into a picture of dumb
confusion. When he had finished his study, I was kneeling
by the fireplace and beating the sooty rug with a broom as
if it were the source of all our troubles. He looked up finally,
and I saw that he had composed himself; his breathing was
regular now, though a thin layer of perspiration still shone
on his upper lip.

He opened his mouth, probably intending to order me out
of the room, but a sharp knock on the door distracted him.
James entered, glanced at the open Bible on the desk, then at
his pale master, and then at me. He frowned, advanced into
the room, and his eyes darted quickly to the marks upon the
mantelpiece. I knew, of course, that James had made those
marks, less than half an hour earlier. But would he suspect
that I had been hiding in the room then? Enough time had
passed between James's exit and his return. I might have
entered the room immediately after he'd gone. I felt his eyes
on me, and I moved quickly in the direction of the fireplace.

"Mrs. Bentney told me to come in here and sweep up the mess, sir," I muttered and bent over the pile of ashes by the hearth.

But the valet had other things on his mind. If he suspected me, he certainly wouldn't show it now. He turned casually to his master as if suddenly recalling a message. "Your father has asked that you meet him in his study, sir, before you dress for the dinner party. He said that it is urgent."

Lord Victor nodded slowly and closed the Bible. "I am tired, James, honest to God I am," he murmured.

"Make sure the fire is lit before you go," James said to me before he closed the door behind them. "Master may wish to retire early tonight."

Lord Victor had not meant that he wished to go to bed; his tone had spoken of a deeper weariness that would not be cured by sleep. James had understood exactly what he meant.

The question was, Why was the valet persecuting this family? Did Lord Victor suspect that his sister had been hurt and now feared the same fate for himself? And if so, why did he not ask for help?

It was possible that the Bible on the table had the answer to my question. I glanced up at the markings again and hesitated. No, I decided, it would be best to write them down now and come back to the book later. The conversation in the library was possibly more important, and I could not risk missing it.

II. IV.III : V.III / XI V.VII/ IV V.VII/II.III. I tore a sheet from a notebook on the desk and quickly copied the symbols, then shoved the paper in my pocket and headed to the study.

I passed James on my way down. He had a preoccupied, distant look in his eyes, and he hurried past me without speaking. He had not stayed for the family meeting, and I was now more anxious to hear what was being said behind the closed library door. When the valet was out of sight, I dropped to my knees and put my ear close to the keyhole. The opening was not big enough to see through, but I could hear the conversation as clearly as if I were in the room.

"I cannot believe it," Lady Hartfield was saying. "How could she behave in this way? I never read such a letter in all my life. I always said that we allowed her too many liberties, did I not?"

There was a murmur of agreement.

"I suppose we must call Mr. Porter and let him know," the earl responded. All the confidence had gone from his tone, and he sounded as weary as his son. "I am also in shock. Still, at least she is safe. I thank heaven for that."

There was a contemptuous sniff from the lady, and the

rustling sound of cloth. I scrambled to my feet and ducked behind the staircase. Presently the library door swung open, and Lady Hartfield swept past me, followed shortly afterward by the earl and then his son. This was my chance. The family would be occupied with dressing for dinner, and I was unlikely to be disturbed. As their footsteps died away, I crept into the room and closed the door behind me.

I did not know what new evidence had just arrived, but it was obvious that I had to examine it myself. Although I was relieved to hear that Lady Rose was well, somehow I could not believe that the case was really over. There was still so much that was unexplained. Why had Lord Victor been afraid? What role did James play in all of this? And finally, how was he linked to my cousin's case?

The surface of the desk was empty, and I prayed that he had left the letter in a drawer. The top one was locked, and my heart sunk with disappointment, but my spirits rose as the bottom drawer slipped open easily. I rummaged through it, searching desperately for the elusive note, but the drawer was stuffed with stacks of bills. I groaned and rose slowly to my feet. I would have to wait for Cartwright to tell me about the earl's news, while I had to be content with reporting smudges on a mantelpiece.

It was then that I saw the fire. A yellow envelope was shivering at the edge of the coals, its edges curled and black, burning before my eyes. I had wasted precious moments hunting through the desk while my last clue was disappearing.

There was no time to think about it. I rushed forward, plunged my hand into the fire, and drew out the singed letter, ignoring the shock of pain that shot through my fingers and up my arm. With a flick of my wrist, I dropped the charred paper to the ground and stomped out the flames, cursing the foolish nobleman and his thoughtlessness. Already my hand was beginning to throb, and I could feel an angry blister forming on my palm.

When the crackling stopped and the snaking fire ring had died, I picked up the brittle envelope and slipped it gingerly into my apron. With a hasty motion I swept the remaining ashes into the hearth and left the study, holding a protective hand over the new treasure in my pocket.

CHAPTER
14

My dear parents,

By now you have no doubt discovered my absence and are wondering what prompted me to leave my home as I did, without an explanation or warning. The truth is, I have tried without success to find my place among you and I am weary of my life. That, at least, cannot come as a surprise. Anyone who knew me also knew of my unhappiness.

What may come as a shock is that I have found love at last, despite everyone's predictions. I know you

*would never approve of my choice as he is below my
station, but I cannot care. He loves me and accepts
me for who I am. By the time you get this letter, we
will be married and on our way to America.*

*I beg that you will not search for me, as I know
that my new life will only make you miserable. Please
burn this letter and forget me; it is all that I ask.*
Your loving
Rose

I stared at this impossible note in blank amazement. It
was as much of a puzzle after the tenth reading as it was
on the first. It had to be authentic, I could not doubt that,
for the girl's parents would surely know their daughter's
handwriting. And yet the script was sloppy and weak; an
educated noblewoman would never have written such a
note. There were splotches of ink across the page and one
section was blurred and unclear. I simply could not believe
that her last message to her parents would be so thoughtless; an earl's daughter would have taken more care with a
dress order. And why would she ask them to burn the letter?
Her elopement would not remain a secret for long. What
purpose would be served by destroying this final memory?

Something was very wrong, I was sure of it. Lady Rose
had been described as awkward by some, high-strung by

others; but no one had ever called her cruel. And this was a letter calculated to inflict pain, to embarrass and wound those who had loved her. I had not known the girl, but I still could not accept it.

I studied the note again with a more critical eye. The ink stains had surprised me most of all. Maids wrote messy letters; their mistresses used blotting paper. I brought my candle closer to the page. The first mark had been made with a thumbnail dipped in ink; I could see the whorls of a partial thumbprint. It might have been an accident, of course, it might have been—

But then I saw the second stain, and I knew that there had been no accident and the letter was a lie. One fingerprint could have been an oversight, but three identical prints across the page?

But what was the significance of the markings? What could I learn from this discovery? I held the page at arm's length in front of me and frowned. The prints had been clearly placed beneath the words *He*, *life*, and *Please*. But this sentence did not make sense in any order. If there was a message in this, it would have been a hasty one, thought of quickly and executed in a moment. It could not be complicated.

That's when I saw it.

The first stain was the largest and the most deliberate,

underlining the entire word. The next two were smaller and placed at the beginning of the words:

HELP.

One pleading word behind a mask of lies. It was the only message of the letter.

And it would be her final farewell, for the man who had forced her to write those words intended that she disappear. *I beg that you will not search for me.* No one would look for her, and her kidnapper would make certain she was never found.

But who had taken her, and why?

And why had the earl burned the letter as she had asked him to do? Was that a natural response to his daughter's last message? Shouldn't he have saved it as a final memory of her—or at least preserved it so Mr. Porter and Cartwright could look at it?

I glanced again at the address on the envelope. The handwriting here was masculine, cramped and awkward, clearly a disguised hand. I knew that only a skilled forger could successfully mask his script. If I could obtain a sample of the criminal's writing, my case would be complete.

Complete. I shivered at the thought. I could hand two slips of paper to Cartwright and say the words, "Our case is now complete."

And he would smile at me and say—

I shook myself and pushed the scene out of my mind. It did not matter what he said, I told myself. I was not doing this for him.

I was doing this to save Adelaide and Lady Rose, and perhaps also to save myself, to prove to myself that I was worth more than a sweet face on the marriage market. But I was certainly not doing this for Cartwright.

No, I did not care what Peter Cartwright thought of me. I could not allow myself to care.

CHAPTER
15

Now that I was certain Lady Rose had been abducted and I had identified James as the most likely suspect, how could I discover where he had taken her? Before the day was out I would need to report something to Cartwright, who was likely waiting anxiously for my message. But he would ask for proof of James's guilt, some evidence that identified him as the man who had addressed and posted the envelope. I would need to get a sample of James's writing. The obvious next step would be to rummage through the valet's room for some scrap or note he had written, but I had no doubt that Agatha's snooping had already put him on his guard, and he likely kept all of his papers hidden away as a security against her prying. I searched for a solution as I descended to the kitchen. The dinner party was under way, and they would be calling for me anyway.

The guests had come for an overnight stay, as their estate was too far for a comfortable nighttime return. In preparation, the bedrooms had been aired and linen laid, coal brought into previously empty hearths and curtains brushed. Sauces had been boiled, fowl roasted, meat joints braised, and puddings set. The silverware had been carefully polished and turned, and the table set for twenty in precisely measured rows.

As the dinner was now drawing to a close, I begged leave to tend to my wounded arm, which had begun to ache. The housekeeper took one look at my weeping skin and indicated the supply room where I might find some clean rags and salves, but warned me to return immediately after I had done. When she had gone, I wrapped my blistered palm in a moistened dressing and tied the ends over my sleeve, then quickly slipped outside to find my little messenger.

Perkins was hovering by the toolshed. I, of course, had no message to relay to Cartwright yet; I wanted to have a complete chain of evidence before I wrote to him. Still, I had to communicate with my messenger that evening, if only to reassure Cartwright that I was doing well and progressing in my investigation.

"I'll check back again, in a couple of hours," he told me with a shrug. "Meantime I'm supposed to give you this."

He handed me a crumpled letter, touched his cap, and disappeared over the hill.

I crouched by the servants' entrance with my note and read it over by the dim gaslight.

My dear assistant,

I have not heard from you for some time, so I must assume that something terribly exciting has occurred that has left you no opportunity to write to me. I know that it is challenging to you to remain focused on your mission when you're surrounded by so many devilishly handsome bachelors, but perhaps you can remember that I am waiting patiently for some news?

I know how much you admire my methods of investigation and how you must be aching to imitate everything I do, but may I remind you that I climbed out of Lady Rose's window in order to clarify a clue? You didn't need to repeat the exercise. But if you felt you had to, did you have to hurl yourself down a tree to do so?

You needn't look so shocked, my friend. Perkins heard your scream and saw you get hoisted back into the house. Who else witnessed your entertaining act, may I ask? Is all of Hartfield now aware that there is a batty housemaid scaling trees outside her master's windows?

While you've been playing at whatever you've been playing at, I have been on James's trail. There are a few points that still need clarifying, and I am work-ing on them now. May I ask if anyone has mentioned the name Mark Fellows, or the squire from Lambley? If they do, please make a note of it.

Your patient servant,

Peter Cartwright

P.S. I would burn this letter if I were you. There are far too many questionable letters floating about in this case, and I don't want to add mine to the pile.

I crushed the paper in my fingers and shoved it roughly into my pocket. I would certainly be burning it when I got a moment free, but now, with the dinner party and the tidy-ing up that would follow, I had no time for anything. It was easy for him to laugh, I thought irritably. He had no other obligations; he was not hampered by his disguise. I was supposed to be both bold and cautious all at once, all while obeying a short-tempered housekeeper.

As I entered the kitchen, I was summoned to relight an extinguished fire in the drawing room. I had just completed my task when the door opened and the ladies entered, resplendent in their silk dinner gowns and eager to share the most current news in gossip and high fashion. A maid of my station was not permitted near the company, so I shrank quietly into the adjoining anteroom and watched them from behind the door. Lady Hartfield swept into the room first, followed by Lady Jane (Lord Victor's fiancée), the Duchess of Wellsborough (the fiancée's mother), and several older relatives of the bride.

The women had contented themselves with polite commentaries on horse breeding and politics throughout dinner to please their male companions. Now, as their husbands relaxed with port and cigars in the other room, the real conversation flowed fast and free. The talk was thick with details about lace prices and milliners, fascinating descriptions about ballroom slippers and bouffant sleeves and frightening tales of gown trains that tore in two when young debutantes backed away from their presentation to the queen.

The subject of clothing was discussed and put to rest, and a brief and awkward silence reigned. My eyes fixed on Lady

Jane during that moment, and I was glad to study her from my dark corner by the door. She was a shiny, soft bubble of a woman, with dimpled skin powdered pink and white, and a head of flaxen curls. She was clearly the only one of the party who was enjoying herself, for the rest of the women appeared drained by the proceedings, though they tried to politely hide the fact. No silence was too short or too awkward but Lady Jane proved ready to fill it with the chirp of her voice. Irrelevant questions about nothing spilled from her lips, directed at everyone and no one.

During the pause, Lady Jane's restless little eyes fixed on a feature of the room and a stream of commentaries flowed forth. "Those velvet drapes are lovely. Wherever did you get them? That's an interesting shade of red. What color would you say it is? What sort of elms are there by the stream? I adore elms. Do the bushes by the front of the home bloom all year or only in the spring? Are you happy with your gardeners? Were they born on the estate, or are they imported?" And so on, until the lady of the house began to droop and look about desperately for some distraction.

I had almost given up hope of hearing anything of interest when Lady Jane leaned over to her future mother-in-law and commented, "Why, I had quite forgotten to ask after Rose, Lady Hartfield! How is she? We heard that she had taken ill! Nothing serious, I hope?"

"Not at all, my dear," replied the elder lady without hesitation. "Her aunt, you know, has been very poorly for several weeks, and Rose insisted on going down to stay with her. Several days ago she came down with a bad chill and has taken to her bed. I just received a letter from her assuring me that it is nothing serious and that she is looking forward to the wedding."

The brazen lie impressed me. Lady Hartfield was planning to preserve appearances to the last, it seemed.

"I am glad," chirped Lady Jane. "I do so long to see her. Did I tell you that I got a letter from her this past Wednesday? She asked if she might come visit me the following day. I wrote back immediately, but I got no answer. My response must have arrived after she had left for her aunt's home."

"I will forward it on to her if you like."

"Oh, it is of no account, Lady Hartfield, for it was she who made the appointment, not I, and now it is quite broken, I think. She wrote that she had something she needed to speak to me about. Can you imagine what it was? The wedding procession, do you think? Was she unhappy with her dress?"

"Oh, not at all, my dear. I am certain she is delighted with it! We all have been so excited about the wedding."

"As have we, my dear," chimed in the duchess. "It is so *good* to see a young man choosing a bride from among his own. It seems that half of the young men these days are choosing not to marry, or are being caught by those vulgar American heiresses. It's caused an alarming shortage of eligible bachelors."

"But, of course, you know what they say, Mother," chimed in Lady Jane. "One wedding brings another." And she glanced significantly at Lady Rose's portrait.

Lady Hartfield smiled patiently and cast about for another topic of conversation. "Have you read anything of interest lately, Jane?" she inquired.

"Yes, indeed, Mother is quite adamant that I read for the improvement of my mind. I don't think she approves of my choice of material, though. What was it you said about my last favorite, Mother? Remember 'The Sign of the Four,' the mystery story?"

"Shocking. No moral value at all. And the detective in it, whom everyone seems to admire so, was worst of all."

"Mother met him a few months ago. She objected to the fact that he was not married," sniffed the bride.

"There is a *crisis*, Jane, and young men ought not to ignore it."

"Well, I read that he was killed, Mother. He got into a fight with someone and was pushed into a waterfall."

"There now! Just as I said! That never would have happened if he had settled down. Jane, please pass the plate of licorice over here. The smell is really quite enticing."

And a sudden thrill went through me, for that platter of sweets had given me the inspiration that I needed. It was a daring plan and very risky, but the key to the mystery could be in my hands that evening. I slipped out of the drawing room and headed for the stairs. A quick visit to the pantry and a few minutes in the lower bedrooms provided me with the tools I needed.

Now I only had to get James to notice me.

CHAPTER

16

EMERGED FROM THE lower bedrooms carrying a tall pile of linen stripped from servants' beds. My hair was tucked inside my cap, held in place with one brave little pin, and the collar of my high-necked dress was missing a rather crucial button. In my pocket I carried a vial of anise oil. I had unwrapped my burned hand, and the blistered flesh smarted painfully as the bandage came away. It was an ugly sight, but it would make my little performance more convincing.

And so I paced the halls and waited for my chance. The passageway that I was guarding was the route from the dining room to the cellar, and I knew that it was just a matter of time before the gentlemen ran out of port and sent the valet for more. My patience was rewarded finally when James stepped out from around the corner, carrying a bottle and a corkscrew. I waited until he was two feet in front of me, and as I moved aside to let him pass, a turn of the ankle brought me tumbling down before him, dirty linen scattering in every direction. As I fell, I pushed the vial from my pocket, and it shattered on the parquet floor, showering us both with broken glass and pungent oil. In the confusion, I managed to knock the cap off my head, the little pin popped out, and my hair came down in a dark mass of curls around my face. The collar button had come open on its own, exposing a few inches of bare neck (and perhaps a trifle more).

I waited until the flustered valet was less than a foot from me, and as he extended his arm to help me up, I lifted my eyes and showed my injured hand to him.

"I'm sorry I'm so clumsy," I gasped, "but it hurts to move my wrist."

Clutching his outstretched arm, I scrambled to my feet, and as I did, I stumbled back over the oil and pulled him forward. Both his shoes were slick with anise now. The easy portion of my plan had passed. It was now time for the daring part.

I held his arm a moment longer and waited, painfully aware of the little patch of white beneath my open collar. His eyes skimmed down my neckline, then traveled farther, to the edge of my chemise. I ducked my head and clutched defensively at my collar, and he flushed to the roots of his blond hair but did not look away.

"I'd better go and get a broom," I gasped, "before anyone sees this mess."

"Why don't you sit down a moment here and collect yourself?" he suggested in a kind tone. "You're looking a bit ragged. I'll clean this up." His eyes had not left my face.

"I—I'm not allowed to sit on any of the furniture," I protested meekly.

He shook his head and sighed. "Of course you're not, how stupid of me," he remarked. He picked up one of the sheets that I had dropped and spread it across the floor. "There we are—that will do for now. You can rest on that."

As I watched him, he gathered up the loose linen and folded it carefully by my feet, then mopped up the anise oil with a cloth square and placed it beside the pile. When he was done, he squatted by my side and regarded me quietly for a moment. I could not think of anything to say to him—but he did not seem to notice my discomfort, just stared at me as if he was expecting me to speak.

I was nervous, and the longer he watched me, the more nervous I became. There was something unnatural in his look, a vague doubt lurking in his eyes. On the surface he was all pleasantness and charm, his full lips curled into an easy smile, a healthy blush still coloring his cheeks. But there was a tension beneath it all, a ripple of a muscle in his neck, a tautness in his posture, a slight tilt of his head toward me. He was waiting, I realized, waiting for me to give something away.

But what exactly was he waiting for? Was he simply charmed by my helpless maiden act? Or was he wondering about me now? Was he questioning my role at Hartfield, my arrival so soon after Lady Rose's disappearance, my presence in Lord Victor's room earlier in the evening? Had I gone too far with my little scheme just now and made myself look suspicious?

I had to act quickly, I realized; I had to do something to throw him off the scent, or my plan would fall apart before I could put it into action. But even as I cast about desperately for a distraction, his hand had already traveled to my hair. Slowly, with almost seductive care, he brushed his finger through a curl beside my ear and plucked a little shard of glass out of the strand. He held it up with a short laugh and then tossed it over his shoulder. "You have to be more careful, little one," he told me playfully. "Especially if you plan on following me."

I felt my face flush dark, and I drew back in embarrassment. There could be only two possible meanings to his joke—and one of them did not bode well for me. There was only one way to look innocent, I realized, and that was to admit my guilt openly and beg him to forgive me.

I lifted my head and met his gaze, then slowly widened my eyes in meek amazement. "How did you *know*?" I asked him in a shocked whisper. "Was it really obvious?"

He relaxed a little and leaned back against the wall. The wary expression had faded somewhat, but I saw that he had not completely let his guard down. "Well, only a little," he admitted with a smirk. "I couldn't help noticing that you happened to be everywhere I was today."

I giggled bashfully and scrambled to my feet. "I'm very sorry about that," I breathed. "Please don't tell anyone that I've been so foolish. I promise not to bother you again."

Before he could respond, I scooped the pile of linen off the floor and backed away from him, still holding one guarded arm across my chest. He grinned at me and opened his mouth to speak but I had already turned and was running down the hall. As I rounded the corner I glanced back and saw that he was still staring after me, lips parted in a pleased, distracted smile.

My plan could have gone far worse, I reflected as I put away the dirty linen. And I'd discovered that playing silly maidservant had more advantages than I had thought. Criminal or not, I now knew for certain that the man was vulnerable to flattery. And truthfully, despite my pity for Agatha, I could not entirely regret my brief flirtation with the dashing valet. He had looked so very captivated in that moment. I had never experienced anything like that before. The men of my acquaintance were too well-bred to show a lady such attention. Even Mr. Cartwright—well, I had no idea what he thought of me. So far he had treated me more like an interesting pet or toy, rather than as a young woman.

I thought about Cartwright's warning as I prepared the final portion of my plan. "You are so innocent and thoughtless, Dora," he had insisted. He had instructed me to be only a naïve observer, a sweet and timid maidservant. This was not turning out as either of us had expected.

My dear James,

I am so hapy that I come to Hartfield now. I am sorry about my clumsyness this evening. I hope we can meet again somtime soon. Peraps after dinner

*tommorrow? By the stables near the greenery. Please
rite if you can come and leave your note by the fowtain.*

The next time he emerged from the dining room, I was
ready with my message. As he passed me, I saw him wink
broadly in my direction. I reached out my arm to stop him,
and he froze in surprise as I extended my note in a shaking
hand. He took it from me without a word, but his fingers
brushed over my wrist in a teasing caress, like a subtle tickle.

I was lucky that no one had seen his gesture, or the rumors
of a brewing romance would have reached the kitchen within
the hour. That would have been a painful and embarrassing
complication for me. I was sorry enough already for betray-
ing Agatha; she did not have to learn that her only friend at
Hartfield was flirting with the man she loved. He was not
worthy of her heart, it was true, but that did not lessen my
treachery or my guilt. The sooner my double role was over,
the better.

His reply came sooner than I expected. The corner of his
note could be seen protruding from beneath the fountain
basin within half an hour of our meeting. *I will be behind
the greenery tomorrow evening. I must speak with you. Yours,
James.*

I had my evidence and my trap was set, I thought, as I ran

to my room with my hard-won prize. By the tradesmen's entrance I ran into Perkins, my little messenger. I had not had time to examine James's note yet, but I was confident enough to call in Cartwright.

"I have a message for you," I told him in a breathless whisper. "Tell Mr. Cartwright to come to Hartfield tomorrow afternoon. I have something to show him."

It was a lovely moment for me. Perkins had caught some of my enthusiasm, and he congratulated me, respect and admiration shining in his widened eyes. Then he fled, and I realized, too late, that in my excitement I had forgotten a portion of my message. I would have to find him in the morning and tell him.

Ten minutes later, I was crouching in the servants' quarters with my two clues: the envelope from Lady Rose's letter and James's note to me. James had dictated Lady Rose's farewell message, I was sure of it, and then mailed it to Hartfield. Now I could identify James as the writer of the envelope by comparing the two scripts. They have to match, I muttered to myself, as I passed the candle from one to the other. They *have* to.

I stared at the scribbles until my eyes went dim, turning them sideways and upside down in my frustration. Then I slipped the papers under my mattress and dropped face-first onto my pillow. I had been so certain, so absolutely certain that I had already crowed my victory to Perkins and he would pass it along to Cartwright. But there was no doubt about it.

The writing did not match.

CHAPTER
17

I NEEDED ONE TINY CLUE, one shred of evidence, something solid that didn't fall to pieces at my touch. And I needed it soon, before my meeting with Cartwright the next day. I couldn't show up with nothing, not after I had boasted about my fantastic progress on the case. There was no time left now, no chance to wait for something grand to tell him. I would have to ignore all of his advice and disregard his rules. I needed to break into James's room that night.

What else could I do? Even if James wasn't involved in

Lady Rose's case, even if he was as loving as Agatha seemed to think he was, wasn't it possible that he was still behind Adelaide's blackmailing? I had at least his initials to go on, didn't I? And what if my cousin's letters were hidden in his room and I uncovered them? I would be no closer to helping the earl's missing daughter, but at least I would have the satisfaction of saving my cousin's marriage. I really had no other choice.

And I realized that now would be the perfect time, before the guests retired to their rooms. James would be busy fetching and carrying all evening for Lord Victor, so I would have a few clear minutes to search the place.

Agatha had pointed out James's chamber to me earlier that morning. I waited until the coast was clear, then slipped down the hallway and into his room. My first action was to locate a hiding place, in case I was interrupted. I had no desire to fall out of a window again and even less desire to try to explain to James what I was doing snooping under his bed. I made a mental note of the spacious wardrobe in the corner and then began the process of snooping under his bed and everywhere else.

Unfortunately for me, within five minutes I was able to confirm only one of my suspicions: that James was too smart to leave anything incriminating lying about. Every unlocked drawer was empty, no scrap of paper, no photograph, no

loose telegram was anywhere to be found. Even his hairbrush
was clean.

And, as luck would have it, less than ten minutes after I
had entered, I was interrupted by the occupant of the room.
This time, at least, I had a plan, and I had climbed into
his wardrobe and was crouching behind his shirts before
the door had opened. It was a good hiding place; peeking
between the wardrobe doors, I had a perfect view of the
entire room while still being hidden in the shadows. The
only danger, of course, was if the valet needed an article of
clothing. It would be over for me then, I knew, for James
was suspicious of me as it was.

The valet entered the room, and I held my breath. He
never turned toward me, however, but headed straight ahead
to the opposite corner, to the chest of drawers beside his
bed. Quickly, he drew out a set of keys and unlocked the
middle drawer, slid it open, and slipped something into his
trouser pocket. From my vantage point I could not see what
he had taken out, for his back was turned to me, but when
he rose again, I caught a passing glimpse of his expression.

It was not one that I would ever have expected to see on
him—or on any criminal. He actually looked frightened at
that moment. There was a grim tension in his jaw, but his
eyes were widened in a fixed stare, as if he had just thought
of something that had alarmed him. Then he was gone,

and I fell back against the wardrobe in limp relief. After his footsteps had died away I stole out into the hallway and scurried to my bedroom.

I slept rather poorly that night, for my disappointment weighed on me like a cold stone upon my chest. I would have nothing to tell Cartwright tomorrow, and I knew that he would make me feel my failure. Or worse, he would want to know why James had written such a note to me, what it meant and what I'd done to bring it all about. It was one thing to admit to a flirtation if I had a result to show him, a little hurrah for me. But now, with this dead end in my hand, how was I to justify my actions to him?

I buried my head under my pillow and tried to fall asleep. The damp and pungent servants' chamber was not helping much. It was difficult to breathe at night, for I shared the windowless room with three extremely dirty maidservants. The girls were allowed one bath a week, but rising before dawn was quite a trial, so that chore was often skipped. I still had not gotten used to the unpleasant odors in my room.

I awoke a few hours later from my troubled slumber with the vague feeling that I was being watched. As my eyes focused slowly in the darkness, I could just make out the trembling figure of Agatha sitting at the corner of my bed. I could not be certain how long she had sat there, but the gutted candle on the night table told of a long, cold vigil. I offered her my blanket, and she wrapped it around her shoulders gratefully. Several minutes passed in silence, the girl sitting there on the bed and studying me while I wondered sleepily what she could possibly want in the middle of the night. As my eyes adjusted to the dark, I saw that her face was swollen and her eyes were bloodshot and weak. She sniffed, wiped the blanket across her cheek, and gave a hic-cupping sigh.

I suddenly remembered my recent flirtation with the valet and I sat up, awakened by a panicked guilt. With a shock of paranoid alarm, I realized that James's note was still beneath my mattress. Had she somehow found it?

"I want to thank you for taking my part with the girls below," Agatha whispered finally. "It was very good of you. Most people wouldn't have done it, not for someone like me."

I breathed an internal sigh of relief and settled back against my pillow. "It weren't nothing—" I began, but she interrupted me with a wave.

"I need to talk to you about something," she said urgently.

At three in the morning? I wondered, but I nodded and murmured, "Of course."

"There's something very wrong with James," she whispered, glancing over her shoulder as if she expected to find him listening at her back.

"What do you mean?" I asked her.

"Something's been bothering him for weeks now, Dora. One moment he's as sweet as honey to me—and the next he's sneaking about like someone is after him. He's in some trouble, I just know it."

"But what's he done?"

She sighed and rubbed her forehead. "Oh, I've seen him do any number of odd things. A fortnight ago I caught a peek at a note that he was reading, but when I looked at it, there wasn't no meaning to it. It was just letters with no meaning."

"What sort of letters?"

"Just X's and V's and lines. No words at all. I asked him what it was, but he told me to mind my own business. And not to sneak up behind him."

"Well, perhaps he was doin' research on Egyptians," I suggested brightly. "They wrote in strange symbols, I heard. Did he have a book open next to the letter?"

I wasn't thinking about Egyptian hieroglyphics, of course. I was hoping she would mention the Bible on Lord Victor's desk, which I suspected was linked to the strange symbols that I'd just seen scrawled over the fireplace.

"Yes, actually—he had a set of Dickens next to him and was glancing back and forth between his letter and the book. But that didn't make no sense to me, neither."

Not the Bible, then, I thought. Why were all of my theories wrong?

"But, Agatha, I still don't understand," I protested after a pause. "Those letters that you saw—that doesn't mean he's guilty of anything."

"Where did he go tonight, then, answer me that!" she demanded, her voice rising. One of my roommates groaned and cursed irritably in her sleep. Agatha bent down to me. "It's what I wanted to talk to you about, actually," she continued in a lower tone. "Earlier this afternoon—he was so kind to me. I met him in Lord Victor's room just before dinner and we talked for a little while. Ah, Dora, if you had only seen him then you would have understood why I love him so. He was so tender and honest. But then, after we had parted, something happened and he became distant again. He'd warned me that he would be. He told me to be patient with him. But I knew something was wrong. So after the dinner party was over I was watching him. He was carrying some towels up to his master's room and then I saw him stop, look out of the window, duck into his room, and then take off out the door, like his life depended on it. He weren't gone but an hour, but when he came back"— she sank her voice to a tremulous hiss—"he had dirt on his trouser knees—and—I saw—I saw *a revolver* bulging from his pocket."

I stared at her in alarm. I realized suddenly that I had seen him do what she'd just described; it was a weapon that he must have taken from his drawer while I watched him from the wardrobe. Was it possible that while I was "rummaging through coal dust," as Cartwright had said, Lady Rose had met her end? Had I really been so close to her killer and yet had failed to stop him? Real tears bit my eyes, and when I reached out to grab Agatha's hands, my own were shaking. I was not acting anymore, and the memory of my little performances in front of Lord Victor and James filled me with disgust. What had I been proud of, after all?

"Where could he have gone?" I asked, trying to keep my voice steady and failing. "I don't know the area so well as you."

She seemed to draw strength from my agitation, as if upsetting her emotional friend had somehow eased her mind. My reaction had at least justified her concern, and she was encouraged by it. She patted me on the back in a kind maternal gesture. "I didn't mean to scare you, Dora, I forgot how young you are. I just needed to talk to somebody so badly. I didn't know what to make of what I saw, and I just couldn't hold it in no longer. But maybe we shouldn't talk of it anymore."

"I'm all right, you just gave me a turn, that's all."

My heart had slowed a little now and I was breathing

normally. My theory did not make sense, I realized. Agatha had said that James had only been gone an hour. But why had his pants been covered in dirt? He couldn't have murdered Rose and then buried her on the Hartfield grounds as I had first imagined; he wouldn't have gotten back that quickly. "Where could he have gone?" I repeated.

She shrugged. "In that direction is Sheffield Green, the tenant village. It's about a twenty-minute walk from here. It's the nearest village to the estate; the others are miles off."

I recognized the area; I had been to their bakery earlier that day. Somewhere in that village lay the key to the mystery, then, and Lady Rose was there, praying for us to find it.

Agatha was plucking at my sleeve, waiting for my attention. I put my new theory away and focused on my friend, who had drifted back into her own thoughts.

"Oh, Dora, I never expected it to come to this," she sighed. "My mother didn't raise me so. She was a good woman, went to church regular, taught me to read and write. She was so proud that a daughter of hers would get such a noble position in a grand estate, and me only seventeen. She said I had quite a career in front of me, that I could work my way up to lady's maid one day, even though I was only from a poor family, and she herself only a cook's assistant. 'Course I didn't pay her any mind, for whoever heard of such a thing? I had my future all planned out, though, from the moment

I got here. And then I met him, and Dora, he was like no one I'd ever seen before. And I couldn't help it; I believed everything he told me. He promised to marry me; we were planning to open a small shop together. But it's all coming apart in front of me now. I realize now that I can't trust him to take care of me—or anybody else."

She wrapped the blanket tighter around her shoulders and sighed.

"I was hoping that perhaps you could help me think of some explanation for his behavior, something that I hadn't thought of," she continued sadly. "But now that I've told you everything, I can hear the truth myself. I can see how blind I've been about him."

She paused here for a moment; a fading hope flickered briefly in her eyes, as if she was still waiting for me to reassure her, to tell her that I had found some magical solution for her, and a happy ending to her story. But I couldn't think of a reasonable lie to tell her.

"Thank you for listening to me," she murmured when I didn't speak. "I have no one to confide in now, except for you. My mother's dead, you see, she died last year. It's better so, or she would have died if she had found out that I had—you understand."

"But, Agatha, he's the guilty one, not you," I told her.

She hesitated for a moment and then glanced over her

shoulder again. "There's something else I wanted to tell you," she whispered. "It's why I woke you, partly. I don't have much time left, possibly. I'm going to be showing soon. And I can't stay here much longer, Dora. You saw how the other girls were mocking me; they all know about me, and I can't bear it anymore. So I've found another position. I just heard this morning from a gentleman in Hampstead. It's an upper housemaid post, not as good as this one, to be sure. But I can't be too choosy now, not in my—condition."

I nodded, and squeezed her hand in sympathy.

"But how—will you work—if—" I glanced significantly at her still-slim figure. She colored and looked away.

"I—have a—friend. She knows of a place—of a man— who helps girls who are—in trouble. I am going to see him in two days—"

I sat quietly, regarding her. What could I say to her? I had heard the whispered horrors of her choice before, but I had never really thought about it at any length. Our minister had ranted about this once, in euphemism, as "immorality and murder" and I had nodded with the congregation. But I couldn't imagine that he was speaking about this girl. And what choice would he have offered her? She was facing a lifetime of shame ending in the workhouse. I could not see any evil in the pathetic form before me. There was no defiance in her features, her head was bowed, her red-rimmed eyes looked meekly to me for forgiveness.

"If anything happens to me—I just wanted someone to know," she continued. "I wanted to tell someone before I went. I thought that maybe you would understand. Afterward, if I am ill, you will stop them gossiping won't you? When I am better I will hand in my notice. If you're ever in London, you can look me up—the Appledore Towers, Hampstead—that's where I'll be. You don't have to, of course. I'll understand if you'd rather not."

"I won't forget you."

Her tired face lit up, and she embraced me, tearfully.

As I put my arms around her, she began to sob in muffled, ragged gasps against my neck, and I held her as she cried, and listened to her pleading murmur, "I'm sorry, oh, my poor mother, I'm so, so sorry," until it died in sleep. Then I laid her head down on my pillow and sat huddled in my blanket, watching her as she dreamed. She had begged for forgiveness for something she could not change, from a mother who could no longer comfort her. That misery, at least, I could understand.

CHAPTER
18

THE FOLLOWING MORNING I found Perkins at our meeting rock by the toolshed and delivered the rest of my message.

Mr. Cartwright—

Meet me at Mulligan's Tavern in Sheffield Green at four this afternoon. Bring a dog with a good sense of smell. Also a Bible.

Dora

P.S. I am no longer writing you long letters. From

now on you will only get instructions. Nothing to mock
in this one, is there?

Perkins took my note, and in turn handed me a letter from
Adelaide, which she had sent through Cartwright. It was a
long, sweet message, and it made me feel guiltier than ever.
There was a good deal of worrying in it, and tearful questions, and pleas for news from me. *Please let me know that I*
was right to send you with that woman. Did Miss Prim give
you my last letter? Dora, I will not sleep until I hear from you,
she'd written. She did not mention the reason for my situation, however; her blackmail case was not anywhere in the
message. Perhaps she was afraid that her letter to me would
miscarry as the others had and end up in the wrong hands,
or perhaps she was so scared for me that her own concerns
had faded into the background. Either way, I had to ease her
mind, and soon. I would write to her the next opportunity,
I vowed. But I'd have to think of something innocent to say
before I did. *Dear Adelaide, I'm about to meet a young man in*
a tavern did not seem appropriate for the occasion.

I tucked her letter in my pocket and rushed off to complete my chores before my appointment with Cartwright.

Our assigned meeting place was located on the north side
of the tenant farmers' village, about a mile from the country

estate. Mulligan's tavern was hardly the sort of place that any respectable young woman would enter, and therefore seemed to be the best choice. It was also ideal because the staff of Hartfield never frequented it, preferring establishments that catered to servants of nobility. I had briefly considered the sitting room at the village inn, but dismissed it when I learned that the innkeeper's wife was Mrs. Bentney's cousin, and that she spent her idle hours ferreting out tidy bits of gossip about everyone she met.

The tavern was a garishly painted hovel wedged between two other seedy establishments. The entire row of shops sagged in the middle and appeared to be supported by a single moldy beam and by the men who gathered there during their lunch hour to sponge away their boredom with beer and bawdy humor. Several workmen tottered about declaring their affection for absent women. At the far end of the room a little girl pushed her unconscious father off his stool and screamed at the barkeep in a shrill voice. A party of stable hands sat in an exclusive, tight circle in the center, smoking and debating the relative merits of various oats. I chose a corner table and ordered a cup of cider, which was delivered to me in a filmy glass by a very friendly ex-mariner with no teeth.

I settled back in my chair and tried to appear at home, and even to enjoy myself a little. After all, young girls from good families did not normally enter taverns; my aunt would have disowned me for even considering such a thing. So perhaps I should have relished the dense smoke and the plaintive tunes from the fiddler in the opposite corner. A bold detective's apprentice would have inhaled the atmosphere, I suppose, and been proud of her new liberty. But, for all my boldness, I could not wait to leave.

Except for two jaundiced hags at a back table, I was the only female customer in the place, and that realization made me quite uncomfortable. In entering the pub, I had left my respectability at the door and was now regarded by all present as a lady of dubious virtue. It was difficult to ignore the workmen by the bar, who leered at me over their drinks and made audible comments about my figure.

After some vain attempts to drain the liquid in my glass, I began a careful study of every character in that place, concerned that perhaps I had overlooked some shadowy figure and missed Cartwright in disguise. It was soon evident that he was late and that the little urchin by the window was in fact young Perkins, with a scarf over his face. He sat quietly, his head down, and pretended not to watch me. The child had obviously been sent to keep an eye on me until his friend arrived.

It was more than just embarrassing; it was insulting to be guarded by a little boy. I was tired of being treated as an innocent, vulnerable child who required constant supervision. And yet, I was just that, I thought with a sting of shame, a country girl from southern England who knew nothing of the world. I glanced again at the fiddler in the corner and the knot of dancers who had gathered near him. A sweaty farmer, on his way to the drunken reel, tripped past my table and upset my chair, knocking me to the ground.

As he extended his hand to me and helped me to my feet, a great shout arose from the group before the bar. I looked up, surprised, and saw that the farmer was bowing to me, as if asking me to dance. My aunt's face flashed across my mind. *Drinking in a tavern is bad enough, but* dancing? I heard her whinny.

But the farmer had grasped my hand now and had twirled me about, ignoring my cry of protest. And now his hands were behind his back and he was capering about in front of me. The fat little musician plucked his strings and began an Irish jig. I shook my head emphatically and scrambled toward my seat. A cry of disappointment erupted from the drunken crowd.

"Come on, lass, give us a dance!"

What was I to do? What would Cartwright think? I was not to be conspicuous, not to draw attention to myself; he had told me that more than once. But what was more conspicuous—a girl who sat stubbornly glaring at a party, or one who went along with the entertainment? What would my character do in such a situation? The crowd was clapping now, circling my chair, whistling with the music. How long could I sit there dumbly watching them? Where was Peter Cartwright when I needed him?

And the music, the melody, was growing louder and more insistent; two more fiddlers had emerged from among the shadows, and the beat of dancing feet drummed steadily through me. I sat staring at the dancers, my fingers gripping the fabric of my skirt, my chair bouncing to the rhythm of the pounding boots. I might have sat that way forever if another of the farmers had not stopped his prancing for a moment and, before I could object, grabbed me by the hands and pulled me up. He wouldn't let go this time but held on to my fingers with a drunken persistence.

I glanced at Perkins again and shrugged helplessly at him. He was no longer pretending not to watch me. The scarf had fallen from his face, and his mouth was hanging open in disbelief. He knew what I was thinking.

I nodded at the farmer and curtsied sweetly, then, smiling my surrender, put my arms behind my back and slowly began to dance. This was no stately ballroom waltz or promenade, but a lively hornpipe jig, which soon led into a frenetic reel. A few years back I had learned the steps from our former gardener (before my aunt dismissed him), and now as the music swelled I found that I still remembered what he'd taught me. The throb of melody was coursing through me, and I danced now as I had never danced before, as no well-bred lady could. The musicians increased the tempo. Accuracy and rhythm were sacrificed to speed as the crowd shouted for more. My embarrassment had melted with the first steps, and now I would not have stopped the song for anyone.

I cannot remember exactly how I ended up singing and dancing on the table. It certainly was not my intention to do any such thing. The crowd in the back had started craning their necks and pushing aside their friends, so a fellow dancer grabbed me by the waist and hoisted me up there to pacify them. I should have gotten down immediately, of course, but the fire of the moment was intoxicating, and I could not stop. And the fiddler had begun "The Jolly Beggar" now, so I joined in at the chorus line. I had already lost my respectability, after all. It could not hurt to sing a little.

I am truly sorry that Cartwright chose to make his entrance in the middle of the song, while I was belting out the naughtiest rhyme.

He was not difficult to recognize, even under his workman's disguise. As he came in through the door, I quickly

glanced away and concentrated on the verse that I was
singing.

> *He took her in his arms and to the bed he ran*
> *Kind sir, she says, be easy now, you'll waken our*
> > *good man.*

From the corner of my eye, I saw Perkins scurry out of the
tavern. Cartwright crossed his arms and advanced toward
me, making his way deliberately through the crowd. I would
not look directly at him. At that moment the rickety bench
on which I was balanced presented a sufficient challenge
without the added distraction of those horrified green eyes.
With every little move, the table groaned and swayed and
threatened to give way.

It was the loose back leg of my "stage" that proved to be
my undoing. I could have ignored my friend's black looks
indefinitely had it not been for that sorry piece of furniture.
An unlucky back step, a crack, a splinter, and a shout, and
I fell from glory. I regret to report that I hit Cartwright on
the way down.

The farmers shouted for more as I scrambled to my feet,
but I shook my head and curtsied, and the crowd melted away,
grumbling. Peter Cartwright gave me a tired look and jerked
his thumb in the direction of a vacant corner. As I settled

there, one of the workmen made a lewd comment about my figure. Cartwright glanced up sharply, fists clenched. A moment later he had remembered himself and settled back, though his pale cheeks stayed dark for quite some time.

I was not sure how to begin. Some explanation of my behavior seemed in order, but the excitement of the dance still lingered in my imagination. A meek apology would have sounded insincere, especially when contrasted with my tousled curls and the flush upon my cheeks.

So I said what I was thinking.

"I'm sorry that I landed on you."

His eyes were expressionless, narrow and quiet. He would not look at me.

"I—they were dancing, and—I could not draw attention to myself—" I paused, embarrassed by his silence. He still had not looked up. The last whispers of my confidence began to fade away, and I cast about for a new approach.

"I've discovered some new evidence!" I concluded desperately.

He plucked a telegram from his jacket pocket. "I suppose you wish to enlighten me about this message, which just arrived this morning. Mr. Porter has been crowing about it since it came. *Have received a communication from our daughter. Please come to estate tomorrow evening to discuss. Lord Hartfield.*'"

I pulled Lady Rose's letter from my pocket. "I have her 'communication' here, actually."

He started and finally met my eyes. "You *stole* it?" he hissed at me. "How could you—they will notice that it's gone!"

"The earl tried to *burn* it," I retorted angrily. "If I hadn't rescued it from the fire, you wouldn't have this clue at all."

He snatched the envelope from my hand, turned it over, and stared for a moment at the blackened edges. I thought he would begin with a commentary about the postmark or an examination of the script, but instead he dropped the paper on the table and crossed his arms. "Show me your other hand, Dora," he demanded.

I had passed the letter to him with my right hand; the left arm I had kept hidden beneath my apron. Reluctantly I extended my injured palm across the table and looked away. Even in the dim light my wound was terrible to see, a discolored swelling above my wrist, crusted scabs by the blistered edge, and a scarlet streak that radiated to my elbow.

He inhaled sharply and caught my hand, and slowly turned it toward the light. "For heaven's sake," he gasped. "What have you done?"

"What else could I do?" I protested. "I had to rescue the letter. At any rate—I'm fine, it doesn't really hurt," I added, even though my fingers had gone numb, and I could feel my pulse shooting raw heat through my palm.

"It doesn't hurt?" he responded with a doubtful frown. "Dora, please, stop being brave, I'm begging you. This really is a serious injury."

"I'm *not* being brave, I barely feel it," I insisted doggedly. "And you needn't fuss at me like a mother hen."

"I'm not—" he began heatedly and then paused. There was no longer any frustration in his expression; his look was still severe, but he appeared bewildered now, and his eyes had widened in real concern. He would not release my hand.

"Listen, Dora. I appreciate what you're doing, I truly do," he continued in a gentler tone. "But you needn't torture yourself like this. I'll find another way to approach this case. I'd rather do that than have you injured or falling ill—"

But I wasn't going to listen to the rest. He was trying to send me home, I realized, to take me off the case before it was finished. I knew that he was truly anxious for me, and it pleased me a little to see the honest worry in his eyes. But there was no way that I would step down now. "No, don't say that, please!" I pleaded, pulling my arm back and tucking it beneath my apron. "Peter, you have to listen to me. My hand is well enough for now, and I promise that I'll tell you if I'm feeling ill. I'll walk away myself if I have to. But you need to trust me just a little. I won't endanger the case, I won't damage your career. *Please*, Peter."

"I don't *care* about my career!" he shot back. "And I don't want you sacrificing yourself for me. I don't want *anyone* sacrificing themself for me!"

"That's very well, then! Because I'm not doing this for you. I'm here for Adelaide and Lady Rose, remember? And the longer we argue about this—the longer I'm away from Hartfield, the more suspicious everyone becomes. So, please, stop fighting me now and just read that note from Lady Rose. I need to know what you think of it."

He shook his head and slowly eased the letter from its envelope. While he studied the paper, I shifted impatiently in my seat and waited to hear his verdict.

"Someone dictated this," he remarked after a few minutes.

I gave him a little smile of triumph. "That is what I thought. But look closer there—Lady Rose had tried to spell out her own message—"

"Yes, the word 'HELP.' I noticed that before I read the letter."

"Oh." My smile faded. "Right. Well, fine, then. I was just making sure you saw that. Very smart of you."

He threw his hands up. "Well?"

"Well, Mr. Cartwright, naturally I wanted to know who dictated the letter—who addressed the envelope. So I obtained this sample of James's writing for comparison."

I thrust the slip of paper across the table. He stared at it for a moment and then shoved it in his pocket. "Well done—but the writing on the envelope doesn't match."

"I know that. Perhaps an accomplice posted it for him."

"That doesn't help us much now, does it? And why did you ask me to bring a Bible?"

"Because James is also sending coded messages to Lord Victor, and I believe I've found the key to them."

I placed my last clue beside the book and described the scene with Lord Victor and the ash stains. As I spoke he turned to page 243 (indicated by the first three Roman numerals in the message), and I began to count, "53/11."

"SHAVE," he read out.

This was not what I had expected. Still, I would not give up hope so soon. "57/4," I continued.

"BLOODY," he responded, a faint grin playing on his lips. I felt my throat constrict. "57/23."

"TURTLE-DOVES." He was snickering now. "Go on."

"No, thank you," I responded, dropping my head onto my arms. "I think 'Shave bloody turtle-doves' is humiliating enough."

"Ah, well, never mind," he replied in a kinder tone, and closed the book. "This code was clearly meant to be deciphered only by people with identical editions. And this is simply not the version that we need."

I sighed and raised my head. "I should have anticipated that. Agatha told me that she saw James thumbing through a set of Dickens once and he had a letter written in code resting next to him. Perhaps he, too, had been trying to decipher the code as we are."

"And he tried every book in the library until he found the right one."

"And yet I am certain that he *wrote* the markings on the mantelpiece," I protested. "James is involved in something guilty, I am sure of it. Agatha told me that she saw him steal away last night and that he returned with dirty trousers and a concealed gun. If we find out where he went last night, I believe it will lead us to the solution."

"With that, at least, I must agree," he responded. "And I suppose that's the reason you requested that I bring a dog?"

I nodded, and a little pride came back into my voice. "James's shoes smell like licorice. I coated them with anise oil yesterday."

I saw that I had finally impressed him. He smiled and rose quickly from the bench. "Then the trail should still be warm for us. I have the dog tied up outside."

I grabbed the Bible and followed him out the door. Lying sprawled out by the bottom step was the animal in question, a speckled, long-haired mutt who was snoring and sighing like an old man after a meal. The dog opened one eye, yawned lazily, and rolled over on his side. "He's rather an ancient fellow, isn't he?" I remarked, patting him behind the ear. "Shall I hold his leash?"

"No, I'll hold him. I have two good arms, and Toby can pull quite hard when he is on the trail."

"Oh, this is Toby?" I exclaimed. "I'd pictured a larger animal." I had read about Toby in "The Sign of the Four." It was somewhat ironic that I had traveled all this way to meet the great detective but had only succeeded in becoming acquainted with his favorite dog. "Shall we go then, Peter?"

But his mood changed again, his expression shifting to one of dawning realization. He had pulled James's note out from his pocket and was now regarding me with narrowed eyes. I could tell that he was about to say something rather unpleasant, and I had a suspicion about what it was going to be.

"Oh, for heaven's sake, what are you worried about now?" I asked him after an uncomfortable pause.

"Well, I can't help wondering about this note from James," he muttered finally, holding out the letter. "Why *exactly* did he request a meeting with you?"

I sighed irritably and snatched the paper from his hand. "I never compromised myself. You needn't glare at me like that."

"I beg your pardon, my dear Miss Joyce, but I think you'll

have to forgive my doubts about your behavior. You see, I'm still a little sore after your last display. This *is* the first time that I've worked with a barroom dancer, after all."

I suppose that he was bound to mention that eventually. In fact I was surprised he hadn't reproached me sooner and instead had allowed himself to be distracted by my wounded arm. But I was too tired to argue with him now, especially since, deep down, I knew that he was right to criticize me for what I'd done.

"The dancing was rather much, I know," I admitted finally, when I realized that he would not speak again. "But it *is* possible for a girl to use her charms without risking anything."

"Oh, really?" he retorted. "And is that how you obtained this note, then? By being charming? And flirting with a suspected *criminal*?"

"Oh, Peter, what do you *want* from me?" I shot back. "You encourage me to lie to Adelaide, dress me in a servant's costume, and send me as a spy to investigate a kidnapping. And yet I am supposed to be discreet, demure, an innocent little shadow beneath the stairs? And you? You can behave in any way you like, and no one says a word! You have no reputation to preserve, and yet for some reason you seem obsessed with guarding mine."

"But we are not the same, Miss Joyce! Why can't you see that?"

"Because I am just as capable as you are, sir. So I wish that you'd stop treating me like a helpless child!"

He frowned and turned away; I saw his hands ball into fists. Then, without warning, without a sound, he swung about and seized me by the shoulders, pushing me roughly up against the tavern wall. My right wrist was pinned against my back; my left shoulder trapped against the hard, cold brick. I fought furiously, trying to pull my arm free from his grasp, kicking savagely at his shins. He could not mean to harm me; I knew that even as I wrestled with him. But he was not allowed to touch me, not like this! I was supposed to be insulted, shaking, horrified. I should have screamed my outrage at him.

But I did not.

The struggle lasted but a moment for his grip relaxed at once and he leaned his face down close to mine. He was still holding me firmly to the wall, but I could feel a gentleness now beneath the iron strength. The fingers about my uninjured wrist were lax, forgiving; he had not touched my wounded arm, even when I had tried to strike him with it. He brought his lips down to my ear; his cheek was so near mine that I could feel its warmth against my own.

"Dora?"

I could not speak. My throat had gone quite dry, and my mouth was now so close to him that I did not dare to move.

"Dora, you know that I would never hurt you?"

I nodded mutely, and leaned back against the wall.

"But if I'd meant to hurt you here, could you have stopped it?"

"Let me go."

"Please answer me."

"I'm going to scream!"

"Just *answer me!*"

I stamped my foot and tried to kick him one more time, not to try to free myself, for I knew that to be useless, but to distract him from my blushing. After a couple of false attempts, my boot finally connected with his knee.

"Ow, Dora, for God's sake!"

I hadn't succeeded in freeing myself, but I stopped struggling for a moment and watched him grit his teeth against the pain. I was sorry to have hurt him, but seeing him uncomfortable made me a little less self-conscious. I could think more clearly now, despite the beating warmth surging through my cheeks.

"What would you like to hear?" I hissed at him. "Yes, if you wanted to—you could have hurt me. You could have strangled me, or beaten me, or done anything else you wished." My voice had sunk into a bitter whisper. "There now, are you satisfied? Or must you humiliate me further and mock my weakness?"

He released me and stepped back, his cheeks darkening with shame.

"I trust I didn't hurt you," he said apologetically after a tense pause. "I was only trying to make a point. I'm glad we understand each other now."

"I don't understand you at all, actually," I responded bitterly. "One moment you're praising me and encouraging me to succeed, and the next you're doing your best to frighten me and trying to shelter me as if you feel responsible for me. Why can't you just make up your mind?"

He sighed and rubbed a hand over his forehead. "I don't know, Dora," he replied after a pause. "But I do realize how frustrating it must be for you. And I'm sorry, really I am." He gave me a timid smile and shrugged his shoulders. "I rather overdid it with that demonstration, didn't I? But you have to understand that I do worry about you—about your safety. Not just because I care about you—but because *I'm* the one who put you in this place. I've encouraged you, just as you pointed out. And if anything was to happen to you, it would be entirely my fault. I didn't appreciate that before, but now I see that I was too hasty, that I didn't think this through properly. Dora, I just—I don't want any more people to suffer because of a selfish decision that I made."

It was a heartfelt apology, sincere and honest, and it made me regret the way I'd spoken to him earlier. And truthfully,

I couldn't help it; one phrase stood out to me from all the rest. Those sweet few words: *not just because I care about you.*

I wanted to hold on to those words, wanted him to speak them again, to tell me more. But of course I could not ask him then. We were moments from tracking James, perhaps minutes from finding Lady Rose. This was clearly not the time for that sort of talk. But I had to say something to him, to laugh off our fight and show him that I'd forgiven him. So I decided to make a careless joke, just to make him smile again.

"You don't want anyone else to suffer because of one of your decisions, Peter?" I teased him. "So, other young girls have sacrificed themselves for you in the past?"

I had expected him to smile and tease me back, to mock me a little and so smooth over our quarrel. So I could not imagine why he suddenly turned pale and stared at me like I'd just slapped him across the face. It was just a momentary reaction, really. I think that he soon realized I'd been joking and that I hadn't meant anything by it; but in that instant I saw a startled hurt flame in his eyes, the flash of an unwilling confession. Then it was gone as quickly as it came.

"Not recently, no," he muttered, and stepped away from me. "All right now, enough of this; it's time to go, don't you agree? It will be dark soon, and I'd prefer not to track at night." He leaned over the dog and held out several cubes of sugar. "Wake up, Toby, wake up!"

There was an irritable iciness to his posture now, and I saw that he had deliberately turned his back to me, as if he were trying to avoid further conversation. I still had no idea what I'd said to upset him so, but there was nothing I could do about it now. He was clearly no longer in the mood to talk. So I decided to carry on as if nothing had occurred between us.

"We should circle the village," I suggested evenly. "Agatha said that James headed toward Sheffield Green, so the dog should be able to pick up the scent close to the border."

Cartwright straightened quickly and shook his head.

"Oh, no. You can return to Hartfield now, Miss Joyce. Toby doesn't need two people pulling at his leash."

I took a rag out from my pocket and crumpled it in my hand. "You have to put Toby on the scent, remember? This is the cloth that I used yesterday to wipe up the anise spill. So you can let me come with you. Or you can to try to force this napkin from my fingers. Just as you wish."

He did not seem surprised or even irritated by my challenge. He appeared too weary to object just then, too tired to even look at me. He shrugged and passed his hand over his face. "Very well. Let's go, then."

I tossed the rag to him, and he allowed the dog to sniff it

for a moment. Then we set off in the direction of the parish church, which stood at the northern corner of the village. At first we walked in silence, for we were both still smarting from our recent tussle. Cartwright limped a little, and I glumly rubbed my wrist every time he looked at me. I wanted to apologize and ask for his forgiveness, but I wasn't sure yet what I'd said to hurt him. Besides, he didn't appear to want to talk about it, as if he'd realized that he had already given too much away by his reaction. It seemed that there was only one safe way to mend the rift that I'd just caused and that was to talk about the case.

"Have you learned anything more about the valet since we last met?" I inquired finally.

"I did," he told me. "Tell me, do you know James's real family name?"

I shook my head. "No, but I assumed Farringdon was not his real name. Footmen and valets are frequently renamed when they enter service. Besides, criminals usually take on pseudonyms."

"He had used the alias James Farringdon when he applied for the post at Hartfield. But I was able to find his hometown, and from there to trace him and learn a little about his family. He was the only son of Mark and Abigail Fellows, of Lambley."

He paused and looked at me expectantly. I bit my lip and

stared fixedly ahead, pretending to be fascinated by Toby's progress.

I had forgotten to ask about Mark Fellows as Cartwright had requested. After I received his letter, I had been so focused on obtaining a sample of James's handwriting that I had ignored the lead he had offered me. Cartwright seemed disappointed by my silence but continued as if I had responded. "Mark Fellows abandoned his family five years ago. He simply disappeared without a trace."

It was then it flashed on me, a comment made by one of the maids about Lord Victor's mysterious older friend. *"He scared off the one friend he had, Mark Fellows, that gray-haired squire from Lambley,"* she had said.

"But Mr. Fellows was well-known at Hartfield!" I exclaimed. "James must have known that his father had been close with the family."

"I am certain that he *did* know. But did Lord Victor know the connection? I indulged in a little gossiping with some Lambley housewives and learned that James had been at school the year his father vanished and that after the investigation was over, James disappeared for a time as well, only resurfacing when his mother died last year."

"What did the police think happened to Mark Fellows?"

"The police thought nothing, as they usually do. Mr. Fellows was known to be something of a philanderer, and it was assumed that he had run off with one of his amours. Lord Victor revealed that Fellows had been thinking of leaving his wife for quite some time. Even the neighbors confirmed that the squire's marriage was unhappy, though they were surprised by such a sudden turn of events. Also, men usually take their belongings with them when they leave their families, but Fellows disappeared with just the clothes upon his back."

"That must have seemed suspicious to the police."

He shrugged his shoulders. "Ah, he must have run off with a rich woman, they theorized, and closed the case."

"But the squire disappeared five years ago. How does Lady Rose's kidnapping fit into this?"

"As for Lady Rose—I believe we are about to learn that connection very soon." Toby had suddenly stiffened and let out an urgent yelp. Nose down to the ground, he bore straight ahead, pulling us toward the western edge of Sheffield Green. We were now on the outskirts of the village, and it was evident that Toby was not leading us to the paved main road but rather to a side dirt path, which led to some of the tenant cottages.

The route that we were taking brought us to a sparsely populated area along the western border of the village. We passed two older houses, and Toby finally stopped near an isolated rundown cottage, which appeared from the outside to be unoccupied. He pulled Cartwright around and around in a circle and then finally took off in the direction of the estate.

My friend pulled the dog back and handed me the leash. "This is as far as James went last night," he whispered, "before he returned to Hartfield. Stay here for a moment while I have a look around."

We were standing about fifty feet away from the house, behind the toolshed. The piggery and stable next to it had clearly been empty for months, and the equipment by the shed was coated with layers of dust and dirt. Cartwright tossed his hat and coat beside me and crept around the side, while I squatted next to the faithful Toby, who had already rolled over and started to snore. I tied the dog's leash to a tree and settled down to wait. Cartwright had not been gone a minute when I suddenly heard a far-off whistling sound coming from beyond the hilltop. As the sound grew nearer, I peeked out from behind the shed and saw that a boy was coming up the path, swinging a wicker basket by his side. The child was heading toward the abandoned house.

As he approached, I realized that I would be too far away to observe him, so I moved forward slowly, crawling along on my hands and knees. An overturned broken wheelbarrow, half covered by wild shrubbery, lay closer to the door, and I scrambled underneath it. Crouching there out of sight, I commanded an excellent view of the doorway and could easily hear everything that passed.

The boy gave three brisk taps with the back of his fist and the door swung open. There was a sound of mumbled greeting from inside, and a dark-bearded man in wrinkled clothing emerged. He looked around him anxiously before fixing his attention on the basket in the boy's hand. "Well, then, what took ye so long?" he demanded.

The boy shrugged. "Sorry, Mr. Ellison. I saw your little girl in the bakery just now, and we got to talkin'."

A shade of alarm passed over the man's face. "Well, what did you talk about?"

There was a crafty look in the child's eyes, and he answered slowly, as if the man's anxiety was a matter of no importance. "We talked of many things. The weather. The church social. Dinner." He raised his chin defiantly, an insolent smirk curling his lips. "But there was something she said that I found a bit surprising."

Ellison grunted and spit a wad of tobacco onto the grass. "And what was that?"

"Well, sir, your daughter seemed to be under the impression that her father was in Southampton, visiting his sick brother."

"And what did you say to her, boy?"

"Ohhhh," crooned the child in a mocking singsong, "I

didn't tell her nothin' different, of course." The boy placed the basket deliberately behind his back and stepped away. "But then I got to thinking—I couldn't help wonderin' what it is you're hidin' out here away from your little girl? And why can't you leave this house to get your own food?"

Ellison shot forward, but the boy darted out of his way, tossing the basket at the man as he went. A moldy roll and a half-eaten apple bounced out and, with a roar of fury, the man lunged for the child again. "Where is the food I paid you for?" he bellowed.

The boy was halfway up a tree before he answered, and he crowed at his opponent from the height. "You didn't pay me enough. There was one pound missing."

"One *pound*? It was two shillings for the rolls and a shilling for the delivery!" roared the man.

"Aye, sir, that was before I started carryin' your little secret around with me. Powerful heavy, it is. That'll cost you extra."

"You stupid brat," growled the man. "There is no secret. My brother has lost his house on account of his gambling and drinking. He came to me for help, half-starved and sick, and I could not bring him home like that. Maddy is only ten, and she thinks the world of her uncle. So I am watching over him in this old cottage until he is well enough to take care of himself. And if you tell Maddy, you'll just be hurting her and not surprising anyone in the village with your tale.

0s Ileah, ssss

So I want my food as we agreed or you won't see another farthing from me."

The boy scrambled down from the branch and rubbed his hands over his dirty knees. With a bowed head and a shamefaced pucker, he whined out a sulky apology and took off down the road. "I'll bring it, sir, I'll bring it," he called over his shoulder. "I have to run an errand for my mum, but I'll be back with it tonight right after supper."

Ellison threw a clod of dirt after the child and cursed under his breath. "What am I expected to do now?" he muttered, tugging absentmindedly at his watch chain and gazing at the deserted road with vacant eyes. He gave the watch an irritable tug, and the chain shot forward and snapped in two. Swearing furiously, he tossed the watch into his coat pocket and vanished back into the cottage, shutting the door noisily behind him.

CHAPTER

19

I STAYED HIDDEN there for some minutes afterward and watched the house, in case the man should reappear. Finally, when I was confident that all was quiet, I crawled slowly out from my hiding place, keeping my eyes fixed on the cottage. Presently Cartwright emerged from behind the house, waved to me, and ducked behind the shed again. I waited impatiently for him, for I was certain we had reached the last part of our journey and I could not wait to hear what our final step would be. When he joined me his expression was indifferent, but his eyes were bright

and focused, his figure tense and poised, like a racer waiting
for his cue.

"You heard him?" I whispered eagerly.

He nodded grimly, and his jaw set. "I could not see inside
the house. There is a locked back entrance, and every window is shuttered and bolted."

"Could we apply to the police to search the house, then?"

"Is that what you would do?"

"We must have grounds for a warrant."

"Do we? Are you prepared to give the case over to the
officials and the public, then?"

"You aren't still concerned about the earl's privacy?"

"No, but I'd rather have my case complete before I hand it
over to Porter. I would like to at least lay eyes on the young
lady and hear her story."

I studied the door for a moment and then turned to face
him. An idea had formed in my mind but I was hesitant to
share it, for its details were somewhat vague, and I did not
wish him to reject it before I could refine it. "I can get in
there" was all I said.

"Absolutely not."

"I shall knock on the door, and Ellison will let me in. He
won't suspect me. I will need two shillings, please."

"No."

Had I proposed scaling the roof and descending through

the chimney, he could not have been more dismissive. He had already turned away from me with an impatient finality, and I saw with a start of horror that he had drawn a pistol from his coat pocket.

"You will stay hidden here, until I return," he demanded, his voice hoarse and dark.

I reached my hand out and touched his sleeve. "Just listen to me for a moment, please. I can get inside there, no violence, no weapon. If we are wrong and Lady Rose isn't there, no one will ever know our error. I will be in the house for less than five minutes, and when I get the opportunity I will unlock one window. Then I shall get him to follow me outside, and you will have your chance to look for her. You will be less than twenty feet away. If anything goes wrong I'll scream."

He turned around slowly, arms crossed over his chest, and studied my face for a moment.

"Please," I added quietly before he answered. "Peter, give me this last chance."

He uncrossed his arms and tossed over two shillings. "Be careful, Dora."

I dropped the coins into my pocket and ran, worried that if I stayed to explain my plan he might change his mind once more. In less than a quarter of an hour I had arrived at the village bakery, and, some minutes later, I was heading

back carrying a basket loaded with sweet-smelling, freshly
baked muffins and warm loaves of bread. I gave three brisk
taps on the cottage door and stood beside the post, out of
view from the front windows. The door swung open and old
Ellison leaned out of the gap. He started at the sight of me
and seemed inclined to shrink back into the house. I smiled
and meekly asked for directions to Hartfield, claiming to be
new to the area and lost. He relaxed a little and stepped farther out onto the terrace. As he lifted his hand to point out
the path back to the estate, I caught a glimpse of his fingers
and I knew suddenly what I would say.

My eyes went wide and I smiled broadly, as if in recognition. "Why, sir, I hadn't recognized you before! Mr. Ellison,
you are looking so much better than the last time I saw
you, sir!"

The alarmed look returned, and he shook his head. "I
don't think we've met before, Miss—"

"Banister, sir! Lizzie Banister! I don't expect you'd remember me, though, for you were terribly ill then. Around
Christmastime, I think it was. I was visiting your neighbors.
I helped take care of you, sir. Ask your little Maddy about
me. She'll remember me, right enough."

He nodded slowly. "I was quite sick then, it's true, and I
doubt I'd have recognized my own mother the state I was in.
I lost two whole weeks. You were visiting with the Saunders

family, then? One of their cousins, are you?"

"Second cousin. How is Maddy, sir? I have been meaning to stop by and tell her I've just gotten a job at the bakery."

"She's well, she's very well." He paused and pulled nervously at his beard. "Listen, dear girl, if you talk to Maddy, you needn't mention that you saw me here today. You see"— he coughed several times and jerked his head in the direction of the house—"I've been here for some time taking care of an old friend who has come down in the world. I wouldn't want my little girl to know about it. Maddy's so young and all, you understand?"

I gave him a reassuring nod. "You needn't worry. I don't tell tales, sir. And I'd never say anything that might bother your little girl." He seemed satisfied and moved back toward the door. I gave a little farewell curtsy and, in doing so, allowed the cloth to fall off my basket. I let him stare hungrily at the uncovered cakes for a moment and then held one out for him. "I've already eaten two," I whispered confidentially. He hesitated, and I laid down my basket and picked up a muffin for myself. "I got some extra, sir, so it's no trouble."

He took the proffered muffin, and I bit into mine. The next moment I was choking and spitting and holding my hand desperately to my throat. Old Ellison sprang to my side and gave a little exclamation of concern. The man seemed genuinely alarmed, not by my crisis, I think, but at the prospect of my collapsing on his doorstep and attracting attention to his suspicious situation. He beat on my back with all the enthusiasm of a concerned parent, and I rewarded his efforts by gasping louder and falling to my knees. As he leaned down to help me, my hand found its way into his coat pocket, and I removed his watch and tucked it in my dress before finally sinking down onto the ground. Ellison looked about wildly for a moment and seemed ready to escape back into the house, but I pulled on his jacket tail and whispered, "Water, please—" and pointed to the cottage door. He looked helplessly toward the doorway, and I used the opportunity to fling his watch into some shrubbery beneath the terrace. My coughing had at this point eased a little, but I was still breathing noisily, and my eyes were watering profusely. The man gave me a last look of exasperation and finally extended his arm to assist me into the house.

Once inside the cottage, I found it more difficult to ignore his agitation than to play my part. His hands were shaking as he lowered me down onto a wooden rocking chair, and he glanced repeatedly toward one of the closed doors at the end of the room. Had I been totally ignorant of his purpose in that house, his behavior alone would have convinced me that there was a guilty secret in the place. I breathed deeply again and repeated my request for water. He nodded distractedly and hurried off to the kitchen.

When he had gone, I darted across the room and quickly unfastened the clasp on one of the windows and the hook between its shutters. I placed my handkerchief upon the sill before closing the unlocked shutters once again. By the time Ellison returned with the water I was again reclining on the chair and breathing noisily. I took several sips, smiled gratefully at him, and after a few minutes declared that I was much improved. He saw me out, and, as I bid him farewell, I inquired innocently about the time. He reached his hand into his pocket, discovered that the watch was missing, and gave a loud exclamation of dismay.

"It's my father's watch!" he moaned. "It must have dropped from my pocket when I was helping you out there."

He hurried from the house, pushing me out in front of him, then dove beneath the bushes in his desperate search. I had to toss the piece in four separate hiding places, but the hunt kept Ellison occupied for a quarter of an hour. I had no idea if Cartwright had broken into the place, and still less if he had found the missing girl. It was absolutely still inside; there was no sign of movement or whisper of voices from within. As I edged closer to the house, Ellison finally climbed out from behind the wheelbarrow, clutching his lost timepiece. I looked desperately toward the door, praying for some signal from my friend, and realized too late that I had not planned for complications.

What if there had been a second man in that house, and Cartwright had walked into a trap? Or was it possible that Ellison was actually caring for a relative as he had claimed? I had just encouraged my friend to break into a house while carrying a weapon, and he would be arrested and imprisoned if he were caught. Even now Ellison was getting closer to the door; his foot was on the step and he was glaring at me from beneath his brows. I had to say something, anything, to make him halt—

"*Stop! Don't move. Hands above your head!*" I heard the words, but I had not shouted them.

In front of me I saw Ellison drop heavily to his knees, his face pinched and livid, his arms extended. Peter Cartwright was standing in the doorway, gun in hand, a length of rope wrapped around one shoulder. Holding the pistol barrel to our prisoner's head, he tossed the twine to me, and I pulled Ellison's hands behind him and knotted the cord around his wrists. He did not resist when Cartwright grasped him by the arm and pulled him to his feet, just glowered dumbly at me as we led him into the house.

"Well, sir, what have you to say?" Cartwright demanded.

Ellison dropped sullenly into a nearby chair and glared at us. "I don't got nothing to say, laddie," he growled, and spat into the corner.

"As I'm sure you understand, you'll be arrested for the kidnapping of Lady Rose."

"What of it, then?" The man spit once more, this time straight in front of him.

The wad of tobacco that had landed on his shoe did not amuse my friend. "Tie him to the chair," he ordered gruffly. "You'll be comfortable there until the police arrive. And I will stay with Lady Rose until her doctor comes to tend to her."

As he spoke, he walked over to the corner door and pushed it open. The room inside was windowless and bare, and on a gray and threadbare blanket a young girl was lying, her eyes closed and chin tucked down. She was dressed in a nightgown and a wrinkled travel cloak; her uncombed hair was gathered back in a damp and matted braid. One arm lay outstretched across the floor, and I could see the raw and blistered wheal across her wrist where her arms had been bound together. She opened her eyes briefly and gazed vacantly at us, her dotlike pupils roving lazily about in drugged confusion. With a little murmur of surprise she lifted her hands into the air, as if she was amazed to find them free, then let them drop again as she drifted off to sleep.

Cartwright knelt by the girl and placed his finger on her wrist. "Go fetch a doctor right away," he told me. "Then run for the police."

I nodded and put my hand out toward the door, my eyes still fixed on the miserable figure of Lady Rose. From the corner of my eye I saw old Ellison start and jerk back in blank surprise, saw Cartwright spin about and freeze, one arm raised in mute alarm. A moment later I felt a cold draft from the open door behind me and the sting of freezing metal on my temple. Someone wrenched me backward, pinning me to him, the crush of a heavy arm tightening across my chest. I could not move or breathe; even as I struggled the muzzle of a revolver bore deeper into my neck and choked me.

"One move and I will kill her."

I recognized the voice, but I could not speak, for the barrel was pressed firmly now beneath my chin. Peter Cartwright had risen slowly off the ground, both palms extended in a gesture of surrender and appeal. "Let her go," he pleaded, his voice high, uncertain. "Let Dora go, James. You have nothing to gain by hurting her."

I felt the arm around me slacken, but the revolver still hovered menacingly about my throat.

"The weapon in your pocket," James directed. "Take it out and kick it over to me. Slowly, now." My heart sank as Cartwright pulled his pistol from his coat and pushed it roughly across the floor. My last hope had now passed into a criminal's hands. Behind me I felt James relax as he tucked his revolver into his belt and plucked the other off the ground. For a fleeting moment I thought of trying to escape while his weapon was down, but I caught Cartwright's eye and paused. He shook his head slightly and I understood that I was to trust him and stay still.

"What have you done to Lady Rose?" James demanded.

What had *we* done? I wanted to shout but the sight of his finger on the trigger kept me silent.

"I am now unarmed," Cartwright replied, ignoring James's question. "Let Dora go and we can talk. I will not say a word while you are holding her."

"I do not need to hear your story. I'm here for Lady Rose."

"Put down the gun."

James wavered for a moment and dropped his hand, but wrapped his other arm about my waist and pinned me to him. "Now talk."

"Let her go, James."

"Not until you tell me who you are."

"Drop your weapon or I will shoot!"

The shout had echoed from behind me, and as James spun around to face the challenge, he let me go, and I toppled to the ground. I looked up to see Mr. Porter standing in the doorway, gun extended, and James on his knees before him, hands crossed behind his head. Peter Cartwright ran over to me and pulled me to my feet, then seized James by the elbows, disarmed him, and shoved him roughly to the ground. Mr. Porter advanced slowly into the room but stopped suddenly as I turned to face him. He let out a noise like a strangled grunt; his mouth dropped open and his brows came down.

"What in Heaven's name are you doing here, Miss—"

"Mr. Porter!" exclaimed Cartwright, stepping up to him and grasping him by the arm. "Thank God you're here! I did just as you directed, sir. But I never expected James to turn up when he did! I am so glad that you thought to follow him. Was it very difficult?"

I stared at him. My friend sounded like a student gasping questions at a teacher's elbow. This was not the boy I knew. It was obvious that Porter had not given any of the orders; Cartwright had engineered the search (with a little help from me) and had stationed his colleague at the house to trail James. And yet he was so humble now, hovering at his master's side like an eager lackey waiting for approval. Porter cleared his throat twice, gave me a final puzzled look and nodded slowly. "It appears that I arrived here just in time, or this young—lady might have suffered for your carelessness. What exactly is she doing here?"

"Oh, she's all right. She will keep following me, though," Cartwright declared. "But, sir, I believe another young girl requires your attention." He stepped aside and pointed to the prostrate form of Lady Rose. Mr. Porter gasped and rushed over to her.

James had sat up and was watching us, studying the sullen Ellison, the unconscious lady, and my face, each in turn. Finally he turned to Cartwright and protested in a plaintive whine, "I am innocent of this."

"Indeed?"

James jabbed his finger in Ellison's direction. "I've never seen that fellow before in all my life. I found out where Lady Rose was being kept, and I came to rescue her."

Cartwright shrugged his shoulders. "I doubt that the police will believe your story. They'll want to know why you threatened an unarmed girl, I think. You certainly do not appear innocent, and I daresay your record is not as clean as you would have us think. However, I believe when I explain our case, you will be more than willing to help us capture the person whom we have all been seeking. If you cooperate with us, perhaps Mr. Porter can convince the authorities to overlook a few things about your past. Or we can step aside and allow the police to arrest you for kidnapping and attempted murder."

James thrust out a defiant lip. "What things in my past are we talking about exactly?"

"Well, for starters, there is the matter of the letters."

A shade of fear passed over the valet's face. "Which letters are you meaning?"

"The ones that Thomas Dyer stole from his mistress and sold to you. Those must, of course, be returned to us."

James seemed surprised by this demand but did not seem inclined to argue. "I'll look into it." There was a hint of sly relief behind his answer. "Anything else, sir?"

"One moment." Cartwright stepped over to his master and, kneeling down beside him, whispered something in his ear. Porter nodded briefly, and his assistant rose and strode over to the door.

"I have to return to the estate now, James," Cartwright told the valet. "You will come with me."

James snorted loudly and clambered to his feet. "Just as you say, sir."

I moved to follow them, but Cartwright turned to me abruptly and raised his eyebrows. "I'm sorry, Dora."

"But—"

"I need you to stay with Lady Rose until her doctor comes. When she wakes up you can attend to her. We have yet to hear her story—"

"But Mr. Porter can—"

"No! I need *you* to be here."

I slumped against the wall. At this crucial moment he was

leaving me behind, and I would miss it all, the capture, the arrest, the final flourish. I would hear about it later, if he remembered to explain it to me, or I might read about it in the papers.

He saw my sour expression and, leaning down, he took my hand in his. "Dora, don't be angry, please. I'm asking you to stay because I need you here. You know that your help has been invaluable to me. And that last trick you used to break into this house—honestly, I'm still trying to work out how you knew that Ellison had been sick on Christmas."

I felt the blood rush to my cheeks. "Oh—that. Well, his fingernails, you see—there was a ridge across his nail-plate. When a man is severely ill, the nail stops growing briefly. The distance of that line from the cuticle allowed me to estimate the date of illness."

"Ah, of course! I did not see that."

"But you were not close enough to him—"

"I was—but I simply did not notice. Well done, Dora."

I forgot my disappointment for a moment. Also my throbbing arm, the case . . .

"Thank you."

He nodded quietly and pulled the sleeve back from my wounded arm. "When the doctor has tended to Lady Rose, I want him to examine your burn. It's looking worse with every passing hour."

He turned away before I could respond and grabbed James by the shoulder. The valet glowered at him but made no protest, and together they left the house.

When they were gone, Ellison smirked at me and shook his head. "You needn't look so cheeky, girl. He just 'got around' you, or didn't you see that?"

"The police will soon be here for you," I told him scornfully and left the room. But Ellison was right, and of course I knew it. I had truly begun to hate our prisoner.

Mr. Porter was kneeling beside Lady Rose when I joined them. He had succeeded in reviving her with some water and a swig of brandy, and he was asking her if she remembered what had happened to her.

"A rag with a strong sharp smell is all I can remember," she told him. "Then I woke up here. My hands were tied, and a man whom I had never seen before was standing over me."

From the next room I heard a clatter, a thud, and the sound of Ellison cursing. "I need some help in here! The blasted chair has fallen over and my face is bleeding. Hello in there!"

Porter gave me a weary look and left to tend to our troublesome prisoner. Lady Rose stared at me for a moment and then pushed herself up against the wall.

"Who are you?" she inquired in a weak voice.

It suddenly occurred to me that I did not know who I was. Was it still necessary to keep up my role as Hartfield scullery maid, or could I tell her that I was working with the detective who had rescued her? I decided to be cautious and reveal nothing about myself until I was certain it was safe.

"My name is Dora Banister, Your Ladyship," I told her. "I'm the new maid at Hartfield Hall."

She half-rose from the blanket as I spoke and looked about the room with growing interest. I held out a bit of muffin and she took it eagerly, and, manners quite forgotten, began to stuff it whole into her mouth. I pulled out another one and offered it to her, but she caught my wrist and turned it over. "What happened to your hand?" she asked me between mouthfuls.

I pulled my arm back and tucked it beneath my apron. "I scalded it on the stove," I responded. "It's nothing really."

In truth, my burn had swelled now, and the wound looked uglier than before. The scarlet streak had darkened to a dusky purple, and though my fingers were still numb, the aching heat across my palm now seemed to radiate through my body. The room was cold and drafty, but a flush of fever warmed my cheeks and a sheen of perspiration glistened on my brow.

"What are you doing here?" she asked after she had finished her second muffin. "And where is that brutish farmer who was starving me?"

"He's tied to a chair out there. We're waiting for the doctor to come and then we'll take you home. Until he arrives, I'm here to take care of you."

Lady Rose glared at me and shook her head. "I don't believe you," she declared finally. "They tried starvation to get me to confess and then drugged me with opium when I refused. They forced me to write a farewell letter to my parents. Perhaps this is another trick. I have never seen you before in all my life. Tell me why I should trust you."

Of course she did not believe me. A maid in my position would not have dared to address her mistress in such an easy way; she would have answered shortly, with great embarrassment and averted eyes. But I had to know what she was hiding, had to understand what her kidnappers had wanted from her.

"You can trust me, Lady Rose," I assured her. "Because I'm working with the man who rescued you, who apprehended James just moments ago in this cottage."

She frowned and reached out for another pastry.

"James, my brother's valet? He found me here? How very poetic. Now we've both unearthed a secret." She smiled to herself and bit deep into the crust.

"You unearthed a secret, Lady Rose?"

She looked startled for a moment, as if realizing for the first time that she had spoken her thoughts out loud. Then she slumped back against the wall and turned her face away from me. "Perhaps I have—or perhaps not. What is it to you?"

"I'm trying to help you," I answered her. "It's obvious that you've been cruelly wronged. These criminals have kidnapped you, mistreated you—starved you, even. Surely you wish them to be brought to justice?"

She turned to me and I saw that she was smiling now, a tired, ironic smile, as if she pitied me for my sad mistake. "Cruelly wronged, you said?" she echoed. "Are you talking about this?" She waved her hand over the squalid room. "This lasted a few days, and I was asleep through most of it. And while I wouldn't want to return here again, I wouldn't say that *this* is how they've wronged me."

"Then, how—?"

"I'm not going to tell you what I know," she interrupted. "I don't know who you are, Miss Dora, but I can see that you aren't meant to be here. And you're obviously not a maid; I noticed that right away. No maid has eyes like yours. And there are no female inspectors that I know of—certainly not at your age. So either you're a criminal—or an actress. Either way, you're not doing what you ought to be."

I smiled to myself. She was certainly right about that, I thought.

"No, I suppose I'm not," I replied. "People have been telling me for years that I'm not behaving as I ought to be. But

I can't say that I regret the choices that I've made."

"Well, then, we're very different," she retorted in a bitter voice. "As I've spent the last few years regretting nearly every choice I've made. All of the blunders, all the embarrassment I've caused." She sighed and sank back farther against the wall. "You see, *I* never expected to be a disappointment."

"Well, no one wants to be a disappointment," I replied softly. "But I can't imagine that anyone thinks of you that way."

"Well, if you believe that, then you must know nothing about me." She laughed shortly. "Nearly everybody else has heard about the earl's clumsy daughter, about Hartfield's social failure. That's how they all describe me, if they remember me at all."

"But you can still change that," I insisted. "You have your family behind you, after all."

"My family?" she shot back. "No, I don't think they will support me. How could they? They'll hate me for uncovering their secret. Still, what else could I do? What would you have done if you'd been me, if you'd been given an opportunity to change your life forever?"

I wasn't certain what she was asking me, of course, but I had to say something, and encourage her to continue. "I suppose that I would have taken the chance," I ventured.

She sighed and turned away. "But what if, by revealing

the truth, you tore down what your family loved most?" she murmured sadly.

How does one respond to a question like that? I could not claim to understand her feelings without revealing details of my own life, without telling her of my own experience. But she did not want to hear my story, even if I'd been willing to tell it then. In fact she did not appear to want any answer from me, for she was no longer looking at me, but instead was gazing off at some point in the distance. She had only wanted to speak out loud, I realized, to voice the question that had plagued her for so long, which she had not dared to share with anyone.

"Perhaps, in the end, you won't have to reveal the secret," I suggested finally. "Perhaps others will do it for you."

She nodded and lay back on the floor. "That might be the best thing after all, I think," she agreed. "But it can't happen that way now. I've hidden it, you see—and no one will find it without me."

That was all she was prepared to say, it seemed, for she had turned her face back to the wall. Her breathing was more regular now, and after a few minutes I saw that she had drifted off to sleep.

I moved away from her and thought about what she'd just said. Several loose clues were beginning to come together in my mind.

Lady Rose had not identified James as her abductor, even though there was no question that the valet knew why his mistress had been kidnapped. Over the last few weeks he had spent hours deciphering a code in the Hartfield library; Agatha had seen him with a coded message. And just now Lady Rose had hinted that James had discovered something, that they had both "unearthed a secret," as she had put it. Flora had mentioned seeing soil under Lady Rose's fingernails; perhaps the girl had literally unearthed it. Had Lady Rose taken something from James and hidden it away for her own purpose? But what had she had taken from him, and, more importantly, where had she concealed it?

And then it came to me. I had noticed something no one else had. Even Cartwright had missed it, for he had searched Lady Rose's room in the beginning and found nothing. But I knew now where it was. I knew where she had hidden her secret before she was abducted.

CHAPTER
20

A S I ROSE TO LEAVE, Mr. Porter stepped into the room and moved to block my path. "One moment, please, young lady. My assistant promised me an explanation later—but I believe I'd like to hear it now. What exactly are you doing here?"

I did not want to justify my presence to this man. I was minutes away from uncovering Lady Rose's secret, moments away from my first success, and this grumpy second-rate detective wanted an accounting *now*? He could apply to his apprentice for an answer.

"Mr. Cartwright needed my assistance, sir. That is why I'm here."

"I beg your pardon?!"

"Mr. Porter, perhaps you ought to speak with him."

"I most certainly intend to speak to him. This has become outrageous. A flirtation is a flirtation, and I do not begrudge a young man his *amours*, however misguided his choice might be. But to put his blind infatuation in front of his career, to intentionally endanger both—"

"Infatuation, sir?! You think that I came to Hartfield dressed like a maidservant in order to wink at your assistant?"

"I do not know what your game is yet, Miss Joyce, and, frankly, I do not care. But when I took that boy on I pledged that I would look after him. I made a promise to myself to do my best by him, to treat him as my own son. And I can honestly say that I've kept that promise. He was doing well with me, and learning a great deal. He was *recovering*, Miss Joyce, faster than anyone could have imagined. And so I think I have a duty now to ask you what you're about and what your relationship is with my young apprentice. I have the right to understand that much!"

"I don't know what you want to hear, sir!" I exclaimed furiously. "Mr. Cartwright asked me to help him!" I was choking on my own anger now, burning crimson with humiliation. "He asked me as a friend, a colleague—as an equal! I realize that you are worried about my involvement in this case, but I've done nothing, *nothing* to shame anyone."

I would have continued in that vein, would have protested my innocence until I had convinced him, but my mind had now suddenly clouded over, and a gray fog had swirled before my eyes. Alarmed, I reached my hands out to steady myself against the wall, and then gasped as a searing pain shot across my arm.

Porter stepped forward and grasped me by the elbow. "Miss Joyce? Are you unwell?" His voice came at me like a distant roar, a muffled rumble without meaning. I shook my head to clear my sight and took a deep breath in. Porter was calling to me now, and I heard myself replying, a dull echo in my head, "I need a moment—please just give me a moment."

I couldn't be sick now; I had come so close! What was the use of all my work if I fell ill when they needed me the most? And I couldn't faint before this man, this overbearing pompous bag! He would smirk at me and then lecture me about a young girl's innocent fragility. I could never live that down. I had to overcome this nausea, the sinking blackness in my head.

A few more breaths brought back some clarity; I shook myself, pulled my shoulders back, and opened my eyes. My vision was slowly returning. I could see Porter's frowning face, and the unpleasant sight helped to clear my mind. He had stepped forward when he'd moved to catch me, and I saw that he was no longer blocking the doorway. My path to Hartfield was now clear.

I gave him an ingratiating smile, took a final deep breath, then quickly dodged past him and headed for the door. He spun about and shouted after me. "Where are you going, girl?"

But I did not stay to answer him; I was already out the door and running toward the Hall. He would not follow me, I knew, for he could not leave Ellison and Lady Rose alone.

It was nearly evening now and the sun had set into a bleak and cloudy sky; a southerly wind bit at my ankles and snapped at my neck as I sped down across the valley. I hid my wounded hand beneath my cloak to shield it from the biting wind. By the time I reached the Hall, my chest burned with every breath I took, and my head throbbed as if a crown of freezing lead had been bound around my temples. Clutching the banister, I pulled myself up to Lady Rose's bedroom and stumbled over to the bookcase.

The wooden clock, the broken one, was still sitting on the shelf, the only silent, lifeless piece in the entire bookcase. The other ceramic clocks each ticked their tunes, mocking their quiet brother. I plucked it off the shelf and pried the base open with my fingers. There was a hollow cavity inside where the mechanism had once been, and there, rolled into a spiral cone, was a single letter. Carefully I eased it from its hiding place and held it up, trying to read the writing by the dimming light.

On one side was a list of *I*'s and *V*'s and *X*'s arranged in neat, short columns. On the reverse, in different handwriting, was the translation of the code.

> *My dearest Mark,*
>
> *By now you understand why we can no longer see each other. It is becoming obvious that he is your son—*

"DORA!" In a moment, the letter was tucked beneath my apron. Agatha was standing by the door, hands on her hips, shaking her head back and forth like an angry schoolteacher. "What are you doing here? They have been looking for you all afternoon!"

"I—the clock is broken!" I blurted out and pointed to the dismantled piece upon the shelf.

"*What?*"

My composure was returning to me now, and I tried again. "I was passing by the room, and I saw this clock lying on the floor. I was tryin' to put it back together."

She looked perplexed and shook her head. "That's where you've been all day?"

I rolled my eyes. "No, 'course not. But listen, I think it

was the workman that was here before that broke it. I saw him near here earlier."

Agatha smiled. "The workman? Ah, the tall one that Flora likes?"

"That's the one."

"He was just in the library talking with James."

"I'll just go and ask him about the clock, then."

"But you won't find him there now."

"Why not?"

"They both left the Hall a few minutes ago."

I was too late. Swallowing my frustration, I turned away from her and peeked out through the window curtain. The grounds were shadowed and quiet. There was no sign of them. "Did they say where they was goin'?"

"Of course not. 'Tisn't my business, is it? And I can't figure out why you think it's yours." Her eyes narrowed, and she raised her chin. "See here, what do you want with James, anyhow?"

There was really no way to answer that without creating further questions. I had to think of something to throw her off the track, or else I would never be allowed to leave. So I decided to tell her what I thought she would want to hear, as I had run out of ideas.

"Listen, Agatha," I whispered miserably. "If I tell you this, you have to swear to me that you won't tell a livin' soul."

She relaxed a little and stepped closer to me. "You've been straight with me, haven't you?" she told me. "So I'll be straight with you."

I wavered for a moment, exhaled slowly and ducked my head. "That workman that was here, that tall one with the green eyes—he's very important to me. You see, the truth is—*I'm in love with him.*"

"In love with him! That's wonderful! Oh, but, Dora, does he know?"

I shook my head and wrung my hands. A shock of pain shot through my palm and real tears started to my eyes. "He asked me to marry him. And, Agatha, I turned him down!"

"Oh, but why?" she breathed. "If you love him so?"

I managed a little hiccup of despair. "Oh, Agatha, I'm such a stupid girl! I didn't know how much I cared for him until I realized that I was going to lose him. He's leaving tomorrow for Ireland. And I will never see him again!"

"Ah, Dora, you poor, poor girl." She clucked her tongue and took my hand. "Don't cry. I think I might know where they went."

I dried my eyes and smiled gratefully at her. This was an unexpected bonus. "You do?"

"I watched them from the window—and then I followed them. Just for a little bit, mind you. Just because I was so worried about James, you understand."

"Of course."

"They headed for the cemetery. Due north. Behind the church."

"The cemetery? But—"

"I can't imagine why, my dear, but I believe that is where they went."

"Thank you, my friend," I told her earnestly. "I cannot tell you what this means to me."

"Good luck," she murmured. "And Godspeed."

I fled before she could wonder why I was seeking my lover in a graveyard, instead of waiting for his return to tell him of my passion.

By the time I reached the church it was nighttime and a light fog had settled on the earth. I wished suddenly that I had brought a dark lantern, for the moon was now my only source of light, and I could not see beyond the iron spikes of the graveyard fence. I stumbled past a tree stump and slipped across a patch of mud, then finally fell upon the gate and pushed it open. All was still within.

I wondered irritably why I had followed Agatha's directions. She had said that they had walked in the direction of the cemetery, but she had not actually seen them there. Perhaps they had changed course or had turned around, and now I would have to find my way back through the dark alone. The place was eerie and forbidding, as cemeteries in the nighttime tend to be, and as I turned to flee I realized that I was shivering from real fear as well as from the cold.

I was only halfway out the gate when I felt a hand upon my shoulder. I opened my mouth to scream, but another hand closed over my lips and pushed me backward. Terrified, I lashed out blindly with my fists, striking desperately at my unknown enemy, in an effort to free myself. Before I could turn to face my attacker, my right arm was pinned behind my back and the hand over my mouth tightened its hold. In a last frantic attempt to escape, I pulled my left elbow forward and with all my strength drove it backward into my assailant's chest.

There was a muffled gasp, and the grip upon my arm loosened. I twisted about to face my opponent. The next moment I had fallen back, shaking with laughter and relief.

"I was not expecting that," muttered Peter Cartwright, rubbing one hand over his right side. "Two bruises in one day, Miss Joyce. Have you no compassion?"

I ran my fingers over my sore jaw. "You put your hand over my mouth."

"You were about to scream and wake the dead. I tried to speak to you but you were too busy thrashing about to listen."

"Where have you been hidden, then?"

"Behind the cherub tombstone in the corner." He pointed

to an angelic stone baby, and I saw a shadow flicker by a wreath of flowers at the base.

"James is with you?"

"And two constables as well. We are expecting company at any moment. I was not, however, expecting you. I distinctly remember telling you—"

"I came to bring you this," I interrupted and pulled the letter from my apron. "This is what Lady Rose had hidden. This letter originally belonged to James."

He snatched it from me and held it up, squinting at the words in the dim moonlight.

"*My dearest Mark,*" he read, and his eyes widened as he skimmed it. "Dora, this is from the earl's first wife, from Lord Victor's mother."

"Yes, it's their family secret—and the reason Lady Rose was kidnapped," I told him.

"But how did you find it—" he began, then shook his head and grasped me by the shoulder. "Never mind, we'll have to discuss that later. Come now, quickly, let's get back into position. He will be here any moment."

We hurried over to the tombstone, crouched beneath the icy shadows, and waited in the darkness. The minutes ticked by slowly, my legs grew stiff and cold; but I did not stir, I would not dare. Behind me I could hear the labored breathing of the heavier constable, the nasal whistle of the smaller one, and the irregular panting of the tense valet. I don't believe Cartwright breathed at all, for he was as silent as the dead. The night air had an oppressive dampness to it. Someone had recently smoked a cigarette, and the smell of tobacco stung my eyes and made my throat constrict. The scent had never bothered me before, but it was suffocating now; my head swam and my vision blurred. I had begun to lean heavily on my companion, and I felt him shift and put his hand across my forehead. His fingers felt like icicles on my skin.

"You're feverish, Dora," he whispered, a shade of concern coloring his voice. I shivered as he spoke and pulled away from him.

"I'm just a little warm, that's all. I ran all the way here."

"Hush, now, someone's coming!" The order came from James, who was hovering above me, having risen from the ground in his excitement.

From beyond the hill a distant thud of footsteps broke the stillness, and the bulky shadow of a man appeared upon the blue, moonlit horizon. He paused a moment by the church and seemed to look about him warily. I heard him sigh and mutter to himself as he paced before the cemetery fence. Then he pushed open the iron gate and stepped out of the shadows toward us so we could see his face.

Lord Hartfield had arrived. Peter Cartwright sprang to

his feet and slipped into view, an index finger to his lips "Your Lordship," he hissed. "We have been expecting you. Do not make a sound, I beg of you."

The earl heaved an exasperated sigh and shuffled over to our hiding place. "What is the meaning of this?" he rumbled at us. "Why have you called me out here in the dead of night, with this absurd little note?" He held up a slip of paper as he spoke. "Where is Mr. Porter? Why did you instruct me to tell no one about this meeting?" He glanced at me and frowned. "And why is the kitchen maid here?"

"Please Your Lordship, everything will be clear in moments. But now I must ask you to remain quiet." Cartwright put a heavy hand upon the earl's shoulder, and the man sank down beside us, sputtering into irritable silence.

And then the real wait began. No more false alarms, no more guessing; I knew that the next person who stepped into the graveyard would be the real criminal, the man whom we were seeking. We were moments from the end.

And then we heard him, a hesitant scraping sound, the creak of the iron gate, and finally the sound of metal hitting dirt. He was digging, grunting with the effort as the shovel bore through rocky earth, sighing as the clods flew loose and landed at our feet. Then he gave a sudden cry of triumph, and I heard a ripping sound and the grinding noise of something heavy being dragged across the ground.

I leaned forward to try to get a better look, but Cartwright pulled me back. He was too late, for I had already seen what lay upon the ground. A thick cloth bag, partially decayed and covered in black soil, had been pulled from a freshly uncovered grave. The seam had burst and the fabric had fallen to the side. Lying there before us was the waxy remainder of a corpse, its skull grinning and twisted upward to the sky, its arms thrown open as if welcoming the moon.

And standing over the unearthed skeleton, a spade clutched in one clenched fist, was Lord Victor, only son and heir of Lord and Lady Hartfield.

For a moment we were paralyzed; no one breathed or moved as we watched the young lord stretch his arms and wipe his brow. Then the earl gave a hoarse cry of disbelief and leapt forward, crashing toward his son like a wounded bull, grabbing at his clothing, and bellowing his name again and again with building anguish.

"What have you done, what have you done to her?" he screamed, and pushed his cowering son against the iron railing. The man's strength was terrifying in his grief, and the son gasped and crumpled under his father's weight. Cartwright had rushed over to the wailing father and was struggling to restrain him as the constables tried to seize the frantic nobleman by the arms. I realized suddenly that the earl believed that this was his daughter on the ground, that he was looking at his child's corpse. He was raining blows upon Lord Victor now, oblivious to our cries or to the huddled, bleeding body of his son.

"It's not her!" I cried, grasping him by the wrist. "Lord Hartfield, listen to me! It isn't her. Your daughter is alive!"

He tossed me to the ground and wailed his fury, and for a moment I thought he had not heard me. But then he froze, his fists still clenched, and I saw the rage drain from his face. His strength now suddenly abandoned him, and he slumped weakly into the policemen's arms. "Not my daughter?" he gasped.

"Your Lordship, it is a man's body, not a woman's."

Cartwright had fallen back, breathing heavily. He leaned briefly over the corpse and then covered it with his coat. "This man's been dead for about five years, judging by the stage of dry decay."

"And Rose?"

"She is alive and recovering now. Mr. Porter is with her."

The heavy constable laid a hand upon Lord Victor's shoulder. "You are hereby under arrest, sir, for the murder of—" He paused here and looked uncertain.

The young lord lifted a swollen face and spit out a clot of blood. "Oh, pray continue, officer," he sneered.

"For the murder of your father." My accusation echoed through the graveyard.

The earl let out a strangled cry and glared at me. "What exactly are you talking about?" he shouted.

James had moved to stand beside his former master, and slowly plucked a letter from his pocket. There was a hard gleam of triumph in his eyes, and he paused for a moment as if savoring the victory. "For the murder of *our* father," he declared solemnly as Lord Victor paled and dropped heavily to his knees. *"My dearest brother."*

There was a deadly confidence in the valet's tone, a determination in his eyes that would not allow a challenge. We were all silent before his charge; no one dared to say a word. Even the earl was quiet, his lips parted in mute dismay, as if a hidden doubt had suddenly come to life before him.

Lord Victor lifted his head and glared at his accuser. "How long have you known?"

"Longer than I have known you," James told him. "Why do you think I applied for the post in the first place? To press your socks? No, I have been planning this for many months, ever since I understood why my father had disappeared. He was a threat to only one man. And that man was his son."

James turned to us. "When my mother died last year, I learned the truth about my family. I found two letters that my father had carefully concealed beneath a loose floorboard in the cellar. They were both written in code, but I

was able to decipher only one of them, because the key to
the second note was no longer in the house. The first letter was addressed to my father and was written by Lady
Gwendolyn Lennox, Lord Victor's mother. It was not an
easy code to decipher, for I did not know which book they'd
used. It turned out, in the end, to be drawn from a copy of
Oliver Twist. The first symbol signified the page, the second,
the line number, the third the actual word. For words and
names that they could not find in the text, they used the first
letter of the word and marked the symbol with a dash.

"'My Dearest Mark,' she had written, 'by now you understand why we can no longer see each other. It is becoming
obvious that he is your son, and my husband cannot know.
Our son's future is in your hands. If you truly love me you
will stay away from us. Yours, Gwen.'

"I knew now that I had a half-brother," James continued,
"a nobleman who lived just miles from my home, and whom
my father had actually befriended before he vanished. I also
knew that my brother would lose everything if this letter
and his real paternity came to light. But was it possible that
Lord Victor was connected to my father's disappearance?

"The answer lay in the second coded letter, which I could
not read. I knew that Lord Victor had written it, because he
had signed his initials on the bottom. I thought it was interesting that my father had told his son about this code, which

he had used so many years ago to communicate with Lord Victor's mother. I knew he must have also told him of their relationship—and so had sealed his own fate. But how could I prove it? The set of books that the two men had used were different, so I could not decipher the second letter. I had to find out what it said. With the help of some connections, I obtained a post at Hartfield as my own brother's valet. And I watched him, and late at night I combed through the library in hopes of discovering the key to my second note. Finally last week I found it. They had used two copies of the same Bible, but I realized, to my frustration, that my father's copy had been buried with my mother when she died. The letter was from Lord Victor to Mark Fellows, a simple request to meet in the cemetery behind the church the very night of my father's disappearance. I now had proof. But would it hold up in a court of law? I did not have a body, and at any rate I was not fond of the authorities, for reasons of my own. And the more I became acquainted with the family, the more I doubted that they would ever turn against their beloved son. It was so unjust, it drove me mad. This selfish murderer was worshipped by everyone; even his stepmother preferred him to her own daughter. Why would they believe me and my wild accusations? I decided I couldn't trust anyone's judgment but my own. *I* would be his downfall and exact my own revenge.

"My plans did not work out exactly as I had hoped, as you all can see. A week ago I caught one of the servant girls looking through my belongings. It was crucial that no one see the letter from Lord Victor's mother, for I had scrawled the translation on the back. Besides, if I was to use it against my master, I would have to hide it somewhere secret and secure. So I decided to bury the letter until I was ready to make use of it. That is when my real troubles began. Lady Rose observed me digging from her window, and when I had gone she unearthed the little box and read the note. What she did next, I admit I do not understand."

But I understood. "It meant everything to her, Lord Hartfield," I told the unhappy nobleman. "All her life she had been second to her brother. And she resented him for it, resented him for his charm, his easy manners, his scorn for her. Now she realized she was your only child, and the knowledge thrilled her. Her mistake was that she told her brother of her plans. In her triumph, she boasted that she knew his secret and told him that she would speak with you when you returned from London. At the time, she only knew that her brother was not the legitimate heir; she had no knowledge of Mark Fellows's murder because James had only buried the first letter and its translation."

Cartwright gave me a brief nod of approval, and I continued. "Lord Victor was now frantic. He had to silence his

sister, but more importantly, he had to destroy her evidence. At the time, he had no idea that the letter had come from James and believed that eliminating Lady Rose was his only recourse. After the girl was asleep, her brother drugged her with chloroform and carried her quickly down the steps and out the front door. He was the only one who could risk taking her through the house, for, if he were caught, he could simply claim that she had fallen ill and that he was assisting her. Ellison, one of the tenant farmers, was offered a handsome sum to convey her to a vacant house at the border of Sheffield Green, which was to become her prison while her brother searched her room. Lord Victor packed a bag of her clothing and placed it in his room, then returned to his sister's bedroom, locked it from the inside with her keys, and left by way of the window, to complete the impression that she had left alone and by that route. He overlooked the rather obvious fact that his sister would have had to be a professional acrobat to complete her escape without leaving a single footprint in the wet mud outside her window. The twenty-pound bag that she was supposed to have carried down the tree made the scenario even more impossible. The following day Lord Victor returned and searched her bedroom. He was very thorough; he even cut open and looked in the featherbed stuffing for the concealed letter, though he rather overdid his part when he removed and burned all

of Lady Rose's correspondence. In his anxiety that no hint of his secret should remain behind, he hastily gathered up every scrap of paper in the room and disposed of it. Then, in desperation, he tried to coax a confession out of his sister, ordering Ellison to withhold food until she told him everything. But she wouldn't do it, so Ellison kept her in a drugged sleep while her brother decided what to do with her.

"Lord Victor tried to mislead us in the beginning, and his lie initially led us to another explanation," I continued. "The girl may have had an accomplice who took her bag down for her and left those marks beneath the tree. Lord Victor himself suggested the identity of this gentleman when he told Mr. Cartwright of the meeting which he had supposedly witnessed between his sister and a mysterious tall suitor. But that little story about his sister's secret meetings rang false to me when I considered that Lord Victor was the *only one* who had witnessed the event. There was also a clue from the very beginning of the case, which pointed us in the right direction. Why did Lord Victor not send up a servant to call his sister when she did not come down for breakfast the morning of her disappearance? That would have been a task for her lady's maid; there was no reason for her mother to look in on her. But Lord Victor knew that the door would be locked, and he acted on the knowledge without realizing it. Another lie that he arranged was the note which he forced

his sister to write, informing her parents of her elopement. If you had studied it carefully, Your Lordship, instead of burning it as he had directed, you would have seen that your daughter had cried for help within the message."

The earl had lifted a tear-stained face to me, and he shook his head sadly at my last statement. "I didn't burn it," he murmured. "My son threw it into the fire after I left the room."

I nodded and looked over at Lord Victor. "I am certain that your son had no intention of ever setting his sister free," I continued. "Once he had found the letter she had hidden, he planned to make certain that she was never found."

"But I suspected that my stolen letter and the girl's disappearance were connected," James put in. "I was just not certain what had happened to her. So I left a message for my master on the mantelpiece, in a code which only he could read. It said 'I will confess.' I saw it terrified him, for he could not imagine how she could have sent the message. But that night, after the dinner party, he sped off to the village to make certain that she was still secure. I saw him slip a revolver into his pocket before he left, and I followed him to the house to see what he would do. I was worried that he planned to harm her, and I was on the point of rushing into the cottage after him when he emerged again and headed back to the estate. I did not dare act upon the knowledge

yet, for I was not certain that I was right, and I did not want
to confront Lord Victor if I was wrong. I decided to return
the following day when it was light and have a better look
around. But this afternoon when I returned, I found that I
was not the only one who had discovered her."

Cartwright smiled and raised his eyebrows. "But, of course,
if we had not been there, the story would still have had a
happy ending, because I assume you intended to return the
girl unharmed and forget the fact that she had taken your
precious letter."

James flinched. "I had nothing against the girl," he retorted,
but some of the confidence had gone out of his manner.

"We will have to take your word on that," Cartwright
replied dryly. "As for tonight's performance, I do admit
that it came about with your kind help. This afternoon
James and I sent Lord Victor another message, which read,
"I know now where you buried him." It was obvious that
Mark Fellows's body was in the cemetery. Their last meeting place was by the graveyard, and what better place to bury
someone without fear of discovery? But I was not certain
of the exact spot. I see now that he chose to inter the body
above another coffin which had been covered earlier that
day. The earth would still have been soft, and the task an
easy one. The question was: Would the young lord take our
bait? He might have chosen to ignore the bluff, or brave it

out. But knowing his determined character, I believed he would appear tonight and try to move the body before it could be discovered and identified, in a last attempt to save himself."

During the explanation, Lord Hartfield had sunk to the ground, his features drawn and distant, his red-rimmed eyes downcast in quiet resignation. Now, as the constable grasped his prisoner by the collar and fastened the cuffs around his wrists, the nobleman let out a strangled moan. "Let me come with him to the station," he whispered.

"One moment!" James cried as the officer hauled Lord Victor to his feet. "I want to ask him one last question. Why did you kill him, *brother*? He would never have betrayed your secret."

The young lord turned around and sneered at his former servant. The constable cleared his throat and began to warn him that "anything he said might be used against him in a court of law," but the prisoner told him to save his breath.

"Your father was a *drunk*," he snarled at James. "He told me about his relationship with my mother while he was intoxicated. I could not trust that sot. I would have been foolish to take that risk."

"I think we've heard enough," the younger officer interjected. "Your Lordship, you may come with us if you like. We can ask the rest of our questions at the station."

"Well, I got some of what I wanted," muttered James as we watched them leave the cemetery.

"Indeed," Cartwright retorted. "Everything but the money that you planned to extract from Lord Victor before you took your 'revenge.'"

"You can't try a man on what he intended to do," James protested.

"No, but you can try him for what he admitted before five witnesses: that he knew his mistress had been kidnapped, knew where she was being held, and yet never intended to alert the authorities. That makes you an accessory, does it not?"

"Maybe so," James murmured in a chastened tone. "But you did promise to ignore that."

"Yes, I suppose I did. But there was a second part to our agreement, if you recall. I believe you have some letters which belong to a Lady Adelaide Forrester, who is a client of mine. I understand you've brought them with you. Hand them over, please. Then you may change your name and disappear, as you intended, and I will not interfere."

The valet scowled and pulled a wrapped bundle from his coat. "There they are. You can look them over if you like."

Cartwright slipped the package into his pocket without a word and then nodded gravely at his opponent. "You may go now, James."

The valet threw him a contemptuous look and then stalked off, his shadow receding into the darkness beyond the graveyard fence. I waited until he had gone and then turned happily to Cartwright. "I can't wait to tell Adelaide that you have her letters—" I began, but he interrupted me before I could finish.

"Dora, I sent a doctor to tend to Lady Rose. I'll ask Perkins to fetch him as soon as she can spare him. We must get you back to London."

"I am all right, I promise you."

"Your wound is infected, your arm has swollen to twice its normal size, and your cheeks are gray. And yet you are still arguing with me. I suppose I should take that as a good sign."

"If that's a good sign, I can offer more along those lines, if you insist."

"Indeed?"

"I would have dealt differently with the earl. You ought to have informed the nobleman that his daughter was still alive *before* you summoned him to a graveyard in the middle of the night. The unveiling of the corpse would have been a little less dramatic, but it might have softened the blow a little. He loved his son. Even after all this is over, I believe he'll love him still, despite everything he's done."

"You're right. It didn't even matter to him that Lord Victor was not his blood. It won't alter how he feels about him."

I nodded silently and looked away. There was something a bit too personal about that statement, something that echoed of my own experience. I could not share that thought with him, however, so I said nothing then. But I could feel him watching me, and after a moment I heard him step closer. When I finally glanced back at him, I saw that he looked frightened, and that he had extended one arm out to me. I tried to speak, tried to make some suggestion about returning to the estate, but I found suddenly that I could not remember any words. My head had again begun to swim, my arm had gone completely numb, and my vision blurred to white. There was a noise like ocean waves roaring in my ears.

"Dora!" Someone was calling out my name, but I could not place the sound. It seemed to be a female voice, and, as I tried to focus, the figure of Agatha appeared before me, smiling happily and waving. I wondered if I was hallucinating, but then I noticed Cartwright's expression, and I realized that he could see her too.

"You've found him! How wonderful! I could not rest until I was sure that you were safe," she chirped.

"Thank you, Agatha, I am very well," I gasped out. I had forgotten to change my accent, but she did not seem to notice.

"Ah, you don't look well at all, my dear," she protested. "And it's no wonder! Such a difficult thing to have to say, and in such a place!" She shuddered and pulled at her cloak. "Sir, I hope you made it easy for her."

"I'm sorry—who are you exactly?" Cartwright inquired.

She gave him a confidential pat. "It's all right, you needn't worry, sir. Your secret's safe with me. She's already told me that you were in love with her."

I had a brief vision of Agatha's complacent grin and Peter Cartwright's startled eyes. Then a wave of nausea hit, and I fell heavily to my knees. Now they were both calling out my name, but I could no longer see them; and finally their voices vanished too and everything went dark.

CHAPTER

21

I DO NOT REMEMBER how I got to London, how I was conveyed to my cousin's home, or how I got the five-inch scar across my arm. The next two days were filled with chloroform dreams and waking nightmares. I remember only faces, cold compresses, and terrifying words.

"Infectious fever."

"Surgery."

"Necrosis."

"Delirium."

And finally, "Amputation."

I remember begging, pleading, crying out for something, trying to bargain with the voices shouting in my head. I remember a sharp steel blade, a pressure on my arm and a searing burn. I remember hearing someone screaming and then realizing that the sound was coming from my lips. I remember a glass bottle, a mask, the smell of chemicals and then darkness, as I slipped smoothly, gratefully into waves of nothing.

CHAPTER
22

WHEN I AWOKE, I did not know where I was. I opened my mouth to call for help, but then I saw the doctor sitting in an armchair near the window and Adelaide hovering by my bedside. When I tried to rise she gently restrained me and placed a cool rag on my brow. I had been ill for three days, she told me, and they had been worried that I would not recover. The doctor had called the surgeon in and they had argued—

My dream came back to me then, the knife, my cry, the pool of blood. A wave of terror choked me, and I was suddenly afraid to know the truth, to see my leaden, useless limb. With my right hand I pulled my blanket back to reveal my left arm, bandaged, swollen—but still whole. The fingers moved, I could still feel them, and shaking, I sank back onto my pillow and whispered my relief.

The doctor had risen from his chair. There was something familiar about his face—the mourning band around his arm; I wondered vaguely if we had met before. "The surgeon thought that we should amputate," he told me gravely. "I disagreed, and so instead I made a linear incision to relieve the pressure in your arm. It worked, but you will have to wear a bandage for quite some time until the wound heals on its own."

He may have said more, but I never heard it; my arm was safe. I breathed my thanks and fell asleep.

I woke several hours later to a dark and empty room. My back was sore, and I sat up slowly to stretch my aching muscles. There was a small tray of toast and water by the bed. My throat was parched and I drank gratefully from the pitcher, draining it in seconds. Slowly, I began to feel my energy returning, and after a few minutes I decided to test my strength.

I took a small turn around my bedchamber, first to my writing desk, then to the fireplace, each time pausing for several minutes to catch my breath. It was frightening to note my weakness; several steps exhausted me, a bold trip to the door left me panting and light-headed. Finally, I settled before the dresser mirror and gazed at my reflection. Two large gray eyes stared back at me, their black hollows startling against the whiteness of my skin; my mass of curls fell in a cloud of tangles around my shoulders. It was not so bad, I told myself, and looked away. I was thinner, certainly, and my skin appeared transparent, but I had been prepared for worse. I wrapped myself in my dressing gown, bound my hair, and sat down before the fireplace. It was nearly dark, the fire in the hearth was dying, and I moved closer to it, holding my numb hands to the glowing embers.

Presently I heard a rustling sound outside, and my cousin entered, carrying a tray of bandages and water. She started when she saw me by the fire and hurried over to sit beside me.

"You should have called for me, Dora, I would have helped you! And the coals are nearly cold! I specifically instructed Mary—"

"Never mind," I told her weakly. "It is rather warm in here." My voice sounded strange and rasping to my ears.

"How does your hand feel now? The doctor injected morphine for the pain before he left, but I'm afraid it may not have been enough. And it's time to change your dressing."

I shrugged and held my arm out to her. "It aches, of course. But I can stand it."

She shook her head and placed my hand upon her knee, then carefully unpinned the bandage and unwrapped my wound. I winced as the dressing came undone. As the cloth slid back, I could see a fresh and ugly scar cutting through the livid marks of my old burn. It was a cherry streak, from mid-arm to wrist, swollen in the middle and gleaming silver in the fire's light.

"Dora, I never heard—what happened to your arm? Mr. Cartwright told me that he received an urgent message from Miss Prim indicating that you'd had a little accident and would require a doctor's care. The two of them conveyed you here, but you were barely lucid by that point."

I shrugged and looked away. The lies that I had told my cousin were far back in my mind; I was not certain what to say. It was a moment before I recalled Miss Prim at all, for I had quite forgotten the outrageous actor who had posed as my temporary guardian.

"I picked up a hot fire iron by mistake. I should have taken better care of it, I know, but it was just a tiny burn. I ignored it until it became infected."

"Well, thank goodness it is healing now. The doctor was very grave at first, and I was terrified. I kept thinking

that if only I had been with you, none of this would have
happened."

"You know that isn't true. And anyway, at least it's over
now."

Adelaide sighed and dipped my bandage in the water
bowl. "Yes, it's over. Mr. Cartwright got my letters back, did
you know that? We have nothing left to fear."

I attempted to look surprised. "Ah, Adelaide, I am so
happy for you. And how wonderful of him! How did he
do it?"

"I know no more than you, my dear. When he brought
you back in that awful state, I was beside myself. At that
point we did not speak about my case, of course. The following morning Mr. Cartwright returned and handed me
my letters. No explanation, no fee, no answer to my questions. He just inquired after you, and when I told him what
the surgeon had recommended, he rushed off and came back
an hour later with his own doctor. God bless him, that good
man saved your arm, my dear."

"And Mr. Cartwright?"

"He came back the next day to ask me if I had had a
chance to check the letters and make certain that they were
all in order. It was rather sweet, I thought, and obviously
unnecessary, for I would have written if anything had been
missing. I told him that I had already burned the letters.

He shuffled about the place for several minutes, asked me some irrelevant questions, didn't answer any of mine, and then finally inquired after you."

"What did you tell him?"

"That you were improving. He thanked me quickly and disappeared. I haven't seen him or Mr. Porter since." She pinned the corner of the bandage to my sleeve and folded up the edges. "There now, that is done. Back to bed now, Dora. I am off to write a letter to Mother to let her know about your progress."

"Aunt Ina knows that I've been sick?"

"Of course she knows! I couldn't keep that hidden, could I? But she knows nothing else."

"Is she coming down to London?"

"No, we will return to Newheath as soon as you are feeling up it. I had planned to stay until the summer, but she thought that you would recover more quickly if you were home. No doubt she's right."

"But the Season?"

"It is a shame to miss, I know. But perhaps we'll make another trip before it ends. And there's always next year—your first real Season."

I did not care about the Season, but I did not want to leave the city—not yet. At that moment I was not sure exactly what I wanted, or what I hoped might happen if I stayed on through the summer, but I could not leave just yet. I did not want it to be over. The blackmail scheme, the Hartfield case, my brief beginning as a detective's assistant—it could not end in teatime in Auntie's parlor. I did not even know the outcome of the case, and there was no one I could ask about it. Not directly, anyway.

"Adelaide," I ventured as she folded up the bandages, "has anything interesting happened while I've been gone? I'm not tired, truly. I'd love to read the papers for a little while before I go to bed."

She shook her head and helped me rise. "No papers now. It's far too late. We can discuss the news at breakfast."

"Ah, please, cousin, just one tiny rumor, one headline, anything. Something current, something that I haven't heard yet. You have no idea how bored I've been with that Miss Prim. She wouldn't let me read the news. She said it tarnishes the soul." I sighed as she led me to my bed. Hopefully, I thought, there had been only one scandal in the papers recently. There was only one that I truly cared about.

Adelaide smiled and pulled the covers back, and her eyes shone with the promise of future gossip. "Well, of course everyone's been talking about the arrest of Lord Victor, the earl of Hartfield's son. I believe you were already ill when that scandal broke."

I endeavored to look shocked. "What was he arrested for?"

"You can't imagine."

"Not—not murder?"

She nodded and pursed her lips. "An old murder that has only just now come to light. There is no word yet on the motive or how the authorities discovered it, but the papers have been buzzing with theories and speculations."

"And his family?"

"Well, his father, the earl, has been most vocal in defending him."

"*Defending* him?"

"Well, of course. Naturally, the man defends his son."

His son. So the officers had not yet spoken to the press about the young man's history. It was certain to come out eventually at the trial. London society feasted on such lurid details; they would certainly gorge themselves on this aristocratic scandal.

"What about the earl's family? Have they spoken up in the son's defense?"

"His stepmother is standing by her husband's side. There is a sister, too, but she has been under a doctor's care for much of the last week. They say she is recovering, but she is not yet well enough to talk to anyone. The shock of the arrest was probably too much for her."

"Ah, of course."

"Well, does that satisfy you for tonight? Or should I rake

through the morning papers for some other heinous crime?"

I smiled and settled back against my pillow. "That is enough for now, I think. I'm just happy that your letters are safe."

"I am happy that *you* are safe. You can't think how worried I have been. I still have no idea how Mr. Porter and Mr. Cartwright managed it."

"Adelaide—you—you haven't spoken to Mr. Porter, have you?"

She frowned and shook her head. "My dear, after your display in his office, I think he has no wish to speak to either of us again. Mr. Cartwright has managed all the details. It was lucky for us that he had such a talented assistant."

"Yes, very lucky. Well, good night, Adelaide."

"Good night."

I should have slept quite well that night. I was still tired from my recent fever, and our conversation had laid my final doubts to rest. Lord Victor was in custody, the drama around Hartfield would play out in the courts and in the papers, and my cousin's letters were now in ashes. I had achieved my purpose, and my journey was now over. And yet I could not rest.

There was one final mystery that I knew I would never solve, a riddle that I had never sought. Why had Peter Cartwright returned to ask about me? I wondered. Was he simply being kind and inquiring after the sick? Or was there some other feeling there?

He had, after all, told me that he "cared about me." I could not forget that. And yet, whatever his feelings were for me, I realized that they would not matter to anyone in the end. I was not to see him anymore. Even after my coming out into society, after my introduction to the marriage market, I knew that I would have to hide my affection for him. I was expected to marry someone settled and established, a fellow with a decent income and a good name. My family would never consider a young apprentice. Adelaide herself had set me an example with her own choice. She had loved her music tutor but had finally "come to her senses" and married a respectable gentleman with a grand estate. Even Adelaide would not take my part in this.

But still, even if he could never show it, I would have liked to know that Peter was fond of me at least, that he would not forget me when I left the city. It would have meant everything to me then.

I built many theories that night, constructed arguments pro and con, and wrestled with my pride and my imagination. I began ten letters and threw ten letters in the fire. *I thought I ought to write to thank you* . . . met a swift demise beneath the coals. I was not feeling particularly thankful, after all. *I am returning soon to Newheath* . . . There seemed no point in writing that; he probably assumed that I was going home. *My cousin tells me that you asked for me* . . . I tore that one in two before I tossed it to the ground. He must not think that I had talked about him as soon as I awoke.

And so on until morning. The only letter that survived the night was the one that said what I was truly thinking. *I know that we will likely never meet again. And I am sorry for it, sorrier than I ever thought I could be.*

But when the sun rose, that message was the last to burn. There was no way to send a note like that.

When I left my room and joined my cousin at the break-fast table, my eyes were sore and heavy, but my heart was calm. I had closed this chapter now and would resume my quiet, simple life, and live out my easy destiny. It was for the best, I told myself. What else was I to do? I could not lead two lives, one corseted existence dancing upon shiny ballroom floors and another dark and raw, dangerous and exciting. There was no way to manage that.

At least, I had not yet found a way.

CHAPTER
23

"I AM THINKING of going to Highgate, Dora."

It was the first time Adelaide had suggested a trip since I'd been ill, and I had no doubt that somehow new parasols and boots would be involved in our expedition. We would return to Newheath the next morning, and it would be unthinkable to greet my aunt without some evidence of our trip into the city. And yet my cousin had not dressed for a day of pleasure. Her suit was dark and somber, her hat a quiet charcoal pancake. And she had not the look of a young wife about to pass the day in joyful spending. Her eyes were distant, bothered; her face was drawn and sad.

"What's in Highgate?" I inquired.

"I want to pay a visit to your grandmother," she replied after a moment.

I stared at her in mute confusion. Both my grandmothers were dead. My mother's mother, our common grandmother, was buried near our church in Newheath. My father's mother, however, Grandmother Joyce, was interred nearby at—

"—Highgate Cemetery?" I exclaimed in disbelief. "But why do you want to go there on the day before we leave?"

"Well," she replied slowly, "no one has visited Grandmother Joyce's grave since your father died. I want to make certain that the groundskeepers are tending to it as they ought. You needn't go if you don't wish to. I shan't be long."

There was something guilty and hesitant about her explanation; she had not met my eyes during our exchange.

"I'll come along if it's all the same to you," I replied indifferently. "I have not left the house in days."

"Just as you like." She shrugged, rising from the table. "I'll have the boy call for our coachman."

It was for the best, I reflected as I dressed. Hours of clucking over ribbons, tulle, and lace would have been difficult to tolerate that morning. I did not really see the point, in any case; who was I trying to attract? A graveyard would fit my temper better than a shopping trip.

We arrived at Swain's Lane later that afternoon. As we entered through the archway, I saw her glance hesitantly at me.

"Dora, I thought—perhaps you would like to take a turn about the grounds without me for a little while? I can meet you at Grandmother Joyce's plot in half an hour."

"Yes, of course," I told her. "Take all the time you like. I won't be far."

She nodded gratefully and hurried off, and I wended my way across the winding lane to Egyptian Avenue. My grandmother was buried near the parish church of St. Michael, and I headed in that direction. Past the Circle of Lebanon, I discovered a path which led to an overlook, where I could see a great expanse of plots below.

There, several yards away, in a corner by a fallen marble angel, I saw my cousin kneeling by a little gravestone. From where I stood I could not see the name upon the plaque, but her attitude was one of weary grief. She seemed to be clutching something to her chest, and as I watched, she placed the item on the ground. I recognized her jeweled trinket box, the one in which she kept her rings. As she pushed open the clasp, I saw that it was filled with ashes. In a sudden gesture my cousin turned the coffer over, and the dust spilled out onto the tombstone and settled in a gray pall over the humid earth. Slowly she drew her kerchief out and pressed it to her eyes; her head was bowed in quiet meditation. I watched her silently for a while and then withdrew in the direction from which I'd come.

I finally understood why we had come to Highgate that afternoon, and why she had asked to be alone. The ashes she had scattered were the ashes of her letters; she was kneeling at her first love's grave. Always practical and ever charming, my cousin would have shocked her family with this unexpected show of romantic yearning, this grief that should have never been. Her mother would have blanched with shame could she have witnessed this; her husband would have turned to ice.

But I understood my cousin's feelings. She had pretended to scorn that past, to have left her first love behind. And yet she had kept those letters with her, even risked discovery, to hold on to that precious memory. She must have truly loved him—she probably loved him still, though he was gone.

I thought of my lost detective hero and my dreams, of Peter Cartwright and my only case. Would those memories be ground to ashes in the coming years? It was impossible to imagine that.

I had wandered back to Swain's Lane while I thought of

Adelaide's letters, and now I was facing the entrance to the eastern section of the cemetery. It was a plainer area, but it seemed more welcoming than the grandiose tombs of the western plots. I decided I would stroll through there for a little while and give Adelaide the privacy she needed. I did not want to visit Grandmother Joyce's plot just yet; I had not been close to her as a child, and, as it had turned out, she was not actually related to me.

And yet there was one grave that I had wanted to visit. But he was not buried here; he was not buried anywhere, unless a churning waterfall counted as a graveyard.

Slowly I knelt down beside the fence and pulled an unmarked stone from underneath the shrubbery. It felt smooth and cold beneath my fingers. With the knuckles of my right hand, I clawed a hole into the soil, placed the stone inside, and slowly sketched a ragged halo around my make-shift tombstone.

It looked small and sad there, my little rock, perched in its shallow pit like an abandoned egg inside a vacant nest. A marble angel looming large beside me cast a frigid shadow across my patch; only a sliver of my stone shone blue and green beneath the fading sun. This would be his gravestone, I decided, a special tribute to my fallen hero. This would be his spot, my secret place, where I, at least, could bury him.

And I could say something to him now, a few short words,

like a little eulogy at a funeral. When it was done I would
return to Adelaide and step into my ordinary life again. It
was not exactly normal to kneel over an empty grave, perhaps, or to talk to someone who wasn't listening to me, but
nothing about this experience had been normal—and in any
case, nobody was watching now. I was alone, with all the
luxury and pain of total privacy. These would be my quiet
stolen minutes, when nobody could judge or scold me.

"Dear detective in the sky," I murmured quietly, my head
bowed over the stone, "I'm going home tomorrow. I know
that you can't care about that now. Perhaps if I had come
a little sooner, it might have mattered to you. Or perhaps
not. But I'd like to think you would have approved of me,
of what I've done over the last few days. I really miss the
thought of you. I miss the hope that my future could have
been a brilliant one—that you might have made it so. But I
don't regret the dream, even if it's gone now. And I want to
thank you for inspiring it."

CHAPTER

24

F I HAD NOT BEEN concentrating so hard on my little prayer, I might have heard the rustling sooner. It was only when Peter Cartwright's shadow fell across my little stone that I finally looked up to see him standing there, half-hidden by the bushes, one hand raised in awkward greeting. By the time I recognized him, he was standing next to me, leaning over the tiny gravestone with a puzzled face. It was too late to hide it now; he had already taken in the scene. I had thought that nothing could have been more mortifying than our first encounter; now I knew what true humiliation was. I sighed and looked sadly up at him, waiting for his judgment, bracing for the final blow to complete my misery. He glanced briefly at the stone again, then once more at my sad face and stretched his arm out to help me rise.

"I did not mean to interrupt your vigil," he told me gravely as I scrambled clumsily to my feet. His voice was quiet; there was no laughter in his eyes. Perhaps, I thought, perhaps he had not understood what he had seen. Perhaps he would not tease me after all. I had not fully recovered from the shock of our unexpected meeting, but now it was my turn to speak.

"Mr. Cartwright—this is a surprise," I ventured, finally. "How did you know that I would be here?"

"I didn't," he responded simply.

"But I don't understand— My cousin brought me with her on a whim, and I wandered off just now to—"

I stopped and shook my head. There was no way to finish that. What was I to say? *To mourn the death of my mysterious father?* There really were no words to fit this scene.

"To say good-bye?" he suggested solemnly. There was no hint of mockery in his question. He leaned down slowly, picked the stone out from its mound, and turned it over in his fingers. "Are you finished with this, then? You're ready to let him go now?"

I opened my mouth to speak and stopped, confused. His

face was somber, his eyes sad and dark, an emerald shade of black. There was no way he could have understood, I reasoned; there was no way he could have guessed. And yet somehow he had, for as I watched him, he stepped closer to me, put his hand gently over my own, and together we set the rock back in its place, beneath the shrubs and out of sight.

"There now," he murmured simply. "Do you feel better?"

I nodded mutely. That silly gesture had helped me somehow, had made me breathe a little easier, though how he could have known, I still did not understand. And why was he here at all? Highgate Cemetery was nowhere near his home.

"Why did you come?" I asked him finally.

But he did not seem to hear me; he was staring past me at something in the distance. Then he turned to me and smiled broadly, as if a new idea had just dawned on him. "Have you ever studied families, Miss Joyce?" he asked me suddenly.

I shook my head. "What sorts of families?"

"I'm talking about hereditary traits, about family likenesses. It's a hobby of mine, you see, tracing those subtle similarities that link sisters to brothers, cousins to cousins, daughters to fathers—" He broke off and stared thoughtfully at me, as if waiting for my reaction.

"And this hobby is useful to you in your criminal investigations?" I ventured, in an innocent voice. I knew quite well what he was trying to say, of course; I was only pretending not to understand him now, hoping to distract him and so steer him from the truth. Though he'd hinted at it ever since we'd met, I did not want him to speak my secret out loud.

"My hobby is more than just a detective's tool, Miss Joyce," he said. "It also helps me make sense of the people whom I meet, and of this great jumbled city around me. I begin to see a unity, hundreds of tiny little bridges connecting solitary beings to one another. It's startling and exciting. I'll show you sometime if you're interested."

"Mr. Cartwright, I don't understand—"

"The hands are very telling, for example, the curvature of the ear, the cheekbone. Even when the figure and the features differ—there are subtle signs—if you look for them. But the eyes are my favorite study." There was a distant smile playing on his lips. "Dora, some people's eyes give everything away."

I could longer pretend to misunderstand what he was saying. And yet I couldn't admit that I understood him, either. I was too ashamed then, not just because my secret was practically on his lips now, but because it had been so easy for him to guess.

"Mr. Cartwright, these theories are truly fascinating," I told him coolly, "but surely you did not wander out to Highgate just to comment on the color of my eyes."

"No, it was not the color but the expression which caught my notice. Particularly when you are concentrating on something. Or glaring furiously at someone, as you were on that morning when we first met. Do you remember?" He smiled, as if recalling a pleasant memory. And I remembered now, that startled look, his odd expression before we parted that day on Baker Street. He had noticed a faint resemblance between myself and his old master, and so had guessed at my secret from the beginning.

"Oh, is that why you looked so pleased, then?" I shot back with a little laugh. "You thought you'd made a brilliant discovery? And so now you've traveled to a graveyard to tell me all about it?" My voice shook a little at the end, but I did not look away. Until the last, I was determined to pretend confidence. If I spoke lightly, if I teased him, perhaps he would not speak my shame.

But he was no longer watching me. His jaw had set in angry lines, and his eyes had narrowed. He was looking past me once again, at some point in the distance. "I did not come to Highgate to see *you*, Miss Joyce," he retorted. "After I returned the letters to your cousin, I assumed that our acquaintanceship was over."

"Oh, I see." I nodded weakly. "I understand."

So he had never meant to speak to me again; he had not wished to see me anymore. He had assumed that it was over. And I'd been wondering if he'd followed me! I was too weary to feel hurt just then, though I was certain that his words would torture me for months to come. I swallowed and moved away from him. "Naturally, it *is* over, sir. Of course it is. I'm sorry, I never meant—" My voice cracked at the apology.

He glanced back at me, his features softening. "One moment—why *did* you think I came here this afternoon? Did you think that I'd been following you? I'm sorry, Dora, I don't mean to disappoint you. But the truth is that I come here fairly often. Especially to this spot."

"I understand."

But I did not. It seemed so strange to me. He was not the brooding, morbid type. And this was one of the cemetery's plainer areas, not nearly as picturesque as Egyptian Avenue or the Circle of Lebanon. I was supposed to ask him to explain, of course. It would have been quite natural to ask, especially for me. But there was something about his look that stopped me. Beneath his quiet statement there was an aching note, like a confession, a hint which he had left for me. I could not speak just then. I had to wait for him.

"No, I do not think you understand at all," he murmured finally. "But I appreciate your patience. You know, sometimes I think that you are so intent on seeing details that you miss

the person standing right in front of you. Good day, Miss
Joyce. I trust you'll have a safe trip home."

He bowed shortly as he spoke, and as he straightened,
the knot of his cravat slipped forward and the scar upon his
neck gleamed red between the edges of his collar. Perhaps
it was the marked whiteness of his skin which made it glow
that way, or maybe it was the spirit of the place, but suddenly the cross was burning like a living thing, angry, bloody,
and unforgiving. And I was staring at it now; even as he put
his hand over the spot to cover it, I could not look away.
Once more his eyes flickered past my shoulder, once more
he paled, and the little cross went livid.

What had I missed? What was he seeing when he looked
past me?

Slowly, without a word, I turned around and tracked his
gaze, beyond a row of ivy-covered graves, over a hedge of red
moss roses, some fifty feet away into the shadows beneath a
weeping willow tree.

There, in a single row stood four small headstones.

Four little crosses.

I could not make out the writing from where I stood, but
somehow I knew that this area belonged to him, that I had
stumbled into his secret sanctuary. Just a few steps would
bring me close enough to read the gravestones. Without

thinking I moved past him toward the spot, stepping through a break between the shrubs. I heard him call my name, heard him call for me to stop, but I did not heed him.

As I approached it, I could see the plot more clearly, a little family of marble crosses, four ivory tombstones gathered comfortably in a private cluster, resting together underneath the willow's pleasant shade. Four gravestones, nearly identical.

Four gravestones, all bearing my friend's surname.

William, Margaret, Trevor, and Charlotte

Cartwright

Four birthdates. Two parents and two children.

His family.

And at the bottom of the stones: four identical engravings.

Died: December 24, 1887

Safe in the hallowed quiet of the past.

All in one day. His parents, brother, and sister gone at once.

How could I have known? How could I have guessed this? What had I heard about him and then forgotten? *I think you know Mr. Cartwright pretty well, so you must remember how miserable he used to be.* Young Perkins had said that about his friend. *Those first few months, I think I only saw him smile once. . . .*

And I was standing there, in the shadow of his tragedy, gaping at his misery, breaking into a grief which he had guarded from everyone he knew, prodding at a mystery which deserved to rest.

He had moved to stand beside me. His head was turned away, and I could not read his face, but I could see that the knuckles on his fingers had gone white and that his hands were trembling at his sides.

"I'm really very sorry," I began. "I hope you can forgive—"

"Please come away from here."

His voice broke, a faded, pleading whisper.

"I did not mean to—"

"Just come away from here."

I had no right to be there. He had tried to warn me, and I had casually ignored him. I needed to leave immediately, without a word. I had to go before he felt obliged to speak again.

I slipped past him quietly, pushing aside the willow branches in my way, and hurried down the winding lane. At the far end of the trail I slowed to catch my breath and looked behind me. Cartwright had followed me up the hill, and he glanced around the garden before settling wearily on a granite bench.

I wavered briefly on the path, waiting for him to say something, waiting for some shrug of forgiveness and understanding. When he did not speak, I crossed the lane and settled down beside him. He gave me a tired look and put his head into his hands.

Some minutes passed in silence. I watched the sun sink deeper into the red horizon; the air was light and cool and smelled of evening. My cousin would be looking for me soon. I could not risk her finding me here, sitting all alone in a secluded area with a young man. But I could not leave him like this.

It was too late now for apologies; he was no longer listening. I needed to turn his mind to other things now, to push away that haunted look. But more importantly, I had to make him trust me once again, to see me as a friend, as someone whose interest in his life ran deeper than simple morbid curiosity. And there was only one way I could think to do that. I had to sacrifice something of my own. I had to tell him the truth about myself.

"Mr. Cartwright?"

No sound at all.

"Peter, please."

He gave a grunting sigh. "Well?"

"The day we met—you asked me why I'd come to London. Do you remember?"

He had been leaning forward, his elbows on his knees, his forehead resting in his palms. At my question he sat up and stared at me, his lips falling open slightly in disbelief. "I asked you more than once. I never really thought you'd answer."

"Well, I'd like to tell you now—if you'd care to listen."

He nodded quietly. "Yes, of course."

"You have to understand that I've carried this secret with me for near four years—and I've never told it to another soul. I cannot imagine what you'll think of me when I tell you."

"Dora—"

"Please don't speak just yet. Just let me finish—and then say what you wish. Or leave me afterward without a word, just as you like."

He nodded again and leaned back slightly. "All right."

I exhaled and looked out into the distance. There was no way to meet his eyes just then. It was best to simply say the truth and have done with it.

"I know you may have guessed a portion of my secret; you've hinted at it more than once, and just now you almost said it out loud." I swallowed hard and closed my eyes. "Peter," I began slowly. "Four years ago I found out that my mother deceived my father before their marriage. When they wed, she may have already been with child."

I had finally said the words. There was no reason now to wait, no need to let the shock sink in. The worst of it was almost over. "I was that child. For years no one suspected the truth, least of all my father, who raised me as his own. A few months before he died, he learned the truth about my mother's past."

No word or sound from my companion. I could not even hear him breathing. It did not matter; I would not look at him. I did not want to see him yet.

"I don't know exactly how he discovered my mother's secret. But when he did, I sensed the change, Peter. I was very young then, not yet twelve, but there was no question in my mind that something awful had suddenly come between my father and me. Even then I was always getting into scrapes, so I thought maybe I had done something to anger him. I tried so hard to work out what it was. And then— those few months before his death I was so careful to behave like the perfect daughter, the one I thought he wanted me to be. Sometimes I would catch him studying me with the strangest expression on his face, like he was seeing me for the first time. And I got quieter and more attentive, hovering by his room, waiting for some sign from him, some hint that the clouds had passed, that all was well between us. I think he tried, Peter, I really do. He was not ill for long before he died, but I think if he'd had more time, he would have made peace with it—with me. I really do believe that. We just never had the chance."

I paused briefly and gazed out over the darkening hilltop. There was just the ending of the story left, and I did not want to tell it. But I knew I could not end at half a truth. I had to tell him about my mother—and about my guilt.

"A few days after my father's death," I continued sadly, "my mother also became ill. They said that she had caught his fever. Her illness lasted a little longer than his—so she had time— Before she died, she wrote me a letter in which she confessed the truth. She told me that she believed my real father is—he was—that my real father was—"

I could not finish it. Why could I suddenly not speak his name? I had built my life around the man. Why could I not just say it, then?

"I know, Dora." He said the words so quietly that at first I did not hear him.

"I'm glad you do," I breathed and finally met his eyes. And now there was no longer any reason to turn away, for I had reached the most difficult portion of the story. His expression was rapt, intent; I could not read disapproval in his look.

"I was not supposed to read the letter, Peter. She had addressed it to me, but she never actually gave it to me. Perhaps she changed her mind at the last moment, or perhaps she only intended for me to see it if she died. But she had not shut the drawer properly, and I noticed it as I sat beside her bed. That evening I stole it from her night table and read it while she slept. And it changed everything for me. Suddenly it seemed to me that every moment of our lives together had been false. And I had lost the one man whom I loved by someone else's wrong, because of a lie which I could not change. I was so angry then, so full of hate. I burst into her room and wailed at her. I told her that she had robbed me and my father, that I was cursed because of her."

I paused here for a minute, waiting for his response. But he stayed silent, as he had promised me he would. "I told her that I would die before I called her 'Mother,'" I finished miserably. "And I will have to, because she died after I left the room, early the next morning. Somehow, in that moment, in that one horrific moment, I managed to destroy a childhood of memories. You wanted to know why I came to London? I came because I wanted to give meaning to the lie behind my birth. I needed someone to make sense of it for me. I wanted to stop regretting my own history, wanted to stop being ashamed of who I was. I needed to belong somewhere."

"You were looking for a calling?"

"I suppose. But mostly—I just didn't want to disappoint again."

He shook his head and frowned. "I don't know how to tell you this—"

"I know what you are going to say," I put in hastily. "You're going to tell me that I need to forgive myself, that it's all buried in the past. I don't want to hear that."

"That's good. Because that is not what I was going to say. I was going to say that I don't think you would have found what you were seeking. Do you remember when I hinted that you've been waiting for a figment of your imagination? My friend, I think *you* would have come away disappointed, not the other way around."

"Why do you say that?"

He seemed to consider for a moment before replying. "Mr. Holmes was the man you've read about: truly brilliant, energetic, generous. But, Dora, he loved his solitude and independence more than anything—more than anyone. He would have been kind to you, no doubt, but your visit would have been very, very short. In the end, you might even have regretted coming up to meet him."

"Oh—I don't want to believe that. I think I would rather have listened to the speech about leaving the past behind."

He smiled and shook his head. "Well, I'm sorry, but I'm hardly the person to lecture you about that. And as for forgiving yourself—Dora, you were not responsible for your family's pain—*you* were not the cause of it—"

His voice had faltered slightly toward the end, but now he stopped completely and slumped back against the bench. I stared at him and thought about his final words. He was no longer talking about me, I was sure of that. He was not even looking in my direction. His last statement had been a private self-reproach, his own bitter hint of guilt.

Was I supposed to ask him what he meant? I had already trod over his privacy; I did not want to pry again. And yet he seemed now to be waiting for me—

And then he answered me before I spoke.

"Dora, you may ask me, if you wish."

"Peter—"

"I'm not angry anymore. I suppose that you were bound to wonder and to stare." He touched the cross upon his neck and looked away. "We've both been poking at each other's secrets, haven't we? But I never thought you would— I hope you don't regret what you have told me?"

"No, I don't."

He nodded briefly as if to reassure himself.

"Dora, perhaps you've guessed already—I don't know. You keep crime journals, do you not? Take another look through them when you get home. The truth is that my family—that they were— It was not an accident, or illness, do you understand?" His voice was soft and hoarse; each word seemed painful to him. I watched him quietly and waited. His gentle manner had been so comforting through my own confession; I hoped that now my silence would encourage him to speak.

"I had a headache that Christmas Eve," he continued after a pause. "Not a real one, mind you. The sort of headache that a child gets when he does not want to do what has been asked of him. We were supposed to visit a family friend that night. The servants had all gone; the house was to be shut up for several days. And at the last minute I put up a fight. I was too ill, the road too long, the night too cold. In truth I simply disliked the family friend's small daughter, who had this habit of following me everywhere and commenting on everything I did. It was nothing really, but it was enough for me, apparently. Have you ever stopped to think how little choices like that one, how insignificant decisions can alter the course of an entire lifetime? For months after that night I had nothing else to think about."

He fell silent for a moment and closed his eyes. I saw his forehead tense, his face go white; a sheen of moisture glimmered on his lip. When he finally continued, it was in a halting, gentle tone, like that of a young boy seeking pardon.

"They stayed back with me, of course. Charlotte, Trevor, and my parents. They could not leave me all alone, especially not on Christmas. Trevor was furious with me. Mother tried to calm him down; she convinced him that we could make our own little celebration. She lit the fire in the drawing room, brought out some sweets and cordials, and we gathered beside the hearth for a midnight family picnic. It was a perfect night, the snowflakes dancing white and pure outside our window, the wind roaring in the chimney, the warmth and crackle of the fireplace. We were laughing soon; my father had a gift for storytelling, and he told us scores of silly tales about his childhood. I think they knew that I'd been faking illness. But I was the youngest, it was Christmas, and so they humored me."

He put one hand over his eyes. "Dora, I was the one who saw them first—"

I had stopped breathing now. I could see what he was seeing in his memory: a dark room, a family in blankets and slippers around a cheerful fire and—

"—Three men. All dressed in black. An older man and his two sons. They had not made a sound in entering the house. I found out later that they'd been tipped off by our new maid. She had left the window in the study open for them. As they walked into the light, I saw a tremor of surprise flash over the old man's face. They had expected to find the place deserted and so had come armed only with their tools and the knife that they had used to slide the shutters open. I called out when I saw them, and the three men froze. Then my father rose to challenge them, and my mother shouted for us to run. I think she had guessed what the men were thinking. The burglars had not turned and fled when they discovered us; that could only mean one thing—they had decided not to leave witnesses behind who could describe them.

"My brother, my sister and I—we all ran. We tried to hide—" He paused here and looked at me for the first time since the beginning of his story. His face was drawn and bloodless, his eyes, hollow, dry, as if he had long ago spent their tears. His voice sank to a pleading whisper. "Dora, please, you can guess what happened next? I don't have to go through it again? At the inquest they made me describe it all—every detail, everything I saw. Please, Dora, I don't want to—"

I put my hand on his. "You didn't have to tell me all of this, Peter. I should never have asked you to."

He stared at me for a long moment and finally shook his head. "It's all right. I'm not sorry that I told you. It's just—" He paused again and plucked absently at the fingers of my glove. "Guilt is a strange feeling, isn't it? You're sorry for your last words to your mother—but no matter what you would have said to her—she would not have lived. You did not change anything when you told her how you felt. And you *had* been wronged too, in a way. But me—Dora, if it hadn't been for me—my family would be alive today. And this"— he ran his fingers over his scar—"I feel more guilty about this than I do anything else."

"But—but why? They tried to hurt you too—"

"No, they didn't," he responded, interrupting me. "I did this to myself. That was how I escaped."

I did not understand what he was saying. How had that helped him? And why did he feel guilty for it? He was looking at me now, not speaking, a question on his face, a tired, silent plea. *Please guess the truth*, his eyes seemed to beg me. *Don't make me say it.*

I was not sure how to begin. The terror of that night seemed to loom before us; I felt it pushing on me, the frozen horror of his memories, like cold fingers around my throat. And then I saw the scene before me, and felt his panic as he tripped, racing down the hall, desperate to escape. "You were trapped," I began slowly, cautiously. "Hiding in a room. There was no way out."

He nodded. "The window was frozen shut."

"Just outside the door—you heard the chaos, you knew what would happen when they found you."

He shut his eyes, and nodded once again.

"And you thought—if you cut yourself, if you pretended— if one of them saw you lying silent on the ground, saw the bloody neck—he might just assume that one of the others had done the deed. In the confusion, in their hurry, they might not check with one another."

"He never even came near me."

"But, Peter, why do you feel guilty about that? Your plan came off, and you survived."

His eyes flew open. He turned angrily to me and pulled his hand away from mine. "Yes, my trick worked very well. And I should be proud of that, should I?" His jaw was clenched and he was speaking now through gritted teeth. "Don't you understand, Dora? I heard *everything*, I even saw—and all I could think then was how to save myself. I was *planning*, working out a strategy. Does that seem natural to you? In those first few minutes, when we were trying to escape, my sister distracted one of the men on purpose. She shouted at him and then fled in the opposite direction so that I had time to hide. *That* was her plan—to sacrifice herself to save her brother. And I? I only managed to make a plan to save myself."

I could not think of a response. He had been only thirteen years old, I reflected sadly. Why did he judge himself so harshly? What else could he have done? Surely someone had comforted him then, reassured him that he could not have saved them? Had there been a friend there to support him when he needed it the most? Or had he truly been surrounded by stern officers and coroners poking at his tragedy, poking him for testimony?

And what was left for me to say to him? He did not want

to hear me babble words of sympathy. He had probably heard them all before.

"Peter—?" I ventured finally after a long silence.

"What, Dora?"

"Did they catch the men who did it?"

"No." He nearly bit the word in half. "The police bungled the case horribly. I was only thirteen at the time, and even I could see that. By the time the inspector thought to call in Sherlock Holmes, weeks later, it was too late. They'd fled the country by then. Still, despite the long delay, Mr. Holmes was able to track their escape route. He found out which ship they'd boarded, and he traced them to New York and from there on to Chicago. But after that the trail went cold."

"And since then there's been no sign of them?"

"Nothing. Not a word or a clue for near four years."

"But they couldn't have just vanished," I protested. "Maybe they were in some accident or were killed during another criminal attempt."

He gave a harsh laugh and shook his head. "It would be nice to think that, wouldn't it? Not a satisfying conclusion, perhaps, but at least an ending, of sorts."

"But you don't believe it?"

"Not for a moment. They're alive, I'm absolutely certain of that."

"I can't imagine how awful that must be," I said, "living

with the knowledge that they were walking free. Especially right after it happened."

"Believe it or not, Dora, the knowledge that they *hadn't* been caught actually supported me at first," he replied. "It's ironic, but it was the thought that those murderers were still alive that helped me survive those first few months."

"How do you mean?"

He didn't answer me right away; he was gazing off into the distance as if he was seeing the memory playing out in front of him. "It was something to hope for, to look forward to," he told me finally. "At the time there didn't seem to be anything else to live for. It wasn't until quite a while later that I grasped the fact that they would never actually be caught. It seemed impossible to me then. If Mr. Holmes hadn't admitted to me that he'd finally come to a dead end, I would never have believed it."

He smiled wryly and shook his head. "When Sherlock Holmes tells you that he's exhausted every option, you have no choice but to accept it. But he promised me that he would never give up until we'd found them. That was exactly how he phrased it, too. Until *we'd* captured them, he said. As if he was including me in the investigation. You may smile if you like, but that one statement helped me more than all the sympathetic nonsense that I'd heard until then."

"No, I can understand that, actually; I think I would have

felt the same," I said. "Mr. Holmes appreciated how guilty and powerless you felt, and so he helped you direct your anger toward a purpose. It gave you a reason to go on."

He nodded thoughtfully. His voice softened, and the tension in his face relaxed a little. "I don't think that he ever imagined I would take it this far, though. But when he saw that I'd become interested in his line of work he encouraged me—in his own way. He would call on me when he needed a young assistant or a messenger boy. It was an unusual sort of kindness, I suppose, but it meant everything to me then."

"You must have been disappointed that he wasn't looking for a permanent assistant," I observed. "I imagine I would have been."

"I was sorry about that, certainly," he replied. "But I was hardly surprised. You didn't know him, Dora, or you wouldn't have expected any different."

"I didn't know him, it is true," I said. "But I wish I had—even if in the end he wouldn't have wanted to know me."

He smiled kindly and shook his head. "I wouldn't think of it like that. I know I told you that he loved his independence. And he could be cold sometimes, especially when he was focused on a case and had forgotten everyone else around him. But that doesn't mean that he was cruel. It rather depended on his mood, I think. Still, even during his warmest moments, he was not what anybody would ever call affectionate—"

"Oh, I know that!" I interjected with a laugh. "I've read the stories, after all."

"Of course you have. So you know what I am talking about, then. Still, I'll never forget that I have him to thank for setting me on this path. I don't know what would have become of me if I hadn't met him. I certainly wouldn't be here now."

"Aren't you forgetting Mr. Porter?" I smiled. "He was the one who took you on. Although I still don't understand why you ever agreed to work for him."

He rolled his eyes. "Oh, honestly, Dora, you needn't look so baffled. That is the least mysterious portion of the tale. Simply put, I could not establish my own practice. I was too young, without experience, without a name. Mr. Porter was a distant relative with a modest practice, some expensive habits, and no capital. I had a small inheritance. So we struck a bargain. I have not had reason to regret my choice."

"Really? Well, I suppose that you know best."

He shrugged. "He is a decent investigator, with some good qualities. And he was my only option at the time. Ah, but if I had known that a budding young detective was soon to descend on London and take the Underworld by storm—"

"Oh, stop it, please. I am hardly a detective, sir. I am hardly much of anything anymore. Tomorrow morning Adelaide and I return to Newheath, and then it's over for me. At least I can look forward to following *your* career—in the papers. I don't suppose our paths will cross again."

"Indeed? No more trips to London? Don't tell me that your aunt intends for you to 'come out' in your little town!"

I rose and walked over to the path. "Well, naturally, Mr. Cartwright, I will be in London for some portion of next Season. But what has that to do with you?"

He got up off the bench and followed me. "Oh, so I'm 'Mr. Cartwright' once again? Very well, *Miss* Joyce, I will not argue with you. Good-bye, then."

"Farewell, sir," I told him simply and extended my hand to him. I was determined to be sensible now. The evening had begun in grim confessions; at least in parting, I hoped to be composed. There would be plenty of time to mourn after he had gone.

He smiled wearily, and swept his cap off. With a respectful, casual bow, he touched his lips briefly to my fingertips, then paused thoughtfully, turned my hand over, and gazed at it as if he meant to read my fortune through my glove. His fingers were barely touching mine but I could feel their warmth as surely as if he held me. And now he was leaning down again, his mouth just inches from my hand, his shallow breathing cool against my skin. I was suddenly conscious of every fiber in the cloth over my palm, every crease across his knuckles, every skip and tremble of my baffled pulse. With a rapid movement, at once careless and deliberate, he pushed the ruffle of my glove aside and pressed his lips against my wrist.

"Promise me," he murmured, his head still bowed over my hand.

I could not answer at that moment; my throat had gone completely dry, and I was afraid that I would squeak if I attempted to reply. A nod was all that I could manage, and even that was stiff and ragged, like a tiny shudder.

How much can race across one's mind in just an instant! Before he spoke again, a hundred questions had already flashed and faded, a hundred hopes had pitched their waves inside of me. What did he want from me? I wondered. What was he about to ask? Would it be something unoriginal and bland like *Promise that you won't forget me?*—a question begging for a declaration while pledging nothing in return? Or, worse yet: *Promise that you will keep our friendship secret.* He did not need to tell me that. And besides, secret friendships did not stop the heart. Or maybe this would be a true confession, a final note of passion that I could carry home with me, which I could then relive each night. *Promise me that you will wait for me. . . . Promise me that one day . . . someday in the future . . .*

I do not know if I gave myself away. I truly hope not. The only comfort that I have when I recall the evening was that he could not have known what I was thinking, what I was wishing for. Indeed, I was struggling so desperately to assume a calm expression that I may have overdone it slightly. I might possibly have scowled at him. He looked up at me before he spoke, and his eyes were quiet, searching, and undecided. I realized suddenly that my hands were shaking, that he would certainly feel my right hand trembling in his own. So I balled my fingers into fists.

He dropped my wrist and stepped away from me, his features smooth, amused.

"Promise me, Miss Joyce?" There was a dangerous lilt behind his smile.

"Yes?"

"Promise me that you'll stop telling the entire world that we're in love? It is *destroying* my reputation."

If there were any words to answer that, I certainly could not find them at that moment.

"But—I never—I *never*—" The rest was lost in gasping sounds.

"Porter nearly sacked me when I got home. Then, after he'd remembered that my departure might actually be bad for business, he settled on a lengthy lecture about propriety. *Propriety!* He said some unfortunate things about your honor, I'm afraid. If he wasn't so much older than me, I might have knocked him down."

I had found my voice by now and a decent store of injured pride. "Mr. Porter's opinions are *not* my concern, sir. I said nothing to support his wild ideas."

"Oh, and I suppose your servant friend at Hartfield— what was her name—Agatha? She came upon the two of us outside the cemetery and *naturally* assumed that you had come out to a graveyard to accept my *marriage proposal*?"

"Well, not naturally, no. I may have led her to believe that we were, that I was—that my *character* was—rather—"

"Overcome with passion?"

"No!"

"Not even a little?" He was grinning wickedly at me through gritted teeth.

"Oh, very well. My character, my *servant* character was hopelessly in love with your rude, impossible, conceited character. That is all."

"I see. And the intrepid Dora Joyce? Untouched and undisturbed, of course?"

I frowned and looked away. "Of course. What did you expect?"

"Very little, I'm afraid."

There was a brief silence, and then far away a distant cry, a voice I knew, shouting out my name. "Ah, that would be your cousin," he said. "I suppose you can always tell her that you got lost. She will be close to frantic. It is very late."

His voice had grown softer as he spoke, and when I turned to face him, I saw that he had begun to walk away from me.

"Farewell, Dora."

The two sounds echoed off each other, Adelaide's urgent tone, and Peter's last good-bye, one growing nearer while the other faded.

"Peter—"

But he had already gone. Around the corner I could see my cousin's black-plumed hat shivering its way toward me, the rustle of her petticoat whispering her hurry and her concern. I called out to her and heard her gasped relief; the tapping heels ticked closer.

"Here I am!" I shouted. "Adelaide, I've been searching everywhere—"

CHAPTER
25

OUR TRIP HOME WAS even quieter than our journey to the cemetery. Both of us stared out of our respective windows. Adelaide did not ask me where I'd disappeared to, and I did not ask her why her eyes were dark and swollen or why she had ash stains on her gloves. We had come to a silent understanding. I was happy to feign ignorance if she returned the favor. So when we entered the house we headed in opposite directions, Adelaide to the parlor and me to my bedroom to pretend to pack.

Before I'd left for Highgate, I had emptied all my dresser drawers and my wardrobe. The pile of skirts and petticoats upon my bed had reached quite an impressive height. I parted the mountain in the middle and burrowed a little den beneath the heap, then crawled into the hole and closed the gap. There was something very comforting about my chintz cocoon; it was so warm and dark and intensely floral, the perfect place to dream about the past and draw back from the future.

I had barely settled on my bed when a faint knock roused me from my thoughts.

"Miss Dora? May I come in?"

"Yes, Mary, I'm awake."

The door creaked open and our housemaid entered, holding a letter on a silver tray.

"I am sorry that I didn't give this to you sooner, miss, but I thought—I thought perhaps you might want to read this on your own. A young man delivered it, you see—"

I smiled and held my hand out. "And you guessed that I might not want anyone to know that I'd received a letter from a gentleman?"

She grinned at me and handed me the envelope. "Was I wrong, miss?"

"No, Mary, you have the best of instincts. Thank you."

I tore it open and a slip of paper fell into my lap.

"Mary," I inquired as she moved to leave the room, "When did this letter come?"

"Oh, hours ago, miss. Before you left for Highgate. There simply wasn't time to give it to you sooner. No private time, I mean."

"I see. Well, thank you, Mary."

"Good day, miss," she replied and shut the door.

I held the letter to the light; the paper shivering in my fingers, the words dancing before my eyes. The message was unsigned and read:

I would have said good-bye, my friend, but then I realized: It is not over yet. This work, this life, it calls to you.

You must come back.

You will come back.

And I will wait until you do.

ACKNOWLEDGMENTS

I am so thankful for the encouragement and support of my family and friends throughout this process.

I want to thank Irene Kraas, my amazing agent, whose faith in me and my first novel never faltered. My wonderful editors at Hyperion: Lisa Yoskowitz and Catherine Onder, who took my raw first draft and helped me shape it and realize its potential. Thank you so much for your hard work and insight.

To my wonderful parents, Irina Elashvili, my first reader and biggest fan, and Ilya Elashvili, whose amazing stories made me want to tell my own; and to my sisters: Anna, Dinah, Sarah, and Tammy.

To my beta readers: It's terrifying to show your work to your friends and family for the first time. Thank you for making it so easy and for giving me the confidence that I needed to continue writing. Clara Chen, Kelly Canale, Yael Levy, Donna Scheier, Rachel Scheier Kaplan, Neil Scheier, and Rhonda Woods, I can't thank you enough.

To Shana Gros, for patiently listening to me kvetch about the ups and downs of this process, thank you my dear friend.

For my daughters, Aviva, Miriam, and Talia, my greatest joys. And for Eric, my husband, I love you.